# THE
# CHARING CROSS
# MYSTERY
## J S FLETCHER

OREON

OREON
Oleander Press
16 Orchard Street
Cambridge
CB1 1JT
United Kingdom

oleanderpress.com

ISBN: 9781909349711

Cover design and typesetting: neorelix

# CONTENTS

Joseph Smith Fletcher (1863 -1935) was a British journalist and writer. He wrote more than 230 books on a wide variety of subjects, both fiction and non-fiction and was one of the leading writers of detective fiction in the "Golden Age". The Charing Cross Mystery is one of his most well known.

# THE
# CHARING CROSS
# MYSTERY

# THE LAST TRAIN EAST

Hetherwick had dined that evening with friends who lived in Cadogan Gardens, and had stayed so late in conversation with his host that midnight had come before he left and set out for his bachelor chambers in the Temple; it was, indeed, by the fraction of a second that he caught the last east-bound train at Sloane Square. The train was almost destitute of passengers; the car which he himself entered, a first-class smoking compartment, was otherwise empty; no one came into it when the train reached Victoria. But at St. James's Park two men got in, and seated themselves opposite to Hetherwick.

Now Hetherwick was a young barrister, going in for criminal practice, in whom the observant faculty was deeply implanted; it was natural to him to watch and to speculate on anything he saw. Because of this, and perhaps because he had just then nothing else to think about, he sat observing the newcomers; he found interest, amusement, and not a little profit in this sort of thing, and in trying to decide whether a given man was this, that, or something else.

Of the two men thus under inspection, the elder was a big, burly, fresh-coloured man of apparently sixty to sixty-five years of age. His closely cropped silvery hair, his smartly trained grey moustache, his keen blue eyes and generally alert and vivacious appearance, made Hetherwick think that he was or had been in some way or other connected with the army; this impression was heightened by an erect carriage, square-set shoulders and something that suggested a long and close acquaintance with the methods of the drill-yard and the parade ground. Perhaps, thought Hetherwick, he was a retired non-commissioned officer, a regimental sergeant-major, or something of that sort; this idea, again, was strengthened by the fact that the man carried a handsome walking-cane, the head of which, either of gold or of silver-gilt, was fashioned like a crown. There was something military, too, about the cut of his clothes; he was a smartly dressed man, from his silk hat, new and glossy and worn a little rakishly on the right side of his head, to his highly polished boots. A well-preserved, cheery-looking, good-humoured sort of person, this, decided Hetherwick, and apparently well satisfied with himself and full of the enjoyment of life, and likely, from all outward sight, to make old bones.

The other man came into a different category. The difference began with his clothes, which, if not exactly shabby, were semi-shabby, much worn, ill-kept and badly put on: he was evidently a careless man, who scorned a clothes-brush and was also indifferent to the very obvious fact that his linen was frayed and dirty. He was a thin, meagre man, of not one-half the respectable, well-fed bulk of his companion; his sallow-complexioned face was worn, and his beard thin and irregular: altogether he suggested some degree of poor circumstances. Yet, in Hetherwick's opinion, he was a person of something beyond ordinary mental capacity; his eyes were large and intelligent, his nose was well-shaped, his chin square and determined. And his ungloved hands were finely moulded and delicate of proportion; the fingers were long, thin and tapering. Hetherwick noticed two facts about those fingers: the first, that they were restless; the second, that they were much stained, as if the man had recently been mixing dyes or using chemicals. And then he suddenly observed that the big man's hands and fingers were similarly stained – blue and red and yellow, in patches.

These men were talking when they entered the compartment; they continued to talk as they settled down. Hetherwick could not avoid hearing what they said.

"Queerest experience I've ever had in my time!" the big man was saying as he dropped into a corner seat. "Tell you, I knew her the instant I clapped eyes on that portrait! After – how many years will it be, now? Ten, I think – yes, ten. Oh, yes! Knew her well enough. When we get to my hotel, I'll show you the portrait – I cut it out and put it aside – and you'll identify it as quick as I did – lay you aught you like on it! No mistaking that!"

This was said in a broad North Country accent, in full keeping, thought Hetherwick, with the burly frame of the speaker. But the other man replied in tones that suggested the born Londoner.

"I think I shall be able to recognise it," he said softly. "I've a very clear recollection of the lady, though, to be sure, I only saw her once or twice."

"Aye, well, a fine-looking woman – and a beauty! – like that's not soon forgotten," declared the other. "And nowadays the years don't seem to make much difference to a woman's age. Anyway, I knew her! – 'That's you, my fine madam,' says I to myself, as soon as ever I unfolded that paper. But, mind you, I kept it to myself! Not a word to my granddaughter, though she was sitting opposite to me when I made the discovery. No – not to anybody! – till tonight. Not the sort of thing to blab about – that!"

"Just so," said the smaller man. "Of course, you'd remember that I was likely to have some recollection of her and of the circumstances.

Odd! – very. And I suppose the next thing is – what are you going to do about it?"

"Oh, well!" replied the big man. "Of course, ten years have elapsed. But as to that, it wouldn't matter, you know, if twenty years had slipped by. Still—"

At that point he sank his voice to the least of a whisper, bending over to his companion, and Hetherwick heard no more. But it seemed to him that the little man, although he appeared to be listening intently, was, in reality, doing nothing of the sort. His long, stained fingers became more restless than ever; twice, before the train came to Westminster, he pulled out his watch and glanced at it; once, after that, Hetherwick caught the nervous hand again shaking towards the waistcoat pocket. And he got an idea that the man was regarding his big, garrulous companion with curiously furtive glances, as if he were waiting for some vague, yet expected thing, and wondering when it would materialise: there was a covert watchfulness about him, and though he nodded his head from time to time as if in assent to what was being whispered to him, Hetherwick became convinced that he was either abstracted in thought or taking no interest. If eyes and fingers were to be taken as indications, the man's thoughts were elsewhere.

The train pulled up at Westminster, lingered its half-minute, moved onward again; the big man, still bending down to his companion, went on whispering; now and then, as if he were telling a good story or making a clever point, he chuckled. But suddenly, and without any warning, he paused, coming to a dead, sharp-cut stop in an apparently easy flow of language. He stared wildly around him: Hetherwick caught the flash of his eye as it swept the compartment, and never forgot the look of frightened amazement that he saw in it; it was as if the man had been caught, with lightning-like swiftness, face to face with some awful thing. His left hand shut up, clutching at his breast and throat; the other, releasing the gold-headed cane, shot out as if to ward off a blow. It dropped like lead at his side; the other arm relaxed and fell, limp and nerveless, and before Hetherwick could move, the big, burly figure sank back in its corner and the eyes closed.

Hetherwick jumped from his seat, shouting to the other man.

"Your friend!" he cried. "Look!"

But the other man was looking. He, too, had got to his feet, and he was bending down and stretching out a hand to the big man's wrist. He muttered something that Hetherwick failed to catch.

"What do you say?" demanded Hetherwick impatiently. "Good heavens! – we must do something! The man's – what is it? A seizure?"

"A seizure!" answered the other. "Yes – that's it – a seizure! He'd had one – slight giddiness – just before we got in. A – the train's stopping, though. Charing Cross? I – I know a doctor close by."

The train was already pulling up. Hetherwick flung open the dividing door between his compartment and the next – he had seen the conductor down there and he beckoned to him.

"Quick!" he called. "Here! – there's a man ill – dying, I think! Come here!"

The conductor came – slowly. But when he saw the man in the corner, he made for the outer door and beckoned to men on the platform. A uniformed official ran up and got in.

"What is it?" he asked. "Gentleman in a fit? Who's with him? Anybody?"

Hetherwick looked round for the man with the stained fingers. But he was already out of the carriage and on the platform and making for the stairs that led to the exit. He flung back a few words, pointing upward at the same time.

"Doctor! – close by!" he shouted. "Back in five minutes! – get him out."

But already there was a doctor at hand. Before the man with the stained fingers had fairly vanished, other men had come in from the adjoining compartments; one pushed his way to the front.

"I am a medical man," he said curtly. "Make way, please."

The other men stood silently watching while the newcomer made a hasty examination of the still figure. He turned sharply.

"This man's dead!" he said in quick, matter-of-fact tones. "Is anyone with him?"

The train officials glanced at Hetherwick. But Hetherwick shook his head.

"I don't know him," he answered. "There was another man with him – they got in together at St. James's Park. You saw the other man," he continued, turning to the conductor. "He jumped out as you came in here, and ran up the stairs, saying that he was going for some doctor, close by."

"I saw him – heard him, too," assented the conductor. He glanced at the stairs and the exit beyond. "But he ain't come back," he added.

"You had better get the man out," said the doctor. "Bring him over to some place on the platform."

A station policeman had come up by that time; he and the railwaymen lifted the dead man and carried him across the platform to a waiting-room. Hetherwick, feeling that he would be wanted, followed in the rear, the doctor with him. It struck Hetherwick with grim irony that as soon as they were off it, the train went on, as if careless and indifferent.

"Good heavens!" he muttered, more to himself than to the man at his side. "That poor fellow was alive, and, as far as I could see, in the very best of health and spirits, five minutes ago!"

"No doubt!" observed the doctor dryly. "But he's dead now. What happened?"

Hetherwick told him briefly.

"And the other man's – gone!" remarked the doctor. "Um! But I suppose nobody thought of detaining him. Now – if he doesn't come back – eh?"

"You don't suspect foul play?" exclaimed Hetherwick.

"The circumstances are odd," said his companion. "I should say the man just died! Died as suddenly as man can die – as if he'd been shot dead or literally blown to fragments. That's from what you tell me, you know. And it may be – a case of poisoning. Will that other man come back? If not—"

By that time Hetherwick was beginning to wonder if the other man would come back. He had not come at the end of ten minutes; nor of fifteen; nor of thirty. But other men had come, hurrying into the drab-walled waiting-room and gathering about the table on which the dead man had been laid. They were mostly officials and police, and presently a police surgeon arrived and with him a police inspector, one Matherfield, who knew Hetherwick. While the two doctors made another examination, this man drew Hetherwick aside. Hetherwick retold his story; this time with full details. Matherfield listened and shook his head.

"That second man won't come back!" he said. "Gone half an hour now. Do you think he knew the man was dead before he cleared out?"

"I can't say," replied Hetherwick. "The whole thing was so quick that it was all over before I could realise what was happening. I certainly saw the other man give the dead man a quick, close inspection. Then he literally jumped for the door – he was out of it and running up the stairs before the train had come to a definite stop."

"You can describe him, Mr. Hetherwick?" suggested the inspector.

"Describe him? – yes. And identify him, too," asserted Hetherwick. "He was a man of certain notable features. I should know him again, anywhere."

"Well, we'll have to look for him," said Matherfield. "And now we'll have to take this dead man to the mortuary and have a thorough examination and see what he's got on him. You'd better come, Mr. Hetherwick – in fact, I shall want you."

Hetherwick went – in the tail of a sombre procession, himself and the two medical men walking together. He had to tell his tale again, to the police surgeon; that functionary, like all the rest who had heard the story, shook his head ominously over the disappearance of the sallow-faced man.

"All an excuse, that," he said. "There's no doctor close by. You didn't get any idea – from their conversation, I mean – of the dead man's identity? Any name mentioned?"

"I heard no name mentioned," answered Hetherwick. "They didn't address each other by name. I've no idea who the man is."

That was what he wanted to know. Somewhere, of course, this dead man had friends. He had spoken of his hotel – there, perhaps, somebody was awaiting his coming; somebody to whom the news of his death would come as a great shock, perhaps, and terrible trouble. And he waited with a feeling that was little short of personal anxiety while the police searched the dead man's pockets.

The various articles which were presently laid out on a side-table were many. There was a purse, well stocked with money; there was loose money in the pockets. There was a handsome gold watch and a heavy chain and locket. There was a pocket-book, stuffed with letters and papers. And there were all the things that a well-provided man carries – a cigar-case, a silver matchbox, a silver pencil-case, a pen-knife, and so on; clearly, the dead man had been in comfortable circumstances. But the articles of value were brushed aside by the inspector; his immediate concern was with the contents of the pocket-book, from which he hastened to take out the letters. A second later he turned to Hetherwick and the two doctors, nodding his head sidewise at the still figure on the table.

"This'll be the name and address," he said, pointing to the envelopes in his hand. "Mr. Robert Hannaford, Malter's Private Hotel, Surrey Street, Strand. Several letters, you see, addressed there, and all of recent date. We'll have to go there – there may be his wife and people of his there. Wonder who he was? – somebody from the provinces, most likely. Well—"

He laid down the letters and picked up the watch – a fine gold-cased hunter – and released the back. Within that was an inscription, engraved in delicate lettering. The inspector let out an exclamation.

"Ah!" he said. "I half suspected that from his appearance. One of ourselves! Look at this – *'Presented to Superintendent Robert Hannaford, on his retirement, by the Magistrates of Sellithwaite.'* Sellithwaite, eh? – where's that, now?"

"Yorkshire," replied one of the men standing close by. "South-West Riding."

Matherfield closed the watch and laid it by.

"Well," he remarked, "that's evidently who he is – ex-Superintendent Hannaford, of Sellithwaite, Yorkshire, stopping at Malter's Hotel. I'll have to go round there. Mr. Hetherwick, as you were the last man to see him alive, I wish you'd go with me – it's on your way to the Temple."

Something closely corresponding to curiosity, not morbid, but compelling, made Hetherwick accede to this request. Presently he and Matherfield walked along the Embankment together, talking of what had just happened and speculating on the cause of Hannaford's sudden death.

"We may know the exact reason by noon," remarked Matherfield. "There'll be a post-mortem, of course. But that other man! – we may get to know something about him here. And I wonder whom we shall find here? Hope it's not his wife...."

# WHOSE PORTRAIT IS THIS?

Malter himself opened the door of his small private hotel; a quiet, reserved man who looked like a retired butler. He was the sort of man who is slow of speech, and he had not replied to Matherfield's guarded inquiry about Mr. Robert Hannaford when a door in the little hall opened, and a girl appeared, who, hearing the inspector's question, immediately came forward as if in answer.

Hetherwick recognised this girl. He had seen her only the previous afternoon in Fountain Court, in company with a man whom he knew slightly – Kenthwaite, a fellow-barrister. Kenthwaite, evidently, was doing the honours – showing her round the Temple; Hetherwick, in fact, in passing them, had overheard Kenthwaite telling his companion something of the history of the old houses and courts around them. And the girl had attracted him then. She was a pretty girl, tall, slim, graceful, and in addition to her undoubted charm of face and figure, she looked to have more than an average share of character and intelligence, and was listening to her guide with obvious interest and appreciation. Hetherwick had set her down as being, perhaps, a country cousin of Kenthwaite's, visiting London, maybe, for the first time. Anyhow, in merely passing her and Kenthwaite he had noticed her so closely that he now recognised her at once; he saw, too, that she recognised him. But there was another matter more pressing than that – and she had gone straight to it.

"Are these gentlemen asking for my grandfather?" she inquired, coming still nearer and glancing from the hotel proprietor to the two callers. "He's not come in—"

Hetherwick was glad to hear that the dead man was the girl's grandfather. Certainly it was a close relationship, but, after all, not so close as it might have been. And he was conscious that the inspector was relieved, too. –

"We're asking about Mr. Robert Hannaford," he said. "Is he your grandfather – ex-Superintendent Hannaford, of Sellithwaite? Just so – well, I'm very sorry to bring bad news about him—"

7

He broke off, watching the girl keenly, as if he wanted to make sure that she would take the news quietly. And evidently reassured on that point, he suddenly went on definitely:

"You'll understand?" he said. "It's – well, the worst news. The fact is –"

"Is my grandfather dead?" interrupted the girl. "If that's it, please say so – I shan't faint, or anything of that sort. But – I want to know!"

"I'm sorry to say he is dead," replied Matherfield. "He died suddenly in the train at Charing Cross. A seizure, no doubt. Was he well when you saw him last?"

The girl turned to the hotel proprietor, who was standing by, evidently amazed.

"Never saw a gentleman look better or seem better in my life than he did when he went out of that door at half-past six o'clock!" he exclaimed. "Best of health and spirits!"

"My grandfather was quite well," said the girl quietly. "I never remember him being anything else but well – he was a very strong, vigorous man. Will you please tell me all about it?"

Matherfield told all about it, turning now and then to Hetherwick for corroboration. In the end he put a question.

"This man that Mr. Hetherwick saw in your grandfather's company?" he suggested. "Do you recognise anyone from that description?"

"No! – no one," answered the girl. "But my grandfather knew people in London whom I don't know. He has been going about a good deal since we came here, three days ago – looking out for a house."

"Well, we shall have to find that man," remarked Matherfield. "Of course, if you'd recognised the description as that of somebody known to you—"

"No," she said again. "I know nobody like that. But now – do you wish me to go with you – to him?"

"It's not necessary – I wouldn't tonight, if I were you," replied Matherfield. "I'll call again in the morning. Meanwhile, leave matters to us and the doctors. You've friends in London, I suppose?"

"Yes, we have friends – relations, in fact," said the girl. "I must let them know at once."

Matherfield nodded and turned to the door. But Hetherwick lingered. He and the girl were looking at each other. He suddenly spoke.

"I saw you this afternoon," he said, "in Fountain Court, with a man whom I know slightly, Mr. Kenthwaite. Is he, by any chance, one of the relations you mentioned just now? Because, if so, he lives close by me. I can tell him, if you wish."

"No," she answered, "not a relative. We know him. You might tell him, if you please, and if it's no trouble."

"No trouble at all," said Hetherwick. "And – if I may – I hope you'll let me call in the morning to hear if there's anything I can do for you?"

The girl gave him a quick, responsive glance.

That's very kind of you," she said. "Yes."

Hetherwick and the police inspector left the little hotel and walked up the street. Matherfield seemed to be in a brown study. Somewhere up in the Strand and farther away down Fleet Street the clocks began striking.

"Seems to me," exclaimed Matherfield suddenly, "seems to me, Mr. Hetherwick, this is – murder!"

"You mean poison?" said Hetherwick.

"Likely! Why, yes, of course, it would be poison. We must have that man! You can't add to your description of him?"

"You've already got everything that I can tell. Pretty full and accurate, too. I should say you oughtn't to have much difficulty in laying hands on him – from my description."

Matherfield made a sound that was half a laugh and half a groan.

"Lord bless you!" he said. "It's like seeking a needle in a bundle of hay, searching for a given man in London! I mean, of course, sometimes. More often than not, in fact. Here's this chap rushes up the stairs at Charing Cross, vanishes – where? One man amongst seven millions of men and women! However—"

Then they parted, and Hetherwick, full of thought, went home to his chambers and to bed, and lay equally thoughtful for a long time before he went to sleep. He made a poor night of it, but soon after eight o'clock he was in Kenthwaite's chambers. Kenthwaite was dressing and breakfasting at the same time – a ready-packed brief bag and an open time-table suggested that he was in a hurry to catch a train. But he suspended his operations to stare, open-mouthed, wide-eyed at Hetherwick's news.

"Hannaford! – dead!" he exclaimed. "Great Scott! – why, he was as fit as a fiddle at noon yesterday, Hetherwick! He and his grand daughter called on me, and I took 'em to lunch – I come from Sellithwaite, you know, so of course I knew them. Hannaford had to go as soon as we'd lunched – some appointment – so I showed the girl round a bit. Nice girl, that – clever. Name of Rhona. Worth cultivating. And the old man's dead! Bless me!"

"I don't think there's much doubt about foul play," observed Hetherwick.

"Looks uncommonly like it," said Kenthwaite. He went on with his double task. "Well," he added, "sorry, but I can't be of any use to Miss Hannaford today – got to go down to a beastly Quarter Sessions case, my boy, and precious little time to catch my train. But tomorrow – perhaps you can give 'em a hand this morning?"

"Yes," answered Hetherwick. "I'm doing nothing. I'll go round there after a while. I'm interested naturally. It's a queer case."

"Queer! Seems so, rather," assented Kenthwaite. "Well – give Miss Hannaford my sympathy and all that, and tell her that if there's anything I can do when I get back – you know what to say."

"She said she'd relations here in London," remarked Hetherwick.

"Cousins – aunts – something or other – over Tooting way, I think," agreed Kenthwaite. "Twenty past eight! – Hetherwick, I'll have to rush for it!"

He swallowed the last of his coffee, seized the bag and darted away; Hetherwick went back to his own chambers and breakfasted leisurely. And all the time he sat there he was pondering over the event of the previous midnight, and especially upon the sudden disappearance of the man with the stained fingers. To Hetherwick that disappearance seemed to argue guilt. He figured it in this way – the man who ran away at Charing Cross had poisoned this other man in some clever and subtle fashion, by means of something which took a certain time to take effect, and, when that time arrived, did its work with amazing swiftness. Hetherwick, in his war service, had seen men die more times than he cared to remember. He had seen some men shot through the brain; he had seen others shot through the heart. But he had never seen any of these men – some of them shot at his very side – die with the extraordinary quickness with which Hannaford had died. And he came to a conclusion: if the man with the stained fingers had poisoned Hannaford, then he was somebody who had a rare and a profound knowledge of poisons.

He went round to Surrey Street at ten o'clock. Miss Hannaford, said the hotel proprietor, had gone with her aunt, a Mrs. Keeley, who had come early that morning, to see her grandfather's dead body – some police official had fetched them. But she had left a message for anyone who called – that she would not be long away. And Hetherwick waited in the little dingy coffee-room; there were certain questions that he wanted to put to Rhona Hannaford, also he wanted to give her certain information.

"Very sad case this, sir," observed the hotel proprietor, hovering about his breakfast-tables. "Cruel end for a fine healthy gentleman like Mr. Hannaford!"

"Very sad," agreed Hetherwick. "You said last night – or, rather, this morning – that Mr. Hannaford was in good health and spirits when he went out early in the evening?"

"The best, sir! He was a cheery, affable gentleman – fond of his joke. Joked and laughed with me as I opened the door for him – never thinking, sir, as I should never see him again alive!"

"You don't know where he was going?"

"I don't, sir. And his granddaughter – clever young lady, that, sir – she don't know, neither. She went to a theatre, along with her aunt, the lady that came early this morning. We wired the bad news to her first thing, and she came along at once. But him – no, I don't know where he went to spend his evening. Been in and out, and mostly out, ever since they were here, three days ago. House-hunting, so I understood."

Rhona Hannaford presently returned, in company with a motherly-looking woman whom she introduced as her aunt, Mrs. Keeley. Then Hetherwick remembered that he had not introduced himself; rectifying that omission, he found that Kenthwaite had told Rhona who he was when he passed them the previous afternoon. He delivered Kenthwaite's message and in his absence offered his own services.

"It's very good of you," said Rhona. "I don't know that there's anything to do. The police seem to be doing everything – the inspector who was here last night was very kind just now, but, as he said, there's nothing to be done until after the inquest."

"Yes," said Hetherwick. "And that is – did he say when?"

"Tomorrow morning. He said I should have to go," replied Rhona.

"So shall I," observed Hetherwick. "They'll only want formal evidence from you. I shall have to say more. I wish I could say more than I shall have to say."

The two women glanced at him inquiringly.

"I mean," he continued, "that I wish I had stopped the other man from leaving the train. I suppose you have not heard anything from the police about him – that man?"

"Nothing. They had not found him or heard of him up to just now. But you can tell me something that I very much want to know. You saw this man with my grandfather for some little time, didn't you?"

"From St. James's Park to Charing Cross."

"Did you overhear their conversation, or any of it?"

"A good deal – at first. Afterwards, your grandfather began to whisper, and I heard nothing of that. But one reason I had for calling upon you this morning was that I might tell you what I did overhear, and another that I might ask you some questions arising out of what I heard. Mr. Hannaford was talking to this man, now missing, about some portrait or photograph. Evidently it was of a lady whom he, your grandfather, had known ten years ago; whom the other man had also known. Your grandfather said that when they got to his hotel he would show the portrait to the other man who, he asserted, would be sure to recognise it. Now, had Mr. Hannaford said anything to you? Do you know anything about his bringing any friend of his to this hotel last night? And do you know anything about any portrait or photograph such as that to which he referred?"

"About bringing anyone here – no! He never said anything to me about it. But about a photograph, or rather about a print of one – yes. I do know something about that."

"What?" asked Hetherwick eagerly.

"Well, this," she answered. "My grandfather, who, as I dare say you know by this time, was for a good many years Superintendent of Police at Sellithwaite, had a habit of cutting things out of newspapers – paragraphs, accounts of criminal trials, and so on. He had several boxes full of such cuttings. When we were coming to town the other day I saw him cut a photograph out of some illustrated paper he was reading in the train, and put it away in his pocket-book – in a pocket-book, I ought to say, for he had two or three pocket-books. This morning I was looking through various things which he had left lying about on his dressing-table upstairs, and in one of his pocket-books I found the photograph which he cut out in the train. That must be the one you mention – it's of a very handsome, distinguished-looking woman."

"If I may see it—" suggested Hetherwick.

Within a couple of minutes he had the cutting in his hand – a scrap of paper, neatly snipped out of its surrounding letterpress, which was a print of a photograph of a woman of apparently thirty-five to forty years of age, evidently of high position, and certainly, as Rhona Hannaford had remarked, of handsome and distinguished features. But it was not at the photograph that Hetherwick gazed with eyes into which surmise and speculation were beginning to steal; after a mere glance at it, his attention fixed itself on some pencilled words on the margin at its sides:

*"Through my hands ten years ago!"*

"Is that your grandfather's writing?" he inquired suddenly.

"Yes, that's his," replied Rhona. "He had a habit of pencilling notes and comments on his cuttings – all sorts of remarks."

"He didn't mention this particular cutting to you when he cut it out?"

"No – he said nothing about it. I saw him cut it out, and heard him chuckle as he put it away, but he said – nothing."

"You don't know who this lady is?"

"Oh, no! You see, there's no name beneath it. I suppose there was in the paper, but he cut out nothing but the picture and the bit of margin. But from what he's written there, I conclude that this is a portrait of some woman who had been in trouble with the police at some time or other."

"Obvious!" muttered Hetherwick. He sat silently inspecting the picture for a minute or two.

"Look here," he said suddenly, "I want you to let me help in trying to get to the bottom of this – naturally you want to have it cleared up. And to begin with, let me have this cutting, and for the present don't tell anyone – I mean the police or any inquirers – that I have it. I'd like to have a talk about it to Kenthwaite. You understand? As I was present at your grandfather's death, I'd like to solve the mystery of it. If you'll leave this to me—"

"Oh, yes!" replied Rhona. "But – you think there has been foul play? – that he didn't die a natural death? – that it wasn't just heart failure or —"

The door of the little coffee-room was opened and Matherfield looked in. Seeing Hetherwick there, he beckoned him into the hall, closing the door again as the young barrister joined him. Hetherwick saw that he was full of news, and instantly thought of the man with the stained fingers.

"Well?" he said eagerly, "laid your hands on that fellow?"

"Oh, him? – no!" answered Matherfield. "Not a word or sign of him – so far! But the doctors have finished their post-mortem. And there's no doubt about their verdict. Poisoned!"

Matherfield sank his voice to a whisper as he spoke the last word. And Hetherwick, ready though he was for the news, started when he got it – the definiteness of the announcement seemed like opening a window upon a vista of obscured and misty distances. He glanced at the door behind him.

"Of course, they'll have to be told, in there," said Matherfield, interpreting his thoughts. "But the thing's certain. Our surgeon suspected it from the first, and he got a Home Office specialist to help at the autopsy – they say the man was poisoned by some drug or other – I don't understand these things – that had been administered to him two or three hours before he died, and that when it did work, worked with absolutely lightning-like effect."

"Yes," muttered Hetherwick thoughtfully. "Lightning-like effect – good phrase. I can testify that it did that!"

Matherfield laid a hand on the door.

"Well," he said, "I'd better tell these ladies. Then – there are things I want to know from the granddaughter. I've seen her – and her aunt – before this morning. I found out that Hannaford brought up and educated this girl, and that she lived with him in Sellithwaite since she left school, so she'll know more about him than anybody. And I want to learn all I can. Come in with me."

# THE POTENTIAL FORTUNE

Elder and younger woman alike took Matherfield's intimation quietly. Rhona made no remark. But Mrs. Keeley spoke impulsively.

"There never was a more popular man than he was – with everybody!" she exclaimed. "Who should want to take his life?"

"That's just what we've got to find out, ma'am," said Matherfield. "And I want to know as much as I can – I dare say Miss Hannaford can tell me a lot. Now, let's see what we do know from what you told me this morning. Mr. Hannaford had been Superintendent of Police at Sellithwaite for some years. He had recently retired on his pension. He proposed to live in London, and you and he, Miss Hannaford, came to London to look for a suitable house, arrived three days ago, and put up at this hotel. That's all correct? Very good – now then, let me hear all about his movements during the last three days. What did he do? Where did he spend his time?"

"I can't tell you much," answered Rhona. "He was out most of the day, and generally by himself. I was only out with him twice – once when we went to do some shopping, another time when we called on Mr. Kenthwaite at his rooms in the Temple. I understood he was looking for a house – seeing house agents and so on. He was out morning, afternoon and evening."

"Did he never tell you anything about where he'd been, or whom he'd seen?"

"No. He was the sort of man who keeps things to himself. I have no idea where he went nor whom he saw."

"Didn't say anything about where he was going last night?"

"No. He only said that he was going out and that I should find him here when I got back from the theatre, to which I was going with Mrs. Keeley. We got back here soon after eleven. But he hadn't come in – as you know."

"You never heard him speak of having enemies?"

"I should think he hadn't an enemy in the world! He was a very kind man and very popular, even with the people he had to deal with as a police-superintendent."

"And I suppose he'd no financial worries – anything of that sort? Nor any other troubles – nothing to bother him?"

"I don't think he'd a care in the world," said Rhona confidently. "He was looking forward with real zest to settling down in London. And as to financial worries, he'd none. He was well off."

"Always a saving, careful man," remarked Mrs. Keeley. "Oh, yes, quite well off – apart from his pension."

Matherfield glanced at Hetherwick, who had listened carefully to all that was asked and answered. Something in the glance seemed to invite him to take a hand.

"This occurs to me," said Hetherwick. He turned to Rhona. "Apart from this house-hunting, do you know whether your grandfather had any business affairs in hand in London? What I'm thinking of is this – from what I saw of him in the train, he appeared to be an active, energetic man, not the sort of man who, because he'd retired, would sit down in absolute idleness. Do you know of anything that he thought of undertaking – any business he thought of joining?"

Rhona considered this question for a while.

"Not any business," she replied at last. "But there is something that may have to do with what you suggest. My grandfather had a hobby. He experimented in his spare time."

"What in?" asked Hetherwick. Then he suddenly remembered the stained fingers that he had noticed on the hands of both men the night before. "Was it chemicals?" he added quickly.

"Yes, in chemicals," she answered with a look of surprise. "How did you know that?"

"I noticed that his hands and fingers were stained," replied Hetherwick. "So were those of the man he was with. Well – but this something?"

"He had a little laboratory in our garden at Sellithwaite," she continued. "He spent all his spare time in it – he'd done that for years. Lately, I know, he'd been trying to invent or discover something – I don't know what. But just before we left Sellithwaite, he told me that he'd solved the problem, and when he was sorting out and packing up his papers he showed me a sealed envelope in which he said were the particulars of his big discovery – he said there was a potential fortune in it and that he should die a rich man. I saw him put that envelope in a pocket-book which he always carried with him."

"That would be the pocket-book I examined last night," said Matherfield. "There was no sealed envelope, nor one of which any seal had been broken, in that. There was nothing but letters, receipts and unimportant papers."

"It is not in his other pocket-books," declared Rhona. "I went through all his things myself very early this morning – through everything that he had here. I know that he had that envelope yesterday

15

– he pulled out some things from his pocket when we were lunching with Mr. Kenthwaite in a restaurant in Fleet Street, and I saw the envelope. It was a stout, square envelope, across the front of which he had drawn two thick red lines, and it was heavily sealed with black sealing-wax at the back."

"That was yesterday, you say?" asked Matherfield sharply. "Yesterday noon? Just so! Then as he had it yesterday at noon, and as it wasn't in his pockets last night and is not among his effects in this house, it's very clear that between, say, two o'clock yesterday and midnight he parted with it. Now then, to whom? That's a thing we've just got to find out! But you're sure he wasn't joking when he told you that this discovery, or invention, or whatever it was, was worth a potential fortune?"

"On the contrary, he was very serious," replied Rhona. "Unusually serious for him. He wouldn't tell me what it was, nor give me any particulars – all he said was that he'd solved a problem and hit on a discovery that he'd worked over for years, and that the secret was in that envelope and worth no end of money. I asked him what he meant by no end of money and he said: 'Well, at any rate, a hundred thousand pounds – in time.'"

The two men exchanged glances; silence fell on the whole group.

"Oh!" said Matherfield at last. "A secret worth a hundred thousand pounds – in time. This will have to be looked into – narrowly. What do you think, Mr. Hetherwick?"

"Yes," answered Hetherwick. "You've no idea, of course, as to whether your grandfather had done anything about putting this discovery on the market – or made any arrangement about selling it? No! Well, can you tell me this: What sort of house did your grandfather want to rent here in London? I mean, do you know what rent he was prepared to pay?"

"I can answer that," remarked Mrs. Keeley. "He told me he wanted a good house – a real good one – in a convenient suburb, and he was willing to go up to three hundred a year."

"Three hundred a year," said Hetherwick. He exchanged a meaning glance with Matherfield. "That," he added, "looks as if he felt assured of a considerable income, and as though he had already realised on his discovery or was very certain of doing so."

"To be sure," agreed Matherfield. "Of course, I don't know what his private means were, but I know what his retiring pension would be – and three hundred a year for rent alone means – a good deal! Um! – we'll have to endeavour to trace that sealed envelope."

"It seems to me, Matherfield," observed Hetherwick, "that the first thing to do is to trace Hannaford's movements last night, from the time he left this hotel until his death in the train."

"We're at that already," replied Matherfield. "We've a small army of men at work. But as we want all the help we can get, I'm going to stir up the newspaper men, Mr. Hetherwick – the Press, sir, is always valuable in this sort of thing! – and I want Miss Hannaford, if she's got one, to give me a recent photograph of her grandfather so that it can appear in the papers. Somebody, you know, may recognise it – somebody who saw him last night with somebody else."

Rhona had a new photograph of the dead man, taken in plain clothes just before he left Sellithwaite, and she gave Matherfield some copies of it. Reproductions appeared in the *Meteor* and other evening papers that night, and in some of the dailies next morning. And, as a result, a man came forward at the inquest, a few hours later, who declared with positive assurance that he had seen Hannaford early in the evening of the murder. His appearance was the only sensational thing about these necessarily only preliminary proceedings before the coroner; until he stepped forward nothing had transpired with which Hetherwick was not already familiar. There had been his own evidence; somewhat to his surprise neither coroner nor police seemed to pay much attention to his account of the conversation about the woman's portrait; they appeared to regard Hannaford's observations as a bit of garrulous reminiscence about some criminal or other. There had been Rhona's – a repetition of what she had told Matherfield and Hetherwick at Malter's Hotel: police and coroner evidently fixed on the missing sealed envelope and its mysterious secret as a highly important factor in the case. Then there had been the expert testimony of the two doctors as to the cause of death – that had been confined to positive declarations that Hannaford died from the administration of some subtle poison, the exact details being left over until experts could tell more at the adjourned proceedings. And the coroner was about to adjourn for a fortnight when a man, who had entered the court and been in conversation with the officials, was put into the witness-box to tell a story which certainly added information and, at the same time, accentuated mystery.

This man was a highly-respectable person in appearance, middle-aged, giving the name of Martin Charles Ledbitter, manager of an insurance office in Westminster, and residing at Sutton, in Surrey. It was his habit, he said, to travel every evening from Victoria to Sutton by the 7.20 train. As a rule he arrived at Victoria just before seven and took a cup of tea in the refreshment-room. He did this on the night before last. While he was drinking his tea at the counter, an elderly man came in and stood by him, whom he was sure beyond doubt was the same man whose photograph was reproduced in some of last night's and some of this morning's newspapers. He had no doubt whatever about this. He first noticed the man's stained fingers as he took up the glass of whisky-and-soda which he had ordered; he had, at the time, wondered at the contrast between those fingers and the general spick-and-spanness of the man and his smart attire; also he had noticed his gold-headed walking-cane and that the head was fashioned like a crown. They stood side by side for some minutes, then the man went out. A minute or two later he saw him again – this time at the right-hand side bookstall; he was there obviously looking out for somebody.

This was the point where the interest really began; everybody in court strained eyes and ears as the coroner put a direct question.

"Looking out for somebody? Did you see him meet anybody?"

"I did!"

"Tell me what you saw."

"I saw this. When I approached the bookstall, to buy some evening papers, the man whom I had seen in the refreshment-room was standing close by. He was looking about him, but chiefly at the entrances to the big space between the offices and the platforms. Once or twice he looked at his watch. It was then – by the station clock – about ten minutes past seven. He seemed impatient; he moved restlessly about. I passed him and went to the bookstall. When I turned round again he was standing a few yards away, shaking hands with another man. From the way in which they shook hands, I concluded that they were old friends, who perhaps had not seen each other for some time."

"Their greeting was cordial?"

"I should call it effusive."

"Can you describe the other man?"

"I can describe a sort of general impression of both. He was a tall man, taller than Hannaford, but not so broadly built. He wore a dark ulster overcoat, with a strap at the back; it was either a very dark blue or a black in colour. He had a silk hat – new and glossy. He gave me the impression of being a smartly-dressed man – smart boots and gloves and that sort of thing – you know the general impression you get at a quick glance. But as to his features, I can't tell you anything."

"Why not?" asked the coroner.

"Because, to begin with, he wore an unusually large pair of blue spectacles, which completely veiled his eyes, and to end with, his throat and chin were swathed in a heavy white muffler, which covered the lower part of his face as well. Between the rim of his hat and the collar of his coat it was all muffler and spectacles!"

The coroner looked disappointed. His interest in the witness seemed to evaporate.

"Did you notice anything else?" he asked.

"Only that the newcomer took Hannaford's arm and that they walked away towards the left-hand entrance hall, evidently in earnest conversation. That was the last I saw of them."

"There's just one question I should like to put to you in conclusion," said the coroner. "You say that you are confident that the photograph in the newspapers is that of the man you saw at Victoria. Now, have you seen the dead man's body?"

"I have. The police took me to see it when I volunteered my evidence."

"And you recognised it as that of the man you saw?"

"Without doubt! There is no question of that in my mind."

Five minutes later the inquest stood adjourned, and those chiefly concerned gathered together in the emptying court to discuss the voluntary witness's evidence. Matherfield manifested an almost cheerful optimism.

"This is better! – much better," he declared, rubbing his hands as if in anticipation of laying them on something. "We know now that Hannaford met, at any rate, two men that night. It's easier to find two men than one!"

Rhona, whom Hetherwick had escorted to the coroner's court, looked at him in astonishment. "How can that be?" she asked.

"Mr. Hetherwick understands," answered Matherfield with a laugh. "He'll tell you."

But Hetherwick said nothing. He was always wondering – always wondering – about the woman whose picture lay in his pocket.

# THE DIAMOND NECKLACE

The conviction that there was more than met the eye in Hannaford's cutting out and putting away the handsome and distinguished woman's photograph grew mightily in Hetherwick's mind during the next few days. He recalled all that Hannaford had said about it in the train in those few short minutes before his sudden death. Why had he been so keen about showing it to the other man? Was he taking the other man specially to his hotel to show it to him – at that time of night? Why did the recollections which his possession of it brought up afford him – obviously – so much interest and, it seemed, amusement? And what, exactly, was meant by the pencilled words in the margin of the cutting? – *Through my hands ten years ago*! Under what circumstances had this woman been through Hannaford's hands? And who was she? The more he thought of it, the more Hetherwick was convinced that there was more importance in this matter than the police attached to it. They had proved utterly indifferent to Hetherwick's account of the conversation in the train – that, said Matherfield, with official superiority, was nothing but a bit of chat, reminiscence, recollection, on the ex-superintendent's part; old men, he said, were fond of talking about incidents of the past. The only significance Matherfield saw in it was that it seemed to argue that whoever the man who had disappeared was, he and Hannaford had known each other ten years ago.

At the end of a week the police had heard nothing of this man. Nor had they made any discovery in respect of the other man whom Ledbitter swore he had seen with Hannaford at Victoria. The best Scotland Yard hands had been hard and continuously at work, and had brought nothing to light. Only one person had seen the first man after he darted up the stairs of Charing Cross calling out that he was going for a doctor; this was a policeman on duty at the front of the Underground Station. He had seen the man run out; had watched him run at top speed up Villiers Street, and had thought no more of it than that he was some belated passenger hurrying to catch a last bus in the Strand. But with that, all news and trace of him vanished. Of the tall man in the big blue spectacles and white muffler there never was any trace, nor any news beyond Ledbitter's. Yet Ledbitter was a thoroughly dependable witness, and there was no doubt that he had seen Hannaford in this man's company. So, without question, Hannaford, during his last few hours of life, had been with two men – neither of whom could be found. Within twenty-four hours of his death several men came forward voluntarily who had had dealings or conversation with Hannaford since his arrival in London. But there was a significant fact about the news which any of them could give – not one knew anything of the tall man seen by Ledbitter, or of the shabby man seen by Hetherwick, or of the secret which Hannaford carried in his sealed packet. The story of that sealed packet had been told plentifully in the newspapers – but nobody came forward who knew anything about it. And when a week had elapsed after the ex-Superintendent's burial, the whole mystery of his undoubted murder seemed likely to become one of the many which are never solved.

But Hetherwick was becoming absorbed in this affair into which he had been so curiously thrown head-first. He had leisure on his hands; also, he was well off in this world's goods, and much more concerned with the psychology of his profession than with a desire to earn money by its practice. From the moment in which he heard that the doctors had found that Hannaford had been poisoned, he felt that here was a murder mystery at the bottom of which he must get – it fascinated him. And all through his speculations and theorisings about it, he was obsessed by the picture in his pocket. Who was that woman – and what did the dead man remember about her?

Suddenly, one morning, after a visit from Matherfield, who looked in at his chambers casually, to tell him that the police had discovered nothing, Hetherwick put on his hat and went round to Surrey Street. He found Rhona Hannaford busy in preparing to leave Malter's Hotel: she was going to live, for a time at any rate, with Mrs. Keeley. Hetherwick went straight to the matter that had brought him.

"That print of a woman's photograph which your grandfather had in his pocket-book," he said, "and that's now in mine. Out of what paper did he cut it? – a newspaper, evidently."

"Yes, but I don't know what paper," answered Rhona. "All I know is that it was a paper which he got by post, the morning that he left Sellithwaite. We were just leaving for the station when the post came. He put his letters and papers – there were several things – in his overcoat pocket, and opened them in the train. It was somewhere on the way to London that he cut out that picture. He threw the paper away – with others. He had a habit of buying a lot of papers, and used to cut out paragraphs."

"Well – I suppose it can be traced," muttered Hetherwick, thinking aloud. He glanced at the evidences of Rhona's departure. "So you're going to live with your aunt?" he said.

"For a time – yes," she answered.

"I hope you'll let me call?" suggested Hetherwick. "I'm awfully interested in this affair, and I may be able to tell you something about it."

"We'd be pleased," she replied. "I'll give you the address. I don't intend to be idle though – unless you call in the evening, you'll probably find me out."

"What are you thinking of doing?" he asked.

"I'm thinking of going in for secretarial work," she answered. "As a matter of fact, I had a training for that, in Sellithwaite. Typewriting, correspondence, accounts, French, German – I'm pretty well equipped."

"Don't think me inquisitive," said Hetherwick, suddenly. "I hope your grandfather hasn't forgotten you in his will – I heard he'd left one!"

"Thank you," replied Rhona. "He hasn't. He left me everything. I've got about three hundred a year – rather more. But that's no reason why I should sit down, and do nothing, is it?"

"Good!" said Hetherwick. "But – if that sealed packet could be found? What was worth a hundred thousand to him, would be worth a hundred thousand to his sole legatee. Worth finding!"

"I wonder if anything will be found?" she answered. "The whole thing's a mystery that I'm not even on the edge of solving."

"Time!" said Hetherwick. "And – patience."

He went away presently, and strolled round to Brick Court, where Kenthwaite had his chambers.

"Doing anything?" he asked, as he walked in.

"Nothing," replied Kenthwaite. "Go ahead!"

Hetherwick sat down, and lighted his pipe.

"You know Sellithwaite, don't you?" he asked when he had got his tobacco well going. "Your town, eh?"

"Born and bred there, and engaged to a girl there," replied Kenthwaite. "Ought to! What about Sellithwaite?"

"Were you there ten years ago?" demanded Hetherwick.

"Ten years ago? No – except in the holidays. I was at school ten years ago. Why?"

"Do you remember any police case at Sellithwaite about that time in which a very handsome woman was concerned – probably as defendant?"

"No! But I was more interested in cricket than in crime, in those days. Are you thinking about the woman Hannaford spoke of in the train to the chap they can't come across?"

"I am! Seems to me there's more in that than the police think."

"Shouldn't wonder. Let's see: Hannaford spoke of that woman as – what?"

"Said she'd been through his hands, ten years ago."

"Well, that's easy! If she was through Hannaford's hands, as Superintendent of Police, ten years ago, that would be at Sellithwaite.

And there'll be records, particulars, and so on at Sellithwaite."

Hetherwick nodded, and smoked in silence for awhile.

"Think I shall go down there," he said at last.

Kenthwaite stared, wonderingly.

"Keen as all that!" he exclaimed.

"Queer business!" said Hetherwick. "Like to solve it."

"Oh, well, it's only a four hours' run from King's Cross," observed Kenthwaite. "Interesting town, too. Old as the hills and modern as they make 'em. Excellent hotel – 'White Bear.' And I'll tell you what, my future's brother is a solicitor there – Michael Hollis. I'll give you a letter of introduction to him, and he'll show you round and give you any help you need."

"Good man!" said Hetherwick. "Write it!"

Kenthwaite sat down and wrote, and handed over the result.

"What do you want to find out, exactly?" he asked, as Hetherwick thanked him, and rose to go.

"All about the woman, and why Hannaford cut her picture out of the paper," answered Hetherwick. "Well – see you when I get back."

He went off to his own chambers, packed a bag, and drove to King's Cross to catch the early afternoon train for the North. At half-past seven that evening he found himself in Sellithwaite, a grey, smoke-laden town set in the midst of bleak and rugged hills, where the folk – if the railway officials were anything to go by – spoke a dialect which, to Hetherwick's southern ears, sounded like some barbaric language. But the "White Bear," in which he was presently installed, yielded all the comforts and luxuries of a first-class hotel: the dining-room, into which Hetherwick turned as soon as he had booked his room, seemed to be thronged by a thoroughly cosmopolitan crowd of men; he heard most of the principal European languages being spoken – later, he found that his fellow-guests were principally Continental business men, buyers, intent on replenishing exhausted stocks from the great warehouses and manufactories of Sellithwaite. All this was interesting, nor was he destined to spend the remainder of his evening in contemplating it from a solitary corner, for he had scarcely eaten his dinner when a hall-porter came to tell him that Mr. Hollis was asking for Mr. Hetherwick.

Hetherwick hastened into the lounge, and found a keen-faced, friendly-eyed man of forty or thereabouts stretching out a hand to him.

"Kenthwaite wired me this afternoon that you were coming down, and asked me to look you up here," he said. "I'd have asked you to dine with me, but I've been kept at my office until just now, and again, I live a good many miles out of town. But tomorrow night—"

"You're awfully good," replied Hetherwick. "I'd no idea that Kenthwaite was wiring. He gave me a letter of introduction to you, but I suppose he thought I wanted to lose no time. And I don't, and I dare say you can tell me something about the object of my visit – let's find a corner and smoke."

Installed in an alcove in the big smoking-room, Hollis read Kenthwaite's letter.

"What is it you're after?" he asked. "Kenthwaite mentions that my knowledge of Sellithwaite is deeper than his own – naturally, it is, as I'm several years older."

"Well," responded Hetherwick. "It's this, briefly. You're aware, of course, of what befell your late Police-Superintendent in London – his sudden death?"

"Oh, yes – read all the newspapers, anyway," assented Hollis. "You're the man who was present in the train on the Underground, aren't you?"

"I am. And that's one reason why I'm keen on solving the mystery. There's no doubt whatever that Hannaford was poisoned – that it's a case of deliberate murder. Now, there's a feature of the case to which the police don't seem to attach any importance. I do attach great importance to it. It's the matter of the woman to whom Hannaford referred when he was talking – in my presence – to the man who so mysteriously disappeared. Hannaford spoke of that woman as having been through his hands ten years ago. That would be some experience he had here, in this town. Now then, do you know anything about it? Does it arouse any recollection?"

Hollis, who was smoking a cigar, thoughtfully tapped its long ash against the edge of his coffee-cup. Suddenly his eyes brightened.

"That's probably the Whittingham case," he said. "It was about ten years ago."

"And what was the Whittingham case?" asked Hetherwick. "Case of a woman?"

"Of a woman – evidently an adventuress – who came to Sellithwaite about ten years ago, and stayed here some little time, in this very hotel," replied Hollis. "Oddly enough, I never saw her! But she was heard of enough – eventually. She came here, to the 'White Bear,' alone, with plenty of luggage and evident funds. I understand she was a very handsome woman, twenty-eight or thirty years of age, and she was taken for somebody of consequence. I rather think she described herself as the Honourable Mrs. Whittingham. She paid her bills here with unfailing punctuality every Saturday morning. She spent a good deal of money amongst the leading tradesmen in the town, and always paid cash. In short, she established her credit very successfully. And with nobody more so than the principal jeweller here – Malladale. She bought a lot of jewellery from Malladale – but in his case, she always paid by cheque. And in the end it was through a deal with Malladale that she got into trouble."

"And into Hannaford's hands!" suggested Hetherwick.

"Into Hannaford's hands, certainly," assented Hollis. "It was this way. She had, as I said just now, made a lot of purchases from Malladale, who, I may tell you, has a first-class trade amongst our rich commercial magnates in this neighbourhood. Her transactions with him, however, were never, at first, in amounts exceeding a hundred or two. But they went through all right. She used to pay him by cheque drawn on a Manchester bank – Manchester, you know, is only thirty-five miles away. As her first cheques were always met, Malladale never bothered about making any inquiry about her financial stability; like everybody else he was very much impressed by her. Well, in the end, she'd a big deal with Malladale, Malladale had a very fine diamond necklace in stock. He and she used to discuss her acquisition of it: according to his story they had a fine old battle as to terms. Eventually, they struck a bargain – he let her have it for three thousand nine hundred pounds. She gave him a cheque for that amount there and then, and he let her carry off the necklace."

"Oh!" exclaimed Hetherwick.

"Just so!" agreed Hollis. "But – he did. However, for some reason or other, Malladale had that cheque specially cleared. She handed it to him on a Monday afternoon; first thing on Wednesday morning Malladale found that it had been returned with the ominous reference to drawer inscribed on its surface! Naturally, he hurried round to the 'White Bear.' But the Honourable Mrs. Whittingham had disappeared. She had paid up her account, taken her belongings, and left the hotel, and the town, late on the Monday evening, and all that could be discovered at the station was that she had travelled by the last train to Leeds, where, of course, there are several big main lines to all parts of England. And she had left no address: she had, indeed, told the people here that she should be back before long, and that if any letters came they were to keep them until her return. So then Malladale went to the police, and Hannaford got busy."

"I gather that he traced her?" suggested Hetherwick.

Hollis laughed sardonically.

"Hannaford traced her – and he got her," he answered. "But he might well use the expression that you mentioned just now. She was indeed through his hands – just as a particularly slippery eel might have been – she got clear away from him."

# THE POLICE RETURN

Hetherwick now began to arrive at something like an understanding of a matter that had puzzled him ever since and also at the time of the conversation between Hannaford and his companion in the train. He had noted then that whatever it was that Hannaford was telling, he was telling it as a man tells a story against himself; there had been signs of amused chagrin and discomfiture in his manner. Now he saw why.

"Ah!" he exclaimed. "She was one too many for him. Then?"

"A good many times too many!" laughed Hollis. "She did Hannaford completely. He strove hard to find her, and did a great deal of the spade-work himself. And at last he ran her down – in a fashionable hotel in London. He had a Scotland Yard man with him, and a detective from our own police-office here, a man named Gandham, who is still in the force – I'll introduce you to him tomorrow. Hannaford, finding that Mrs. Whittingham had a suite of rooms in this hotel – a big West End place – left his two men downstairs, or outside, and went up to see her alone. According to his own account, she was highly indignant at any suspicions being cast upon her, and still more so, rose to a pitch of most virtuous indignation when he told her that he'd got a warrant for her arrest and that she'd have to go with him. During a brief interchange of remarks she declared that if her bankers at Manchester had returned her cheque unpaid it must have been merely because they hadn't realised certain valuable securities which she'd sent to them, and that if Malladale had presented his cheque a few days later it would have been all right. Now, that was all bosh! – Hannaford, of course, had been in communication with the bankers; all they knew of the lady was that she had opened an account with them while staying at some hotel in Manchester, and that she had drawn all but a few pounds of her balance the very day on which she had got the necklace from Malladale and fled with it from Sellithwaite. Naturally, Hannaford didn't tell her this – he merely reiterated his demand that she should go with him. She assented at once, only stipulating that there should be no fuss – she would walk out of the hotel with him, and he and his satellites could come back and search her belongings at their leisure. Then Hannaford – who, between you and me, Hetherwick, had an eye for a pretty woman! – made his mistake. Her bedroom opened out of the sitting-room in which he'd had his interview with her; he was fool enough to let her go into it alone, to get ready to go with him. She went – and that was the very last Hannaford ever saw of her!"

"Made a lightning exit, eh?" remarked Hetherwick.

"She must have gone instantly," asserted Hollis. "A door opened from the bedroom into a corridor – she must have picked up hat and coat and walked straight away, leaving everything she had there. Anyway, when Hannaford, tired of waiting, knocked at the door and looked in, his bird was flown. Then, of course, there was a hue-and-cry, and a fine revelation. But she'd got clear away, probably by some side door or other exit, and although Hannaford, according to his own account, raked London with a comb for her, she was never found. Vanished!"

"And the necklace?" inquired Hetherwick.

"That had vanished too," replied Hollis. "They searched her trunks and things, but they found nothing but clothing. Whatever she had in the way of money and valuables she'd carried off. And so Hannaford came home, considerably down in the mouth, and he had to stand a good deal of chaff. And if he found this woman's picture in a recent paper – well, small wonder that he did cut it out! I should say he was probably going to set Scotland Yard on her track! – for, of course, there's no time-limit to criminal proceedings."

"This is the picture he cut out," observed Hetherwick, producing it from his pocket-book. "But you say you never saw the woman?"

"No, I never saw her," assented Hollis, examining the print with interested curiosity. "So, of course, I can't recognise this. Handsome woman! But you meet me at my office – close by – tomorrow morning, at ten, and I'll take you to our police-station. Gandham will know!"

Gandham, an elderly man with a sphinx-like manner and watchful eyes, laughed sardonically when Hollis explained Hetherwick's business. He laughed again when Hetherwick showed him the print.

"Oh, aye, that's the lady!" he exclaimed. "Not changed much, neither! Egad, she was a smart 'un, that, Mr. Hollis! – I often laugh when I think how she did Hannaford! But you know, Hannaford was a soft-hearted man. At these little affairs, he was always for sparing people's feelings. All very well – but he had to pay for trying to spare hers! Aye, that's her! We have a portrait of her here, you know."

"You have, eh?" exclaimed Hetherwick. "I should like to see it."

"You can see it with pleasure, sir," replied the detective. "And look at it as long as you like." He turned to a desk close by and produced a big album, full of portraits with written particulars beneath them. "This is not, strictly speaking, a police photo," he continued. "It's not one that we took ourselves, ye understand – we never had the chance! No! – but when my lady was staying at the 'White Bear,' she had her portrait taken by Wintring, the photographer, in Silver Street, and Wintring was that suited with it that he put it in his window. So, of course, when her ladyship popped off with Malladale's necklace, we got one of those portraits, and added it to our little collection. Here it is! – and you'll not notice so much difference between it and that you've got in your hand, sir."

There was very little difference between the two photographs, and Hetherwick said so. And presently he went away from the police-office wondering more than ever about the woman with whose past adventures he was concerning himself.

"May as well do the thing thoroughly while you're about it," remarked Hollis, as they walked off. "Come and see Malladale – his shop is only round the corner. Not that he can tell you much more than I've told you already."

But Malladale proved himself able to tell a great deal more. A grave, elderly man, presiding over an establishment which Hetherwick, unaccustomed to the opulence of provincial manufacturing towns, was astonished to find outside London, he ushered his visitor into a private room, and listened to the reasons they gave for calling on him. After a close and careful inspection of the print which Hetherwick put before him, he handed it back with a confident nod.

"There is no doubt whatever – in my mind – that that is a print from a photograph of the woman I knew as the Honourable Mrs. Whittingham," he said. "And if it has been taken recently, she has altered very little during the ten years that have elapsed since she was here in this town."

"You'd be glad to see her again, Mr. Malladale – in the flesh?" laughed Hollis.

The jeweller shook his head.

"I think not," he answered. "No, I think not, Mr. Hollis. That's an episode which I had put out of my mind – until you recalled it."

"But – your loss?" suggested Hollis. "Close on four thousand pounds, wasn't it?"

Mr. Malladale raised one of his white hands to his grey beard and coughed. It was a cough that suggested discretion, confidence, secrecy. He smiled behind his moustache, and his spectacled eyes seemed to twinkle.

"I think I may venture a little disclosure – in the company of two gentlemen learned in the law," he said. "To a solicitor whom I know very well, and to a barrister introduced by him, I think I may reveal a little secret – between ourselves and to go no further. The fact of this matter is, gentlemen – I had no loss!"

"What?" exclaimed Hollis. "No – loss?"

"Eventually," replied the jeweller. "Eventually! Indeed, to tell you the truth plain, I made my profit, and – er, something over."

Hollis looked his bewilderment.

"Do you mean that – eventually – you were paid?" he asked.

"Precisely! Eventually – after a considerable interval – I was paid," replied Mr. Malladale. "I will tell you the circumstances. It is, I believe, common knowledge that I sold the diamond necklace to Mrs. Whittingham for three thousand, nine hundred pounds, and that the cheque she gave me was dishonoured, and that she cleared off with the goods and was never heard of after she escaped from Hannaford. Well, two years ago, that is to say, eight years after her disappearance, I one day received a letter which bore the New York postmark. It contained a sheet of notepaper on which were a few words and a few figures. But I have that now, and I'll show it to you."

Going to a safe in the corner of his parlour, the jeweller, after some searching, produced a paper and laid it before his visitors. Hetherwick examined it with curiosity. There was no name, no address, no date; all that appeared was, as Malladale had remarked, a few words, a few figures, typewritten: –

```
Principal ............... £ 3,900
8 years' Interest @ 5% ..... £ 1,560
                             ------
                  £ 5,460
```

Draft £5,460 enclosed herein: kindly acknowledge in London *Times*.

"Enclosed, as is there said, was a draft on a London bank for the specified amount," continued Mr. Malladale. "£5,460! You may easily believe that at first I could scarcely understand this: I knew of no one in New York who owed me money. But the first figures – £3,900 – threw light on the matter – I suddenly remembered Mrs. Whittingham and my lost necklace. Then I saw through the thing – evidently Mrs. Whittingham had become prosperous, wealthy, and she was honest enough to make amends; there was my principal, and eight years' interest on it. Yet, I felt somewhat doubtful about taking it – I didn't know whether I mightn't be compounding a felony? You gentlemen, of course, will appreciate my little difficulty?"

"Um!" remarked Hollis in a non-committal tone. "The more interesting matter is – what did you do? Though I think we already know," he added with a smile.

"Well, I went to see Hannaford, and told him what I had received," answered the jeweller. "And Hannaford said precisely what I expected him to say. He said 'Put the money in your pocket, Malladale, and say nothing about it!' So – I did!"

"Each of you feeling pretty certain that Mrs. Whittingham was not likely to show her face in Sellithwaite again, no doubt!" observed Hollis. "Very interesting, Mr. Malladale. But it strikes me that whether she ever comes to Sellithwaite again or not, Mrs. Whittingham, or whatever her name may be nowadays, is in England."

"You think so?" asked the jeweller.

"Her picture's recently appeared in an English paper, anyway," said Hollis.

"But pictures of famous American ladies appear in English newspapers," suggested Mr. Malladale. "I have recollections of several. Now my notion is that Mrs. Whittingham, who was a very handsome and very charming woman, eventually went across the Atlantic and married an American millionaire! That's how I figured it. And I have often wondered who she is now."

"That's precisely what I want to find out," said Hetherwick. "One thing is certain – Hannaford knew! If he'd been alive he could have told us. Because in whatever paper it was that this print appeared there would be some letterpress about it, giving the name, and why it appeared at all."

"You can trace that," remarked Hollis.

"Just so," agreed Hetherwick, "and I may as well get back to town and begin the job. But I think with Mr. Hollis," he added, turning to the jeweller, "I believe that the woman is here in England: I think it possible, too, that Hannaford knew where. And I don't think it impossible that between the time of his cutting out her picture from the paper and the time of his sudden death he came in touch with her."

"You think it probable that she, in some way, had something to do with his murder – if it was murder?" asked Mr. Malladale.

"I think it possible," replied Hetherwick. "There are strange features in the case. One of the strangest is this. Why, when Hannaford cut out that picture, for his own purposes, evidently with no intention of showing it to anyone else, did he cut it out without the name and letterpress which must have been under and over it?"

"Queer, certainly!" said Hollis. "But, you know, you can soon ascertain what that name was. All you've got to do is to get another copy of the paper."

"Unfortunately, Hannaford's granddaughter doesn't know what particular paper it was," replied Hetherwick. "Her sole recollection of it is that it was some local newspaper, sent to Hannaford by post, the very morning that he left here for London."

"Still – it can be traced," said Hollis. "It was in some paper – -and there'll be other copies."

Presently he and Hetherwick left the jeweller's shop. Outside, Hollis led his companion across the street, and turned into a narrow alley.

"I'll show you a man who'll remember Mrs. Whittingham better than anybody in Sellithwaite," he said, with a laugh. "Better even than Malladale. I told you she stayed at the 'White Bear' when she was here? Well, since then the entire staff of that eminent hostelry has been changed, from the manager to the boots – I don't think there's a man or woman there who was there ten years ago. But there's a man at the end of this passage who was formerly hall-porter at the 'White Bear' – Amblet Hudson – and who now keeps a rather cosy little saloon-bar down here: we'll drop in on him. He's what we call a bit of a character, and if you can get him to talk, he's usually worth listening to."

# SAMPLES OF INK

Hollis led the way farther along the alley, between high, black, windowless walls, and suddenly turning into a little court, paused before a door set deep in the side of an old half-timbered house.

"Queer old place, this!" he remarked over his shoulder. "But you'll get a glass of as good a port or sherry from this chap as you'd get anywhere in England – he knows his customers! Come in."

He led the way into a place the like of which Hetherwick had never seen – a snug, cosy room, panelled and raftered in old oak, with a bright fire burning in an open hearth and the flicker of its flames dancing on the old brass and pewter that ornamented the walls. There was a small bar-counter on one side of it; and behind this, in his shirt-sleeves, and with a cigar protruding from the corner of a pair of clean-shaven, humorous lips, stood a keen-eyed man, busily engaged in polishing wine-glasses.

"Good morning, gentlemen!" he said heartily. "Nice morning, Mr. Hollis, for the time o' year. And what can I do for you and your friend, sir?"

Hollis glanced round the room – empty, save for themselves. He drew a stool to the bar and motioned Hetherwick to follow his example.

"I think we'll try your very excellent dry sherry, Hudson," he answered. "That is, if it's as good as it was last time I tasted it."

"Always up to standard, Mr. Hollis, always up to standard, sir!" replied the bar-keeper. "No inferior qualities, no substitutes, and no trading on past reputation in this establishment, gentlemen! As good a glass of dry sherry here, sir, as you'd get where sherry wine comes from – and you can't say that of most places in England, I think. Everything's of the best here, Mr. Hollis – as you know!"

Hollis responded with a little light chaff; suddenly he bent across the bar.

"Hudson!" he said confidentially. "My friend here has something he'd like to show you. Now, then," he continued, as Hetherwick, in response to this, had produced the picture, "do you recognise that?"

The bar-keeper put on a pair of spectacles and turned the picture to the light, examining it closely. His lips tightened; then relaxed in a cynical smile.

"Aye!" he said, half carelessly. "It's the woman that did old Malladale out of that diamond necklace. Of course! – Mistress Whittingham!"

"Would you know her again, if you met her – now?" asked Hollis.

The bar-keeper picked up one of his glasses and began a vigorous polishing.

"Aye!" he answered, laconically. "And I should know her by something else than her face!"

Just then two men came in, and Hudson broke off to attend to their wants. But presently they carried their glasses away to a snug corner near the fire, and the bar-keeper once more turned to Hollis and Hetherwick.

"Aye!" he said confidentially. "If need were, I could tell that party by something else than her face, handsome as that is! I used to tell Hannaford when he was busy trying to find her that if he'd any difficulty about making certain, I could identify her if nobody else could! You see, I saw a deal of her when she was stopping at the 'White Bear.' And I knew something that nobody else knew."

"What is it?" asked Hetherwick.

Hudson leaned closer across the counter and lowered his voice.

"She was a big, handsome woman, this Mrs. Whittingham," he continued. "Very showy, dressy woman; fond of fine clothes and jewellery, and so on; sort of woman, you know, that would attract attention anywhere. And one of these women, too, that was evidently used to being waited on hand and foot – she took her money's worth out of the 'White Bear,' I can tell you! I did a deal for her, one way or another, and I'll say this for her: she was free enough with her money. If it so happened that she wanted things doing for her, she kept you fairly on the go till they were done, but she threw five-shilling pieces and half-crowns about as if they were farthings! She'd send you to take a sixpenny telegram and give you a couple of shillings for taking it. Well, now, as I say, I saw a deal of her, one way and another, getting cabs for her, and taking things up to her room, and doing this, that, and t'other. And it was with going up there one day sudden-like, with a telegram that had just come, that I found out something about her – something that, as I say, I could have told her by anywhere, even if she could have changed her face and put a wig on!"

"Aye – and what, now?" asked Hollis.

"This!" answered Hudson with a knowing look. "Maybe I'm a noticing sort of chap – anyhow, there was a thing I always noticed about Mrs. Whittingham. Wherever she was, and no matter how she was dressed, whether it was in her going-out things or her dinner finery, she always wore a band of black velvet round her right forearm, just above the wrist, where women wear bracelets. In fact, it was a sort of bracelet, a strip, as I say, of black velvet, happen about two inches wide, and on the front a cameo ornament, the size of a shilling, white stone or something of that sort, with one of these heathen figures carved on it. There were other folk about the place noticed that black velvet band, too – I tell you she was never seen without it; the chambermaids said she slept with it on. But on the occasion I'm telling you about, when I went up to her room with a telegram, I caught her without it. She opened her door to see who knocked – she was in a dressing-gown, going to change for dinner, I reckon, and she held out her right hand for what I'd brought her. The black velvet band wasn't on it, and for just a second like I saw what was on her arm!"

"Yes?" said Hollis. "Something – remarkable?"

"For a lady – aye!" replied Hudson, with a grim laugh. "Her arm was tattooed! Right round the place where she always wore this black velvet band there was a snake, red and green, and yellow, and blue, with its tail in its mouth! – wonderfully done, too; it had been no novice that had done that bit of work, I can tell you! Of course, I just saw it, and no more, but there was a strong electric light close by, and I did see it, and saw it plain and all. And that's a thing that that woman, whoever she may be, and wherever she's got to, can never rub off, nor scrub off! – she'll carry that to the day of her death."

The two listeners looked at each other.

"Odd!" remarked Hollis.

Hetherwick turned to the bar-keeper.

"Did she notice that you saw that her arm was tattooed?" he asked.

"Nay, I don't think she did," replied Hudson. "Of course, the thing was over in a second. I made no sign that I'd seen aught particular, and she said nought. But – I saw!"

Just then other customers came in, and the bar-keeper turned away to attend to their wants. Hollis and Hetherwick moved from the counter to one of the snug corners at the farther end of the room.

"Whoever she may be, wherever she may be – as Hudson said just now," remarked Hollis, "and if this woman really had anything to do with the mysterious circumstances of Hannaford's death, she ought not to be difficult to find. A woman who carries an indefaceable mark like that on her arm, and whose picture has recently appeared in a newspaper, should easily be traced."

"I think I shall get at her through the picture," agreed Hetherwick. "The newspaper production seems to have been done from a photograph which, from its clearness and finish, was probably taken by some first-class firm in London. I shall go round such firms as soon as I get back. It may be, of course, that she's nothing whatever to do with Hannaford's murder, but still, it's a trail that's got to be followed to the end now that one's started out on it. Well! That seems to finish my business here – as far as she's concerned. But there's another matter – I told you that when Hannaford came to town he had on him a sealed packet containing the secret of some invention or discovery, and that it's strangely and unaccountably missing. His granddaughter says that he worked this thing out – whatever it is – in a laboratory that he had in his garden. Now then, before I go I want to see that laboratory. As he's only recently left the place, I suppose things will still be pretty much as he left them at his old house. Where did he live?"

"He lived on the outskirts of the town," replied Hollis. "An old-fashioned house that he bought some years ago – I know it by sight well enough, though I've never been in it. I don't suppose it's let yet, though I know it's being advertised in the local papers. Let's get some lunch at the 'White Bear,' and then we'll drive up there and see what we can do. You want to get an idea of what it was that Hannaford had invented?"

"Just so," assented Hetherwick. "If the secret was worth all that he told his granddaughter it was, he may have been murdered by somebody who wanted to get sole possession of it. Anyway, it's another trail that's got to be worked on."

"I never heard of Hannaford as an inventor or experimenter," remarked Hollis. "But there, I knew little about him, except in his official capacity: he and his granddaughter, and an elderly woman they kept as a working housekeeper, were quiet sort of folk. I knew that he brought up his granddaughter from infancy, and gave her a rattling good education at the Girls' High School, but beyond that, I know little of their private affairs. I suppose he amused himself in this laboratory you speak of in his spare time?"

"Dabbled in chemistry, I understand," said Hetherwick. "And, if it hasn't been dismantled, we may find something in that laboratory that will give us a clue of some sort."

Hollis seemed to reflect for a minute or two.

"I've an idea!" he said suddenly. "There's a man who lunches at the 'White Bear' every day – a man named Collison; he's analytical chemist to a big firm of dyers in the town. I've seen him in conversation with Hannaford now and then. Perhaps he could tell us something on this point. Come on! This is just about his time for lunch."

A few minutes later, in the coffee-room of the hotel, Hollis led Hetherwick up to a bearded and spectacled man who had just sat down to lunch, and having introduced him, briefly detailed the object of his visit to Sellithwaite. Collison nodded and smiled.

"I understand," he said, as they seated themselves at his table. "Hannaford did dabble a bit in chemistry – in quite an amateur way. But as to inventing anything that was worth all that – come! Still, he was an ingenious man, for an amateur, and he may have hit on something fairly valuable."

"You've no idea what he was after?" suggested Hetherwick.

"Of late, no! But some time ago he was immensely interested in aniline dyes," replied Collison. "He used to talk to me about them. That's a subject of infinite importance in this district. Of course, as I dare say you know, the Germans have been vastly ahead of us as regards aniline dyes, and we've got most, if not all, of the stuff used, from Germany. Hannaford used to worry himself as to why we couldn't make our own aniline dyes, and I believe he experimented. But, with his resources, as an amateur, of course, that was hopeless."

"I've sometimes seen him talking to you," observed Hollis. "You've no idea what he was after, of late?"

"No. He used to ask me technical questions," answered Collison. "You know, I just regarded him as a man who had a natural taste for experimenting with things. This was evidently his hobby. I used to chaff him about it. Still, he was a purposeful man, and by reading and experiment he'd picked up a lot of knowledge."

"And, I suppose, it's within the bounds of possibility that he had hit on something of practical value?" suggested Hetherwick.

"Oh, quite within such bounds! – and he may have done," agreed Collison. "I've known of much greater amateurs suddenly discovering something. The question then is – do they know enough to turn their discovery to any practical purpose and account?"

"Evidently, from what he told his granddaughter, Hannaford did think he knew enough," said Hetherwick. "What I want to find out from a visit to his old laboratory is – what had he discovered?"

"And as you're not a chemist, nor even a dabbler," remarked Hollis, with a laugh, "that won't be easy! You'd better come with us after lunch, Collison."

"I can give you a couple of hours," assented Collison. "I'm already curious – especially if any discovery we can make tends to throw light on the mystery of Hannaford's death. Pity the police haven't got hold of the man who was with him," he added, glancing at Hetherwick. "I suppose you could identify him?"

"Unless he's an absolute adept at disguising himself, yes – positively!" replied Hetherwick. "He was a noticeable man."

An hour later the three men drove up to a house which stood a little way out of the town, on the edge of the moorland that stretched towards the great range of hills on the west. The house, an old-fashioned, solitary place, was empty, save for a caretaker who had been installed in its back rooms to keep it aired and to show it to possible tenants. The laboratory, a stone-walled, timber-roofed shed at the end of the garden, had never been opened, said the caretaker, since Mr. Hannaford locked it up and left it. But the key was speedily forthcoming, and the three visitors entered and looked round, each with different valuings of what he saw.

The whole place was a wilderness of litter and untidiness. Whatever Hannaford had possessed in the way of laboratory plant and appliances had been removed, and now there was little but rubbish – glass, whole and broken, paper, derelict boxes and crates, odds and ends of wreckage – to look at. But the analytical chemist glanced about him with a knowing eye, examining bottles and boxes, picking up a thing here and another there, and before long he turned to his companions with a laugh, pointing at the same time to a table in a corner which was covered with and dust-lined pots.

"It's very easy to see what Hannaford was after!" he said. "He's been trying to evolve a new ink!"

"Ink!" exclaimed Hollis incredulously. "Aren't there plenty of inks on the market?"

"No end!" agreed Collison with another laugh, and again pointing to the table. "These are specimens of all the better-known ones – British, of course, for no really decent ink is made elsewhere. But even the very best ink, up to now, isn't perfect. Hannaford perhaps thought, being an amateur, that he could make a better than the known best. Ink! – that's what he's been after. A superior, perfectly-fluid, penetrating, permanent, non-corrosive writing-ink – that's been his notion, a thousand to one! I observe the presence of lots of stuff that he's used."

He showed them various things, explaining their properties and adding some remarks on the history of the manufacture of writing-inks during the last hundred years.

"Taking it altogether," he concluded, "and in spite of manufacturers' advertisements and boasting, there isn't a really absolutely perfect writing-fluid on the market – that I know of, anyway. If Hannaford thought he could make one, and succeeded, well, I'd be glad to have his formula! Money in it!"

"To the extent of a hundred thousand pounds?" asked Hetherwick, remembering what Rhona had told him. "All that?"

"Oh, well!" laughed Collison, "you must remember that inventors are always very sanguine; always apt to see everything through rose-coloured spectacles; invariably prone to exaggerate the merits of their inventions. But if Hannaford, by experiment, really hit on a first-class formula for making a writing-ink superior in all the necessary qualities to its rivals – yes, there'd be a pot of money in it. No doubt of that!"

"I suppose he'd have to take out a patent for his invention?" suggested Hetherwick.

"Oh, to be sure! I should think that was one of his reasons for going to London – to see after it." assented Collison. He looked round again, and again laughed. "Well," he said, "I think you know now – you may be confident about it from what I've seen here – what Hannaford was after! Ink – just ink!"

Hetherwick accepted this judgment, and when he left Sellithwaite later in the afternoon on his return journey to London, he summed up the results of his visit. They were two. First, he had discovered that the woman of whom Hannaford had spoken in the train was a person who ten years before had been known as Mrs. Whittingham, appeared to be some sort of an adventuress, and, in spite of her restitution to the jeweller whom she had defrauded, was still liable to arrest, conviction, and punishment – if she could be found. Second, he had found out that the precious invention of which Hannaford had spoken so confidently and enthusiastically to his granddaughter and the particulars of which had mysteriously disappeared, related to the manufacture of a new writing-ink, which might, in truth, prove a very valuable commercial asset. So far, so good; he was finding things out. As he ate his dinner in the restaurant car he considered his next steps. But it needed little consideration to resolve on them. He must find out all about the woman whose picture lay in his pocketbook – what she now called herself; where she was; how her photograph came to be reproduced in a newspaper; and, last, but far from least, if Hannaford, after seeing the reproduction, had got into touch with her or given information about her. To the man in the train Hannaford had remarked that he had said nothing about her until that evening – yes, but was that man the only man to whom he had spoken? So much for that – and the next thing was to find out somehow what had become of the sealed packet which Hannaford undoubtedly had on him when he went out of Malter's Hotel on the night of his death.

# BLACK VELVET

Next morning, and before calling on either Kenthwaite or Rhona Hannaford, Hetherwick set out on a tour of the fashionable photographers in the West End of London. After all, there were not so many of them, so many at any rate of the very famous ones. He made a hit and began to work methodically. His first few coverts were drawn blank, but just before noon, and as he was thinking of knocking off for lunch, he started his fox. In a palatial establishment in Bond Street the person to whom he applied, showing his picture, gave an immediate smile of recognition.

"You want to know who is the original of this?" he said. "Certainly! Lady Riversreade, of Riversreade Court, near Dorking."

Hetherwick had no deep acquaintance with Debrett nor with Burke, nor even with the list of peers, baronets and knights given in the ordinary reference books, and to him the name of Lady Riversreade was absolutely unknown – he had never heard of her. But the man to whom he had shown the print, and who now held it in his hand, seemed to consider that Lady Riversreade was, or should be, as well known to everybody as she evidently was to him.

"This print is from one of our photographs of Lady Riversreade," he said, turning to a side table in the reception-room in which they were standing and picking up a framed portrait. "This one."

"Then you probably know in what newspaper this print appeared?" suggested Hetherwick. "That's really what I'm desirous of finding out."

"Oh, it appeared in several," answered the photographer. "Recently. It was about the time that Lady Riversreade opened some home or institute – I forget what. There was an account of it in the papers, and naturally her portrait was reproduced."

Hetherwick made a plausible pre-arranged excuse for his curiosity, and went away. Lady Riversreade! – evidently some woman of rank, or means, or position. But was she identical with the Mrs. Whittingham of ten years ago – the Mrs. Whittingham who did the Sellithwaite jeweller out of a necklace worth nearly four thousand pounds and cleverly escaped arrest at the hands of Hannaford? And if so...

But that led to indefinite vistas; the main thing at present was to find out all that could be found out about Lady Riversreade, of Riversreade Court, near Dorking. Hetherwick could doubtless have obtained considerable information from the fashionable photographer, but he had carefully refrained from showing too much inquisitiveness. Moreover, he knew a man, one Boxley, a fellow club-member, who was always fully posted up in all the doings of the social and fashionable world and could, if he would, tell him everything about Lady Riversreade – that was, if there was anything to tell about her. Boxley was one of those bachelor men about town who went everywhere, knew everybody, and kept himself fully informed; he invariably lunched at this particular club, the Junior Megatherium, and thither Hetherwick presently proceeded, bent on finding him.

He was fortunate in running Boxley to earth almost as soon as he entered the sacred and exclusive portals. Boxley was lunching and there was no one else at his table. Hetherwick joined him, and began the usual small-talk about nothing in particular. But he soon came to his one point.

"Look here!" he said, at a convenient interval. "I want to ask you something. You know everybody and everything. Who is Lady Riversreade, who's recently opened some home or institution, or hospital or something?"

"One of the richest women in England!" replied Boxley promptly. "Worth a couple of millions or so. That's who she is – who she was, I don't know. Don't suppose anybody else does, either. In this country, anyhow."

"What, is she a foreigner, then?" asked Hetherwick. "I've seen her portrait in the papers – that's why I asked you who she is. Doesn't look foreign, I think."

"I can tell you all that is known about her," said Boxley, "and that's not much. She's the widow of old Sir John Riversreade, the famous contractor – the man who made a pot of money building railways, and dams across big rivers, and that sort of thing, and got a knighthood for it. He also built himself a magnificent place near Dorking, and called it Riversreade Court – just the type of place a modern millionaire would build. Now, old Sir John had been a bachelor all his life, until he was over sixty – no time for anything but his contracts, you know. But when he was about sixty-five, which would be some six or seven years ago, he went over to the United States and made a rather lengthy stay there. And when he returned he brought a wife with him – the lady you're inquiring about."

"American, then?" suggested Hetherwick.

"Well, he married her over there, certainly," said Boxley. "But I should say she isn't American."

"You've met her – personally?"

"Just. Run across her once or twice at various affairs, and been introduced to her, quite casually. No, I don't think she's American. If I wanted to label her, I should say she was cosmopolitan."

"Woman of the world, eh?"

"Decidedly so. Handsome woman – self-possessed – self-assured – smart, clever. I think she'll know how to take care of the money her husband left her."

"Leave her everything?"

"Every penny! – except some inconsiderable legacies to charitable institutions. It was said at the time – it's two years since the old chap died – that she's got over two millions."

"And this institution, or whatever it is?"

"Oh, that! That was in the papers not so long since."

"I'm no great reader of newspapers. What about it?"

"Oh, she's started a home for wounded officers near Riversreade Court. There was some big country house near there empty – couldn't really be sold or let. She bought it, renovated it, fitted it up, stuck a staff of nurses and servants in, and got it blessed by the War Office. Jolly nice place, I believe, and she pays the piper."

"Doing the benevolent business, eh?"

"So it appears. Easy game, too, when you've got a couple of millions behind you. Useful, though."

Boxley went away soon after that, and Hetherwick, wondering about what he had learned, and now infinitely inquisitive about the identity of Lady Riversreade with Mrs. Whittingham, went into the smoking-room, and more from habit than because he really wanted to see it, picked up a copy of *The Times*. Almost the first thing on which his glance lighted was the name that was just then in his thoughts – there it was, in capitals, at the head of an advertisement:

"LADY RIVERSREADE'S HOME FOR WOUNDED OFFICERS, SURREY. – Required at once a Resident Lady-Secretary, fully competent to undertake accounts and correspondence and thoroughly trained in shorthand and typewriting; a knowledge of French and German would be a high recommendation. Application should be made personally any day this week between 10.00 a.m. and 12.00 p.m., and 3.00 p.m. and 5.00 p.m., to Lady Riversreade, Riversreade Court, Dorking."

Hetherwick threw the paper aside, left the club, and at the first newsagent's he came to bought another copy. With this in his hand he jumped into a taxi-cab and set off for Surrey Street, wondering if he would find Rhona Hannaford still at Malter's Hotel. He was fortunate in that – she had not yet left – and in a few minutes he was giving her a full and detailed account of his doings since his last interview with her. She listened to his story about Sellithwaite and his discoveries of that morning with a slightly puzzled look.

"Why are you taking all this trouble?" she asked suddenly and abruptly. "You're doing more, going into things more, than the police are. Matherfield was here this morning to tell me, he said, how they were getting on. They aren't getting on at all! – they haven't made one single discovery; they've heard nothing, found out nothing, about the man in the train or the man at Victoria – they're just where they were. But you – you've found out a lot! Why are you so energetic about it?"

"Put it down to professional inquisitiveness, if you like," answered Hetherwick, smiling. "I'm – interested. Tremendously! You see – I, too, was there in the train, like the man they haven't found. Well, now – now that I've got to this point I've arrived at, I want you to take a hand."

"I? In what way?" exclaimed Rhona.

Hetherwick pulled out *The Times* and pointed to the advertisement.

"I want you to go down to Dorking tomorrow morning and personally interview Lady Riversreade in response to that," he said. "You've all the qualifications she specifies, so you've an excellent excuse for calling on her. Whether you'd care to take the post is another matter – what I want is that you should see her under conditions that will enable you to observe her closely."

"Why?" asked Rhona.

"I want you to see if she wears such a band as that which Hudson told Hollis and myself about," replied Hetherwick. "Sharp eyes like yours will soon see that. And – if she does, then she's Mrs. Whittingham! In that case, I might ask you to do more – still more."

"What, for instance?" she inquired.

"Well, to do your best to get this post," he answered. "I think that you, with your qualifications, could get it."

"And – your object in that?" she asked.

"To keep an eye on Lady Riversreade," he replied promptly. "If the Mrs. Whittingham of ten years ago at Sellithwaite is the same woman as the Lady Riversreade of Riversreade Court of today, then, in view of your grandfather's murder, I want to know a lot more about her! To have you – there! – would be an immense help."

"I'm to be a sort of spy, eh?" asked Rhona.

"Detective, if you like," assented Hetherwick. "Why not?"

"You forget this," she remarked. "If this Lady Riversreade is identical with the Mrs. Whittingham of ten years ago, she'd remember my name – Hannaford! She's not likely to have forgotten Superintendent Hannaford of Sellithwaite!"

"Exactly – but I've thought of that little matter," replied Hetherwick. "Call yourself by some other name. Your mother's, for instance."

"That was Featherstone," said Rhona.

"There you are! Go as Miss Featherstone. As for your address, give your aunt's address at Tooting. Easy enough, you see," laughed Hetherwick. "Once you begin it properly."

"There's another thing, though," she objected. "References! She'll want those."

"Just as easy," answered Hetherwick. "Give me as one and Kenthwaite as the other. I'll speak to him about it. Two barristers of the Middle Temple! – excellent! Come! – all you've got to do is to work the scheme out fully and carry it out with assurance, and you don't know what we might discover."

Rhona considered matters awhile, watching him steadily.

"You think that – somehow – this woman may be at the back of the mystery surrounding my grandfather's murder?" she suddenly asked.

"I think it's quite within the bounds of probability," he answered.

"All right," she said abruptly. "I'll go. Tomorrow morning, I suppose?"

"Sooner the better," agreed Hetherwick. "And, look here, I'll go down with you. We'll go by the 10.10 from Victoria, drive to this place, and I'll wait outside while you have your interview. After that we'll get some lunch in Dorking – and you can tell me your news."

Next morning found Hetherwick pacing the platform at Victoria and on the look-out for his fellow-companion. She came to him a little before the train was due to leave, and he noticed at once that she had discarded the mourning garments in which he had found her the previous afternoon; she now appeared in a smart tailor-made coat and skirt, and looked the part he wanted her to assume – that of a capable and self-reliant young business woman.

"Good!" he said approvingly, as they went to find their seats. "Nothing like dressing up to it. You're all ready with your lines, eh? – I mean, you've settled on all you're going to say and do?"

"Leave that to me," she answered with a laugh, "I shan't forget the primary object, anyway. But I've been wondering – supposing we come to the conclusion that this Lady Riversreade is the Mrs. Whittingham of ten years ago? What are you going to do then?"

"My ideas are hazy on that point – at present," confessed Hetherwick. "The first thing, surely, is to establish identity. Don't forget that the main thing to do at Riversreade Court is to get a good look at Lady Riversreade's right wrist, and see what's on it!"

Riversreade Court proved to be some distance from Dorking, in the Leith Hill district; Hetherwick chartered a taxi-cab and gave his companion final instructions as they rode out. Half an hour's run brought them to the house – a big, pretentious, imitation Elizabethan structure, set on the hill-side amongst a grove of firs and pines, and having an ornamental park laid out between its gardens and terraces and the high road. At the lodge gates he stopped the driver and got out.

"I'll wait here for you," he said to Rhona. "You ride up to the house, get your business done, and come back here. Be watchful now – of anything."

Rhona nodded reassuringly and went off; Hetherwick lighted his pipe and strolled about admiring the scenery. But his thoughts were with Rhona; he was wondering what adventures she was having in the big mansion which the late contractor had built amidst the woods. And Rhona kept him wondering some time; an hour had elapsed before the cab came back. With a hand on its door, he turned to the driver:

"Go to the 'White Horse' now," he said. "We'll lunch there, and afterwards you can take us to the station. Well?" he continued, as he got in and seated himself at Rhona's side. "What luck?"

"Good, I should say," answered Rhona. "She wears a broad black velvet band on her right wrist, and on the outer face is a small cameo. How's that?"

"Precisely!" exclaimed Hetherwick. "Just what that bar-keeper chap at Sellithwaite described. Wears it openly – makes no attempt at concealment beneath her sleeve, eh?"

"None," answered Rhona. "She was wearing a smart, fashionable, short-sleeved jumper. She'd a very fine diamond bracelet on the other wrist."

"And she herself," asked Hetherwick. "What sort of woman is she?"

"That's a very good photograph of her that my grandfather cut out of the paper," replied Rhona. "Very good, indeed! I knew her at once. She's a tall, fine, handsome, well-preserved woman, perhaps forty, perhaps less. Very easy, accustomed manner; a regular woman of the world I should think. Quite ready to talk about herself and her doings – she told me the whole history of this Home she's started and took me to see it – it's a fine old house, much more attractive than the Court, a little way along the hillside. She told me that it was her great hobby, and that she's devoting all her time to it. I should say that she's genuinely interested in its welfare – genuinely!"

"She impressed you?" suggested Hetherwick.

"I think, from what I saw and heard, that she's a good-natured, probably warm-hearted, woman. She spoke very feelingly of the patients she's got in her Home, anyhow."

"And the post – the secretaryship?"

"I can have it if I want it – of course, I told her I did. She examined me pretty closely about my qualifications – she herself speaks French and German like a native – and I mentioned you and Mr. Kenthwaite as references. She's going to write to you both today. So – it's for you to decide."

"I suppose it's really for you!"

"No! – I'm willing, eager, indeed, to do anything to clear up the mystery about my grandfather's murder. But – I don't think this woman had anything to do with it. In my opinion – and I suppose I've got some feminine intuition – she's honest and straightforward enough."

"And yet it looks as if she were certainly the Mrs. Whittingham who did a Sellithwaite jeweller to the tune of four thousand pounds!" laughed Hetherwick. "That wasn't very honest or straightforward!"

"I've been thinking about that," said Rhona. "Perhaps, after all, she really thought the cheque would be met, and anyway, she did send the man his money, even though it was a long time afterwards. And again – an important matter! – Lady Riversreade may not be Mrs. Whittingham at all. More women than one wear wristlets of velvet."

"But – the portrait!" exclaimed Hetherwick. "The positive identity!"

"Well," answered Rhona, "I'm willing to go there and to try to find out more. But, frankly, I think Lady Riversreade's all right! First impression, anyhow!"

The cab drew up at the "White Horse," and Hetherwick led Rhona into the coffee-room. But they had hardly taken their seats when the manager came in.

"Does your name happen to be Hetherwick, sir?" he inquired. "Just so – thank you. A Mr. Mapperley has twice rung you up here during the last hour – he's on the phone again now, if you'll speak to him."

"I'll come," said Hetherwick. "That's my clerk," he murmured to Rhona as he rose. "I told him to ring me up here between twelve and three if necessary. Back in a minute."

But he was away several minutes, and when he came to her again, his face was grave. "Here's a new development!" he said, bending across the table and whispering. "The police have found the man who was with your grandfather in the train! Matherfield wants me to identify him. And you'll gather from that that they've found him dead! We must lunch quickly and catch the two-twenty-four."

45

# FLIGWOOD'S RENTS

Hetherwick went to the hotel telephone again before he had finished his lunch, and as a result Matherfield was on the platform at Victoria when the two-twenty-four ran in. He showed no surprise at seeing Hetherwick and Rhona together; his manifest concern was to get Hetherwick to himself and away from the station. And Hetherwick, seeing this, said good-bye to Rhona with a whispered word that he would look in at Malter's Hotel before evening; a few minutes later he and Matherfield were in a taxi-cab together, hastening along Buckingham Palace Road.

"Well?" inquired Hetherwick. "This man?"

"I don't think there's any doubt about his being the man you saw with Hannaford," replied Matherfield. "He answers to your description, anyway. But I'll tell you how we came across his track. Last night a man named Appleyard came to me – he's a chap who has a chemist's shop in Horseferry Road, Westminster – a middle-aged, quiet sort of man, who prefaced his remarks by telling us that he very rarely had time to read newspapers or he'd have been round to see us before. But yesterday he happened to pick up a copy of one of last Sunday's papers, and he read an account of the Hannaford affair. Then he remembered something that seemed to him to have a possible connection with it. Some little time ago he advertised for an assistant – a qualified assistant. He'd two or three applications which weren't exactly satisfactory. Then, one evening – he couldn't give any exact date, but from various things he told us I reckoned up that it must have been on the very evening on which Hannaford met his death – a man came and made a personal application. Appleyard described him – medium-sized, a spare man, sallow-complexioned, thin face and beard, large dark eyes, very intelligent, superior manner, poorly dressed, and evidently in low water —"

"That's the man, I'll be bound!" exclaimed Hetherwick. "Did he give this chemist his name?"

"He did – name and address," answered Matherfield. "He said his name was James Granett, and his address Number 8, Fligwood's Rents,

Gray's Inn Road – Holborn end. He told Appleyard that he was a qualified chemist, and produced his proofs and some references. He also said that though he'd never had a business of his own he'd been employed, as, indeed, the references showed, by some good provincial firms at one time or another. Lately he'd been in the employ of a firm of manufacturing chemists in East Ham – for some reason or other their trade had fallen off, and they'd had to reduce their staff, and he'd been thrown out of work, and had had the further bad luck to be seriously ill. This, he said, had exhausted his small means, and he was very anxious to get another job – so anxious that he appeared to come to Appleyard on very low terms. Appleyard told him he'd inquire into the references and write to him in a day or two. He did inquire, found the references quite satisfactory, and wrote to Granett engaging him. But Granett never turned up, and Appleyard heard no more of him until he read this Sunday paper. Then he felt sure Granett was the man, and came to me."

"I shouldn't think there's any doubt in the case," remarked Hetherwick. "But before we go any further, a question. Did Appleyard say what time it was when this man came to him that evening?"

"He did. It was just as he was closing his shop – nine o'clock. Granett stopped talking with him about half an hour. Indeed, Appleyard told me more. After they'd finished their talk, Appleyard, who doesn't live at the shop, locked it up, and he then invited Granett to step across the street with him and have a drink before going home. They had a drink together in a neighbouring saloon bar, and chatted a bit there; it would be nearly ten o'clock, according to Appleyard, when Granett left him. And he remembered that Granett, on leaving him, went round the corner into Victoria Street, on his way, no doubt, to the Underground."

"And in Victoria Street, equally without doubt, he met Hannaford," muttered Hetherwick. "Well, and the rest of it?"

"Well, of course, as soon as I learnt all this, I determined to go myself to Fligwood's Rents," replied Matherfield. "I went, first thing this morning. Fligwood's Rents is a slum street – only a man who is very low down in the world would ever dream of renting a room there. It's a sort of alley or court on the right-hand side of Gray's Inn Road, going up – some half-dozen squalid houses on each side, let off in tenements. Number 8 was a particularly squalid house! – slatternly women and squalling brats about the door and general dirt and shabbiness all round. None of the women about the place knew the name of Granett, but after I'd described the man I wanted they argued that it must be the gentleman on the top back; they added the further information that they hadn't seen him for some days. I went up a filthy stair to the room they indicated; the door was locked and I couldn't get any response to my repeated knockings. So then I set out to discover the landlord, and eventually unearthed a beery individual in a neighbouring low-class tavern. I got out of him that he had a lodger named Granett, who paid him six shillings a week for this top back room, and he suddenly remembered that Granett hadn't paid his last week's rent. That made more impression on him than anything I said, and he went with me to the house. And to cut things short, we forced the door, and found the man dead in his bed!"

"Dead!" exclaimed Hetherwick. "Dead – then?"

"Dead then – yes, and he'd been dead several days, according to the doctors," replied Matherfield grimly. "Dead enough! It was a poor room, but clean – you could see from various little things that the man had been used to a better condition. But as regards himself – he'd evidently gone to bed in the usual way. His clothes were all carefully folded and arranged, and by the side of the bed there was a chair on which was a half-burnt candle and an evening newspaper."

"That would fix the date," suggested Hetherwick.

"Of course, it did – and it was the same date as that on which Hannaford died," answered Matherfield. "I've made a careful note of that circumstance! Everything looked as if the man had gone to bed in just his ordinary way, read the paper a bit, blown out his light, dropped off to sleep, and died in his sleep."

"Yes! – and from what cause, I wonder?" exclaimed Hetherwick.

"Precisely the same idea occurred to me, knowing what I did about Hannaford," said Matherfield. "However, the doctors will tell us more about that. But to wind up – I had a man of mine with me, and I left him in charge while I got further help, and sent for Appleyard. Appleyard identified the dead man at once as the man who had been to see him. Indeed, on opening the door, we found Appleyard's letter, engaging him, lying with one or two others, just inside. So that's about all, except that I now want to know if you can positively identify him as the man you saw with Hannaford, and that I also want to open a locked box that we found in the room, which may contain something that will give us further information. Altogether, it's a step forward."

"Yes," admitted Hetherwick. "It's something. But there's spade-work to be done yet, Matherfield. I don't think there's any doubt, now, that Granett encountered Hannaford after he left Appleyard – and that indicates that Granett and Hannaford were old acquaintances. But, supposing they met at, or soon after, ten o'clock – where did they go, where did they spend their time between that and the time they entered my compartment at St. James's Park?"

"That would be – what?" asked Matherfield.

"It was well after midnight – mine was the last train going east, anyway," said Hetherwick. "I only just caught it at Sloane Square. But we can ascertain the exact time, to a minute. Still, those two, meeting accidentally, as I conclude they did, must have been together two or three hours. Where? – at that time of night. Surely there must be some way of finding that out! Two men, each rather noticeable – somebody must have seen them together, somewhere! It seems impossible that they shouldn't have been seen."

"Aye, but in my experience, Mr. Hetherwick, it's the impossible that happens!" rejoined Matherfield. "In a bee-hive like this, where every man's intent on his own business, ninety-nine men out of a hundred never observe anything unless it's shoved right under their very eyes. Of course, if we could find out if and where Hannaford and Granett were together that night, and where Granett went to after he slipped away at Charing Cross, it would vastly simplify matters. But how are we going to find out? There's been immense publicity given to this case in the papers, you know, Mr. Hetherwick – portraits of Hannaford, and details about the whole affair, and so on, and yet we've had surprisingly little help and less information. I'll tell you what it is, sir – what we want is that tall, muffled-up chap who met Hannaford at Victoria! Who is he, now?"

"Who, indeed!" assented Hetherwick. "Vanished! – without a trace."

"Oh, well!" said Matherfield cheerfully, "you never know when you might light on a trace. But here we are at this unsavoury Fligwood's Rents."

The cab pulled up at the entrance to a dark, high-walled, stone-paved alley, which at that moment appeared to be full of women and children; so, too, did the windows on either side. The whole place was sombre and evil-smelling, and Hetherwick felt a sense of pity for the unfortunate man whose luck had been bad enough to bring him there.

"A murder, a suicide, or a sudden death is as a breath of heaven to these folk!" said Matherfield as they made their way through the ragged and frowsy gathering. "It's an event in uneventful lives. Here's the place," he added, as they came to a doorway whereat a policeman stood on guard. "And here are the stairs – mind you don't slip on 'em, for the wood's broken and the banisters are smashed."

Hetherwick cautiously followed his guide to the top of the house. There at another door stood a second policeman, engaged when they caught sight of him in looking out through the dirt-obscured window of the landing. His bored countenance brightened when he saw Matherfield; stepping back he quietly opened the door at his side. And the two newcomers, silent in view of the task before them, tiptoed into the room beyond.

It was, as Matherfield had remarked, a poor place, but it was clean and orderly, and its occupant had evidently tried to make it as habitable and comfortable as his means would allow. There were one or two good prints on the table; half a dozen books on an old chest of drawers; in a cracked vase on the mantelpiece there were a few flowers, wilted and dead. Hetherwick took in all this at a glance; then he turned to Matherfield, who silently drew aside a sheet from the head and shoulders of the rigid figure on the bed, and looked inquiringly at his companion. And Hetherwick gave the dead man's face one careful inspection and nodded.

"Yes!" he said. "That's the man!"

"Without doubt?" asked Matherfield.

"No doubt at all," affirmed Hetherwick. "That is the man who was with Hannaford in the train. I knew him instantly."

Matherfield replaced the sheet and turned to a small table which stood in the window. On it was a box, a square, old-fashioned thing, clamped at the corners.

"This seems to be the only thing he had that's what you may call private," he observed. "It's locked, but I've got a tool here that'll open it. I want to know what's in it – there may be something that'll give us a clue."

Hetherwick stood by while Matherfield forced open the lock with an instrument which he produced from his pocket, and began to examine the contents of the box. At first there seemed little that was likely to yield information. There was a complete suit of clothes and an outfit of decent linen; it seemed as if Granett had carefully kept these in view of better days. There were more books, all of a technical nature, relating to chemistry; there was a small case containing chemical apparatus, and another in which lay a pair of scales; in a third they found a microscope.

"He wasn't down to the very end of his resources, or he'd have pawned these things," muttered Matherfield. "They all look good stuff, especially the microscope. But here's more what I want – letters!"

He drew forth two bundles of letters, neatly arranged and tied up with tape. Unloosing the fastenings and rapidly spreading the envelopes out on the table, he suddenly put his finger on an address.

"There you are, Mr. Hetherwick," he exclaimed. "That's just what I expected to find out – though I certainly didn't think we should discover it so quickly This man has lived at Sellithwaite some time or other. Look there, at this address – *Mr. James Granett, 7, Victoria Terrace, Sellithwaite, Yorkshire*. Of course! – that's how he came to know and be with Hannaford. They were old acquaintances. See, there are several letters."

Hetherwick took two or three of the envelopes in his hand and looked closely at them. He perceived at once what Matherfield had not noticed.

"Just so!" he said. "But what's of far more importance is the date. Look at this – you see? That shows that Granett was living at Sellithwaite ten years ago – it was of that time that Hannaford was talking to him in the train."

"Oh, we're getting at something!" assented Matherfield. "Now we'll put everything back, and I'll take this box away and examine it thoroughly at leisure." He replaced the various articles, twisted a cord round the box, knotted it, and turned to the dead man's clothes, lying neatly folded on a chair close by. "I haven't had a look at the pockets of those things yet," he continued. "I'll just take a glance – you never know."

Hetherwick again watched in silence. There was little of interest revealed until Matherfield suddenly drew a folded bit of paper from one of the waistcoat pockets. Smoothing it out he uttered a sharp exclamation.

"Good!" he said. "See this? A brand new five pound note! Now, I'll lay anything he hadn't had that on him long! Got it that night, doubtless. And – from whom?"

"I should say Hannaford gave it to him," suggested Hetherwick.

But Matherfield shook his head and put the note in his own pocket.

"That's a definite clue!" he said, with emphasis. "I can trace that!"

# THE MEDICINE BOTTLE

Hetherwick went away from the sordid atmosphere of Fligwood's Rents wondering more than ever at this new development; he continued to wonder and to speculate all the rest of that day and most of the next. That Granett's sudden death had followed on Hannaford's seemed to him a sure proof that there was more behind this mystery than anybody had so far conceived of. Personally, he had not the slightest doubt that whoever poisoned Hannaford had also poisoned Granett. And he was not at all surprised when, late in the afternoon of the day following upon that of the visit to Dorking, Matherfield walked into his chambers with a face full of news.

"I know what you're going to tell me, Matherfield," said Hetherwick, motioning his visitor to an easy chair. "The doctors have held a post-mortem on Granett, and they find that he was poisoned."

Matherfield's face fell; he was robbed of his chance of a dramatic announcement.

"Well, and that's just what I was going to tell you," he answered. "That's what they do say. Same doctors that performed the autopsy on Hannaford. Doesn't surprise you?"

"Not in the least," replied Hetherwick. "I expected it. They're sure of it?"

"Dead certain! But, as in Hannaford's case, they're not certain of the particular poison used. However – also as in his case – they've submitted the whole case to two big swells in that line, one of 'em the man that's always employed by the Home Office in these affairs, and the other that famous specialist at St. Martha's Hospital – I forget his name. They'll get to work; they're at work on the Hannaford case now. Difficult job, I understand – some very subtle poison, probably little known. However, I believe we've got a clue about it."

"A clue – about the poison?" exclaimed Hetherwick. "What clue?"

"Well, this," answered Matherfield. "After you'd gone away from Fligwood's Rents yesterday afternoon, and while I was making arrangements for the removal of the poor chap's body, I took another careful look round the room. Now, if you noticed things as closely as all that, you may have observed that Granett's bed was partly in a sort of alcove – the head part. In the corner of that alcove, or recess, just where he could have set them down by reaching his arm out of bed, I found a bottle and a glass tumbler. The bottle was an ordinary medicine bottle – not a very big one. It had the cork in it and about an inch of fluid, which, on taking out the cork, I found to be whisky, and, I should say by the smell, whisky of very good quality. But I noticed that there was the very slightest trace of some sort of sediment at the bottom. There was a trace of similar sediment in the bottom of the tumbler. Now, of course, I put these things up most carefully, sealed them, and handed them over to the doctors. For it was very evident to me – reconstructing things, you know – that Granett had mixed himself a drink, a nightcap, if you like to call it so, from that bottle on getting into bed, and then had put bottle and glass down by his bed-head, in the corner. And just as I mean to trace that five-pound note, Mr. Hetherwick, so I mean to trace that bottle!"

"How?" asked Hetherwick, closely interested. "And to what, or whom?"

"To the chemists where it came from," answered Matherfield. "It came from some chemist's, and I'll find which!"

"There are hundreds of chemists in London," said Hetherwick. "It's a stiff proposition."

"It's going to be done, anyway," asserted Matherfield. "And it mayn't be such a stiff job as it at first looks to be. See here! There were labels on that bottle, both of 'em torn and defaced, it's true, but still with enough on them to narrow down the field of inquiry. I've had the face of the bottle photographed – here's a print of the result."

He brought out a photographic print, roughly finished and mounted on a card, and handed it over to Hetherwick, who took it to the light and examined it carefully. It showed the front of the medicine bottle, with a label at the top and another at the bottom. Each had been torn, as if to obliterate names and addresses, but a good deal of the lettering was left.

```
+----------------------------+
       C. A    , Esq.,
     The mix  re as before
        No. A.1152
+----------------------------+
```

```
+-----------------------------+
    Note.--This medicine has
    been dispensed by a fully
    qualified Chemist with the
         to possible drugs
         is guaranteed
            wishes of
            the Pres-


            M.P.S.
            St. W.C.
+-----------------------------+
```

"That bottom label's the thing, Mr. Hetherwick," remarked Matherfield. "Let me get that hiatus filled up with the name and address of the chemist, and I'll soon find out who C. A. blank, Esquire, is! The chemist is one in the West Central district; he's a member of the Pharmaceutical Society; he'll have somebody whose initials are C. A. on his books; he'll recognise the number A.1152 of the prescription. It's a decided clue; and even if there are, as there undoubtedly are, scores of chemists in the West Central district, I'll run this one down!"

Hetherwick handed back the photograph and began to pace up and down the room. Suddenly he turned on his visitor, his mind made up to tell him what he himself had been doing.

"Matherfield," he said, dropping into his chair again and adopting a tone of confidence, "what do you make of this? I mean – what's your theory? Is it your opinion that the deaths of these two men are – so to speak – all of a piece?"

"That is my opinion!" answered Matherfield with an emphatic nod. "I've no more doubt about it than I have that I see you, Mr. Hetherwick. All of a piece, to be sure! Whoever poisoned Hannaford poisoned Granett! I'll tell you how I've figured it out since the doctors told me, only a couple of hours since, what their opinion is about Granett. This way: Hannaford and Granett knew each other at Sellithwaite ten years ago. That night when Granett left Appleyard in Horseferry Road and turned into Victoria Street, he met Hannaford – accidentally."

"Why accidentally?" asked Hetherwick.

"Well, that's what I think," said Matherfield. "I've figured in that way. Of course, it may have been by appointment. But anyway, they met – we know that. Now then, where did they spend their time between then and the time they got into your carriage at St. James's Park? We don't know. But here comes in an unknown factor – what about the strange man at Victoria, the man muffled to his eyes? Two things suggest themselves to me, Mr. Hetherwick. Did Hannaford take Granett to see that man, or did Hannaford and Granett meet at that man's? For I think that man, whoever he is, is at the bottom of every thing."

"Why should they meet at that man's?" asked Hetherwick.

"Well," answered Matherfield, "I think that secret of Hannaford's has something to do with it. He had the sealed packet on him when he left Malter's Hotel; it had disappeared when we searched his clothing after his death. Now, the granddaughter says it had to do with chemicals. Suppose the tall, muffled man was a chap whose business opinion on this secret Hannaford wanted, and that they met at Victoria and went to the man's rooms somewhere in that district? Suppose Granett – another man in the chemistry line – came there, knowing both? Supposing the muffled man poisoned both of 'em, to keep the secret to himself? Do you see what I'm after? Very well! There you are. The thing is to hunt out that man, whoever he is. I wish I knew what Hannaford's secret was, though – its precise nature."

"Matherfield," said Hetherwick, "I'll tell you! You've been very confidential with me; I'll be equally so with you, on condition that we work together from this. The fact is, I've been at work. I'm immensely interested in this case. Ever since I saw Hannaford die in that train and in that awfully mysterious fashion it's fascinated me, and I'm going to the very end of it. Now I'll tell you all I've been doing, and what I've discovered. Listen carefully."

He went on to tell his visitor the whole details of his visit to Sellithwaite, of the results of his investigations there, and of Rhona's doings and observations at Riversreade Court. Matherfield listened in absorbed silence.

"Is Miss Hannaford going to this secretaryship, then?" he demanded abruptly, at the end of Hetherwick's story. "Is it settled?"

"Practically, yes," replied Hetherwick. "I heard from Lady Riversreade this morning; so did Mr. Kenthwaite. We gave Miss Hannaford – to be known to Lady Riversreade as Miss Featherstone – very good recommendations for the post, and I expect that as soon as she's had our letters, Lady Riversreade will telephone to Miss Hannaford that she's to go at once. Then – she'll go."

"To act as – spy?" suggested Matherfield.

"If you put it that way, yes," assented Hetherwick. "Though, from what she saw of her yesterday, Miss Hannaford formed a very favourable opinion of Lady Riversreade. However, I'm so certain that somehow or other, perhaps innocently, she's connected with this affair, that we mustn't lose any chance."

"And Miss Hannaford will report anything likely to you?" asked Matherfield.

"Just so! Miss Hannaford's duties don't include any Sunday work; on Sunday she'll come to town, and if there's anything to tell, she'll tell it – to me. She's a smart, clever girl, Matherfield, and she'll keep her eyes open."

Matherfield nodded, and for a while sat silent, evidently lost in his own thoughts.

"Oh, she's a clever girl, right enough!" he said suddenly. "Um! I wonder who this Lady Riversreade really is, now?"

"This Lady Riversreade!" laughed Hetherwick. "A multi-millionairess!"

"Aye, just so; but who was she before her marriage? If she is the woman who was known as Mrs. Whittingham—"

"Can there be any doubt about it after what I found out?"

"You never know, Mr. Hetherwick! Lord bless you! They talk about the long arm of coincidence. Why, in my time I've known of things that make me feel there's nothing wonderful about the most amazing coincidence! But – if Lady Riversreade used to be Mrs. Whittingham, then I'd like to know all about Mrs. Whittingham until she became Lady Riversreade, and who she was before she was Mrs. Whittingham, if she ever was Mrs. Whittingham!"

"Stiff job, Matherfield," said Hetherwick. "I think we shall have enough to do to keep an eye on Lady Riversreade."

"You anticipate something there?" suggested Matherfield.

"I think something may transpire," replied Hetherwick.

Matherfield got to his feet.

"Well," he said, "keep me informed, and I'll keep you informed. We've something to go on – Lord knows what we shall make out of it!"

"You're doing your best to trace the tall man?" asked Hetherwick.

"Best!" exclaimed Matherfield with an air of disgust. "We've done our best and our better than best! I've had special men all round that Victoria district; I should think every tall man in that part's been eyed over. And I believe that Mr. Ledbitter has so got the thing on his brain that he's been spending all his spare time patrolling the neighbourhood and going in and out of restaurants and saloons looking for the man he saw – of course, without result!"

"All the same," said Hetherwick, "that man is – somewhere!"

Matherfield went away, and except at the inquest on Granett – whereat nothing transpired which was not already known – Hetherwick did not see him again for several days. He himself progressed no further in his investigations during that time. Rhona Hannaford betook herself to Riversreade Court, as secretary to its mistress's Home, and until the Sunday succeeding his departure Hetherwick heard nothing of her. Then she came up to town on the Sunday morning and, in accordance with their previous arrangement, Hetherwick met her at Victoria, and took her to lunch at a neighbouring hotel.

"Anything to tell?" he asked, when they had settled down to their soup. "Any happenings?"

"Nothing!" answered Rhona. "Everything exceedingly proper, business-like, and orderly. And Lady Riversreade appears to me to be a model sort of person – her devotion to that Home and its inmates is remarkable! I don't believe anything's going to happen, or that I shall ever have anything to report."

"Well, that'll have its compensations," said Hetherwick. "Leave us all the more time for ourselves, won't it?"

He gave her a look to which Rhona responded, shyly but unmistakably; she knew, as well as he did, that they were getting fond of each other's society. And they continued to meet on Sundays, and three or four went by, and still she had nothing to tell that related to the mystery of Hannaford and Granett.

Three weeks elapsed before Matherfield had anything to tell, either. Then he walked into Hetherwick's chambers one morning with news in his face.

"Traced it!" he said. "Knew I should! That five-pound note – brand new. Only a question of time to do that, of course."

"Well?" inquired Hetherwick.

"It was one of twenty fivers paid by the cashier of the London and Country Bank in Piccadilly to the secretary of Vivian's," continued Matherfield. "Date – day before Hannaford's death. Vivian's, let me tell you, is a swell night club. Now then, how did that note get into the hands of Granett? That's going to be a stiff 'un!"

"So stiff that I'm afraid you mustn't ask me to go in at it," agreed Hetherwick good-humouredly. "I must stick to my own line – when the chance comes."

The chance came on the following Sunday, when, in pursuance of now established custom, he met Rhona. She gave him a significant look as soon as she got out of the train.

"News – at last!" she said, as they turned up the platform. "Something's happened – but what it means I don't know."

# THE MYSTERIOUS VISITOR

The head-waiter in the restaurant to which Hetherwick and Rhona repaired every Sunday immediately upon her arrival now knew these two well by sight, and forming his own conclusions about them, always reserved for them a table in a quiet and secluded corner. Hither they now proceeded, and had scarcely taken their accustomed seats before Rhona plunged into her story.

"I expect you want to know what it's all about, so I won't keep you waiting," she said. "It was on Friday – Friday morning – that it happened, and I half thought of writing to you about it that evening. Then I thought it best to tell you personally today – besides, I should have had to write an awfully long letter. There are things to explain; I'd better explain them first. Our arrangements down there at Riversreade, for instance. They're like this: Lady Riversreade and I always breakfast together at the Court, about nine o'clock. At ten we go across the grounds to the Home. There we have a sort of formal office – two rooms, one of which, the first opening from the hall, I have, the other, opening out of it, is Lady Riversreade's private sanctum. In the hall itself we have an ex-army man, Mitchell, as hall-porter, to attend to the door and so on. All the morning we are busy with letters, accounts, reports of the staff, and that sort of thing. We have lunch at the Home, and we're generally busy until four or five o'clock. Got all that?"

"Every scrap!" replied Hetherwick. "Perfectly plain."

"Very well," continued Rhona. "One more detail, however. A good many people, chiefly medical men and folk interested in homes and hospitals, call, wanting to look over and to know about the place – which, I may tell you in parenthesis, costs Lady Riversreade a pretty tidy penny! Mitchell's instructions as regards all callers are to bring their cards to me – I interview them first; if I can deal with them, I do; if I think it necessary or desirable, I take them in to Lady Riversreade. We have to sort them out – some, I am sure, come out of mere idle curiosity; in fact, the only visitors we want to see there are either medical men who have a genuine interest in the place and can do something for it, or people who are connected with its particular inmates. Well, on Friday morning last, about a quarter to twelve, as I was busy with my letters, I heard a car come up the drive, and presently Mitchell came into my room with a card bearing the name *Dr. Cyprian Baseverie*. Instead of being an engraved card as, by all the recognised standards, it should have been, it was a printed card – that was the first thing I noticed."

"Your powers of observation," remarked Hetherwick admiringly, "are excellent, and should prove most useful."

"Thank you for the compliment! – but that didn't need much observation," retorted Rhona with a laugh. "It was obvious. However, I asked Mitchell what Dr. Baseverie wanted; Mitchell replied that the gentleman desired an interview with Lady Riversreade. Now, as I said before, we never refuse doctors, so I told Mitchell to bring Dr. Baseverie to me. A moment later Dr. Baseverie entered. I want to describe him particularly, and you must listen most attentively. Figure, then, to yourself a man of medium height, neither stout nor slender, but comfortably plump, and apparently about forty-five years of age, dressed very correctly and fashionably in a black morning coat and vest, dark striped trousers, immaculate as to linen and neckwear, and furnished with a new silk hat, pearl-grey gloves and a tightly rolled gold-mounted umbrella. Incidentally, he wore a thin gold watch-chain, white spats and highly polished shoes. Got that?"

"I see him – his clothes and things, I mean," assented Hetherwick. "Fashionable medico sort, evidently! But – himself?"

"Now his face," continued Rhona. "Imagine a man with an almost absolutely bloodless countenance – a face the colour of old ivory – lighted by a pair of peculiarly piercing eyes, black as sloes, and the pallor of the face heightened by a rather heavy black moustache and equally black, slightly crinkled hair, thick enough above the ears but becoming sparse and thin on the crown. Imagine, too, a pair of full, red lips above a round but determined chin and a decidedly hooked nose, and you have – the man I'm describing!"

"Um!" said Hetherwick reflectively. "Hebraic, I think, from your description."

"That's just what I thought myself," agreed Rhona. "I said to myself at once, 'Whatever and whoever else you are, my friend, you're a Jew!' But the creature's manner and speech were English enough – very English. He had all the well-accustomed air of the medical practitioner who is also a bit of a man of the world, and I saw at once that anybody who tried to fence with him would usually come off second-best. His explanation of his presence was reasonable and commonplace enough: he was deeply interested in the sort of cases we had in the Home, and desired to acquaint himself with our methods and arrangements and so on. He made use of a few technical terms and phrases which were quite beyond my humble powers, and I carried in his card to Lady

Riversreade. Lady Riversreade is always accessible when there's a doctor in the case, and in two minutes Dr. Baseverie was closeted with her."

"That ends the first chapter, I suppose?" said Hetherwick. "Interesting – very! A good curtain! And the next?"

"The events of the second chapter," replied Rhona, "took place in Lady Riversreade's room, and I cannot even guess at their nature. I can only tell of things that I know. But there's a good deal in that. To begin with, although Dr. Baseverie had said to me that he desired to see the Home – which, of course, in the ordinary way meant his being either taken round by Lady Riversreade or by our resident house physician – he was not taken round. He never left that room from the moment he entered it until the moment in which he left it. And he remained in it an entire hour!"

"With Lady Riversreade?"

"With Lady Riversreade! She never left it, either. Nor did I go into it; she hates me to go in if she has anybody with her at any time. No! – there those two were together, from ten minutes to twelve until five minutes to one. Yet the man had said that he wanted to look round!"

"Is there any other way by which they could have left that room?" suggested Hetherwick. "Another door – or a French window?"

"There is nothing of the sort. The door into my room is the only means of entrance or exit to or from Lady Riversreade's. No – they were there all the time."

"Did you hear anything?"

"Nothing! The house in which Lady Riversreade set up this Home is an old, solid, well-built one – none of your modern gimcrack work in it! – it's a far better house than the Court, grand as that may be. All the doors and windows fit – I never heard a sound from the room."

"Well," asked Hetherwick, after due meditation, "and at the end of the hour?"

"At the end of the hour the door suddenly opened and Dr. Baseverie appeared, hat, gloves and umbrella in hand. He half turned as he came out and said a few words to Lady Riversreade. I heard them. He said, 'Well, then, next Friday morning at the same time?' Then he nodded, stepped into my room, closed the door behind him, made me a very polite, smiling bow as he passed my desk, and went out. A moment later he drove off in the car – it had been waiting at the entrance all that time."

"I suppose that's the end of chapter two," suggested Hetherwick. "Is there more?"

"Some," responded Rhona. "During the hour which Dr. Baseverie had spent with Lady Riversreade I had been very busy typing letters. When he had gone I took them into her room, so that she could sign them. I suppose I was a bit curious about what had just happened and may have been more than usually observant – anyway, I felt certain that the visit of this man, whoever he is, had considerably upset Lady Riversreade. She looked it."

"Precisely how?" inquired Hetherwick.

"Well, I couldn't exactly tell you. Perhaps a man wouldn't have noticed it. But being a woman, I did. She was perturbed – she'd been annoyed, or distressed, or surprised, or – something. I saw signs which, as a woman, were unmistakable – to a woman. The man's visit had been distasteful – troubling. I'm as certain of that as I am that this is roast mutton."

"Did she say anything?"

"Not one word. She was unusually taciturn – silent, in fact. She took the letters in silence, signed them in silence. No, on reflection, she never spoke a word while I was in the room. I took the letters away and began putting them in their envelopes. Soon afterwards Lady Riversreade came through my room and went out, and I saw her go across the grounds to the Court. She didn't turn up at the usual luncheon at the Home, and I didn't see her again that afternoon. In fact, I didn't see her again that day, for when I went home to the Court at five o'clock, Lady Riversreade's maid told me that her mistress had gone up to town and wouldn't be home until late that night. I went to bed before she returned."

"Next morning?" suggested Hetherwick.

"Next morning she was just as usual, and things went on in the usual way."

"Did she ever mention this man and his visit to you?" asked Hetherwick.

"No – not a word of him. But I found out something about him myself on Friday afternoon."

"What? Something relevant?"

"May be relevant to – something. I was wondering about him – and his printed card. I thought it odd that a medical man, so smartly dressed and all that, should present a card like that – not one well printed, a cheap thing! Besides, it had no address. I wondered – mere inquisitiveness, perhaps – where the creature came from. Now, we've a jolly good lot of the usual reference books there at the Home – and there's a first-class right up-to-date medical directory amongst them. So I looked up the name of Dr. Cyprian Baseverie. I say, looked it up – but I didn't do that – for it wasn't there! He's neither an English, nor a Scottish, nor an Irish medical man."

"Foreigner, then," said Hetherwick. "French, perhaps, or – American."

"May be an Egyptian, or a Persian, or a Eurasian, for anything I know," remarked Rhona. "What I know is that he's not on the list in that directory, though from his speech and manner you'd think he'd been practising in the West End all his life! Anyway, that's the story. Is there anything in it?"

Hetherwick picked up his glass of claret by its stem and looked thoughtfully through the contents of the bowl.

"The particular thing is – the extent and quality of Lady Riversreade's annoyance, or dismay, or perturbation, occasioned by the man's visit," he said at last. "If she was really very much upset—"

"If you want my honest opinion as eye-witness and as woman," remarked Rhona, "Lady Riversreade was very much upset. She gave me the impression that she'd just received very bad, disconcerting, unpleasant news. After seeing and watching her as she signed the letters I had no doubt whatever that the man had deliberately lied to me when he said he wanted to see the Home and its working – what he really wanted was access to Lady Riversreade."

"Look here!" exclaimed Hetherwick suddenly "Were you present when this man went into Lady Riversreade's room?"

"Present? Of course I was! I took him in – myself."

"You saw them meet?"

"To be sure!"

"Well, then, you know! Were they strangers? Did she recognise him? Did she show any sign of recognition whatever when she set eyes on him?"

"No, none! I'm perfectly certain she'd never seen the man before in her life! I could see quite well that he was an absolute stranger to her."

"And she to him?"

"Oh, that I don't know! He may have seen her a thousand times. But I'm sure she'd never seen him."

Hetherwick laid down his knife and fork with a gesture of finality.

"I'm going to find out who that chap is," he answered. "Got to!"

"You think his visit may have something to do with this?" asked Rhona.

"May, yes. Anyway, I'm not going to let any chance go. There's enough mystery in what you tell me about the man to make it worth while following him up. It must be done."

"How will you do it?"

"You say he said that he was going there again next Friday at the same time? Well, the thing to do, then, is to watch and follow him when he goes away."

"I'm afraid I'm no use for that! He'd know me."

"Nor am I! – I'm too conspicuous," laughed Hetherwick. "If I were a head and shoulders shorter, I might be some use. But I've got the very man – my clerk, one Mapperley. He's just the sort to follow and dog anybody and yet never be seen himself. As you'll say, when you've the pleasure of seeing him, Mapperley's the most ordinary, commonplace chap you ever set eyes on – pass absolutely unnoticed in any Cockney crowd. But he's as sharp as they make 'em, veiling a peculiar astuteness under his eminently undistinguished features. And what I shall do is this – I'll give Mapperley a full and detailed description of Dr. Cyprian

Baseverie: I've memorised yours already; Mapperley will memorise mine. Now Baseverie, whoever he may be, will probably go down to Dorking by the 10.10 from here; so will Mapperley. And after Mapperley has once spotted his man, he'll not lose sight of him."

"And he'll do – what?" asked Rhona.

"Follow him to Dorking – watch him – follow him back to London – find out where he goes when he returns – run him to earth, in fact. Then he'll report to me – and we shall know more than we do now, and also what to do next."

"I wonder what it's all going to lead to?" said Rhona. "Pretty much of a maze, isn't it?"

"It is," agreed Hetherwick. "But if we can only get a firm hold on a thread—"

"And that might break!" she laughed.

"Well, then, one that won't break," he said. "There are several loose ends lying about already. Matherfield's got a hold on one or two."

He went to see Matherfield next morning and told him the story that he had heard from Rhona. Matherfield grew thoughtful.

"Well, Mr. Hetherwick," he said, after a pause, "it's as I've said before – if this Lady Riversreade is mixed up in it, the thing to do is to go back and get as full a history as can possibly be got of her antecedents. We'll have to get on to that – but we'll wait to see what that clerk of yours discovers about this man. There may be something in it – in the meantime I'm hard at work on my own clues."

"Any luck?" asked Hetherwick.

"Scarcely that. But, as I say, we're at work. The five-pound note is a difficult matter. Given in change, of course, at Vivian's Night Club – but they tell me there that it's no uncommon thing to change ten, twenty, and even fifty-pound notes for their customers – it's a swell lot who forgather there – and of course they've no recollection whatever about that particular note or night. Still, the fact remains – that note came through Vivian's, and through one of its frequenters, to Granett, and I'm in hopes."

"And the medicine bottle?" suggested Hetherwick.

"Ah, there is more chance!" responded Matherfield, with a lightening eye. "That's only a question of time! I've got a man going round all the chemists in the West Central district – stiff job, for there are more of 'em than I believed. But he's bound to hit on the right one eventually. And then – well, we shall have a pretty good idea, if not positive proof, as to how Granett got hold of the stuff that poisoned him."

"I suppose there's no doubt that there was poison in that bottle?" inquired Hetherwick.

"According to the specialists, none," replied Matherfield. "And in the glass too. What sort of poison, I don't know – you know what these experts are – so mysterious about things! But they have told me this – the stuff that settled Granett was identical with that which finished off

Hannaford. That's certain."

"Then it probably came from the same source," said Hetherwick.

"Oh, my notion is that the man or men who poisoned one man poisoned the other," exclaimed Matherfield. "And at the same time. At least, I think Granett got his dose at the same time – probably carried it off in his pocket and drank it when he got home. But – we shall trace that bottle! Let me know what you find out about this man Baseverie, Mr. Hetherwick – every little helps."

Hetherwick duly coached Mapperley in the part he wanted him to play, and Mapperley, with money in his pockets and a pipe in his mouth, lounged off to Victoria on the following Friday morning. His principal saw nothing and heard nothing of him all that day.

# LADY RIVERSREADE

As Hetherwick was breakfasting next morning, Mapperley, outwardly commonplace and phlegmatic as ever, walked into his room.

"Brief outline first, Mapperley," commanded Hetherwick, instinctively scenting news. "Details later. Well?"

"Spotted him at once at Victoria," said Mapperley. "Followed him down there. He was at Riversreade an hour. Then went back to Dorking – had lunch at 'Red Lion.' He stopped there till four o'clock, lunching and idling. Went back to town by the 4.29, arriving 6.05. I followed him then to the Café de Paris. He dined there and hung about till past ten. And then he went to Vivian's Night Club."

Hetherwick pricked up his ears at that. Vivian's Night Club! – Here, at any rate, seemed to be a link in the chain of which Matherfield believed himself to hold at least one end. The five-pound note found on Granett had been traced to Vivian's Night Club: now Mapperley had tracked Lady Riversreade's mysterious visitor to the same resort.

"To Vivian's Night Club, eh, Mapperley?" he said. "Let's see? – where is that?"

"Entrance is in Candlestick Passage, off St. Martin's Lane," replied Mapperley with promptitude. "Club's on first floor – jolly fine suite of rooms, too!"

"You've been in it?" suggested Hetherwick.

"Twice! Not last night, though. You didn't give me any further orders than to see where he went finally, after returning to town. So, when I'd run him to earth at Vivian's, I went home. I argued that if he was wanted further, Vivian's would find him."

"All right, Mapperley. But before that? You followed him to Riversreade Court?"

Mapperley grinned widely.

"No! – I did better than that. I was there before him – much better that, than following. I spotted him quick enough at Victoria, and made sure he got into the 10.10. Then I got in. As soon as we got to Dorking, I jumped out, got outside the station and chartered a taxi and drove off to

65

Riversreade Court. I made the driver hide his cab up the road: I laid low in the plantation opposite the entrance gates. Presently my lord came along and drove up to the house. He was there the best part of an hour; then he drove off again towards Dorking. I followed at a good distance: kept him in sight, all the same. He got out of his conveyance in the High Street: so did I. He went into the Red Lion: so did I. He had lunch there: so had I. After that he lounged about in the smoking-room: I kept an eye on him."

"I suppose he didn't meet anybody?"

"Nobody!"

"Well, and at the Café de Paris? Did he meet anybody there?"

"He exchanged a nod and a word here and there with men – and women – that came in and went out. But as to any arranged meeting, I should say not. I should say, too, that he was well known at the Café de Paris."

"Did he seem to be a man of means? You know what I mean?"

"He did himself very well at lunch and dinner, anyway," said Mapperley, with another grin. "Bottle of claret at Dorking, and a pint of champagne at the Café de Paris – big cigars, too. That sort of man, you know."

Hetherwick considered matters a moment.

"How do you get in to this Vivian's Night Club?" he asked suddenly.

"Pay!" answered Mapperley laconically. "At the door. Some nonsense about being proposed, but that's all bosh! Two of you go – say Brown and Smith. Brown proposes Smith and Smith proposes Brown. All rot! Anybody can get in – with money."

"And what goes on there?"

"Dancing! Drinking! Devilry! Quite respectable, though," replied Mapperley. "Been no prosecutions, anyway – so far."

"What time does it open?"

"Nine o'clock," answered Mapperley, with a suggestive grin. "In the old days it didn't open till after the theatres. But now – earlier."

"Really not a night-club at all – in the old acceptation of the term," suggested Hetherwick. "Evening, really?"

"That's about it," agreed Mapperley. "Anyhow, it's Vivian's."

For the second time in the course of his investigations, Hetherwick's thoughts turned to Boxley. Boxley's love of intimate acquaintance with all sides of London life had doubtless led him to look in at Vivian's: he would ask Boxley for some further information. And he looked up Boxley at the club.

Boxley knew Vivian's well enough – innocent and innocuous now, said Boxley, what with all these new regulations and so on: degenerated, indeed – or improved, just whichever way you regarded it – into a supper club and that sort of thing. Dancing? – oh yes, there was dancing, and so on – but things had altered.

"Well, I don't want to dance there, nor to go there at all, for that matter, unless I'm obliged to," said Hetherwick. "What I want to know is something about a man who, I believe, frequents the place – a somewhat notable man."

"Describe him!" commanded Boxley.

Hetherwick retailed Rhona's description of Baseverie: Boxley nodded.

"I know that man – by sight," he said. "Seen him there. I believe he's something to do with the proprietorship: that place is owned by a small syndicate. But I don't know his name. I've seen him outside too – round about Leicester Square and its purlieus."

Hetherwick went from Boxley to Matherfield and told him the result of Mapperley's work.

"I know Vivian's, of course," said Matherfield. "Been in there two or three times lately in relation to this five-pound note. Don't remember seeing this man, though. But in view of what your clerk says, I'd like to see him. Come with me. We'll go tonight."

"Make it Monday," suggested Hetherwick. "Tomorrow, Sunday, I shall be meeting Miss Hannaford again, and before we go to Vivian's I'd like to know if she has anything to tell about the last visit of Baseverie to Riversreade Court – the visit that Mapperley watched yesterday. She may have."

"Monday night then," agreed Matherfield. "I don't know what we can expect, but I'd certainly like to know who this man is and why he goes to Lady Riversreade."

"No good, you may be sure!" said Hetherwick. "But we'll ferret it out – somehow."

"Odd, that things seem to be centring round Vivian's!" mused Matherfield. "The fiver – and now this. Well – Monday evening then? – perhaps Miss Hannaford can supply a bit of extra news tomorrow."

Hetherwick, meeting Rhona at Victoria next day, found his arm grasped in Rhona's right hand and himself twisted round.

"If you want to see Lady Riversreade in the flesh, there she is!" whispered Rhona. "Came up by the same train – there, going towards the bookstall; a tall man with her!"

At that moment Lady Riversreade turned to speak to a porter who was carrying some light luggage for her, and Hetherwick had a full and good view of her face and figure. A fine, handsome, capable-looking woman, he said to himself, and one that once seen would not easily be forgotten.

"Who's the man?" he asked, looking from Lady Riversreade to her companion, a tall, bronzed man of military appearance, and apparently of about her own age.

"Major Penteney," replied Rhona promptly. "He's a friend of hers, who takes a tremendous interest in the Home – in fact, he acts as a sort of representative of it here in town. He's often down at the Court – I believe he's in love with her."

"Well-matched couple," observed Hetherwick, as the two people under notice moved away towards the exit. "And what's Lady Riversreade come up for?"

"Oh, I don't know that," replied Rhona. "She never tells me anything about her private doings. I heard her say that she was going to Town this morning and shouldn't be back until Tuesday, but that's all I know."

"That man, Baseverie, came again on Friday?" suggested Hetherwick. "But I know he did – Mapperley watched him. Anything happen?"

"Nothing – except that Lady Riversreade told me that if Dr. Baseverie called he was to be brought in to her at once," answered Rhona. "He came at the same time as before, and was with her an hour."

"Any signs on her part of being further upset?" asked Hetherwick.

"No – on the contrary she seemed quite cool and collected after he'd gone," said Rhona. "Of course she made no reference to his visit."

"Has she never mentioned him to you?"

"Never! In spite of the fact that his professed object was to see the Home and the patients, he's seen neither."

"Which shows that that was all a mere excuse to get speech with her!" muttered Hetherwick. "Well – we're going to find out who this Dr. Baseverie is! Matherfield and I intend to get in touch with him tomorrow night."

But when the next night came Hetherwick's plans about the visit to Vivian's were frustrated by an unexpected happening, and neither he nor Matherfield as much as crossed the threshold of the night-club in Candlestick Passage. They went there at ten o'clock: that, said Matherfield, was a likely hour – between then and eleven-thirty the place would be full of its habitual frequenters: the notion was to mingle unobtrusively with whatever crowd chanced to be there and to keep eyes and ears open for whatever happened to transpire.

Candlestick Passage, unfamiliar to Hetherwick until that evening, proved to be one of the many narrow alleys which open out of St. Martin's Lane in the neighbourhood of the theatres. It wore a very commonplace, not to say shabby complexion, and there was nothing in its atmosphere to suggest adventure or romance. Not was there anything alluring about the entrance to Vivian's, which was merely a wide, double doorway, ornamented by two evergreen shrubs set in tubs and revealing swing-doors within, and a carpeted staircase beyond. Hetherwick and Matherfield, however, never reached swing-doors or staircase: as they approached the outer entrance a tall woman emerged, and without so much as a look right or left turned down the passage towards the street. She paid no attention to the two men as she walked quickly past them – but Hetherwick softly seized his companion's arm.

"Lady Riversreade, by all that's wonderful!" he exclaimed under his breath. "That woman!"

Matherfield turned sharply, gazing after the retreating figure.

"That," he said incredulously, "coming out of here? Certain?"

"Dead sure!" affirmed Hetherwick. "I knew her at once – I'd had a particularly good look at her, yesterday. That's she!"

"What's she doing at Vivian's?" muttered Matherfield. "Queer, that!"

"But she's going away from it," said Hetherwick. "Come on! – let's see where she goes. We can easily come back here. But why not follow her first?"

"Good!" agreed Matherfield. "Come on then! Easily keep her in sight."

Lady Riversreade at that moment was turning out of the passage, to her left hand. When the two men emerged from it, she was already several yards ahead, going towards St. Martin's Church. Her tall figure made her good to follow, but Matherfield kept Hetherwick back; no use, he said, in pressing too closely on your quarry.

"Tall as she is and tall as we are," he whispered, as they threaded in out of the crowds on the pavement, "we can spot her at twenty yards. Cautiously, now – she's making for the cab rank!"

They watched Lady Riversreade charter and enter a taxi-cab: in another minute it moved away. But it had scarcely moved when Matherfield was at the door of the next cab on the rank.

"You saw that cab go off with a tall woman in it?" he said to the driver. "There! – just rounding the corner, know its driver? Right! – follow it carefully. Note where it stops, and if the woman gets out. Drive slowly past wherever that is, and then pull up a bit farther on. Be sharp, now – this is—" he bent towards the man and whispered a word or two: a second later he and Hetherwick were in the cab and across the top side of Trafalgar Square.

"This is getting a bit thick, Mr. Hetherwick," remarked Matherfield. "Your clerk tracks his man to Vivian's on Friday night, we find Lady Riversreade coming out of Vivian's on Monday night. Now I shouldn't think Lady Riversreade, whom we hear of chiefly as a humanitarian, a likely sort of lady to visit Vivian's!"

"She came out of Vivian's, anyway!" replied Hetherwick.

"Then, of course, she'd been in!" said Matherfield. "But why? I should say – to have a meeting with Baseverie, or with somebody representing him, or having something to do with the business that took him to Riversreade Court. What business is it? Has it anything to do with our business? However, there's Lady Riversreade in that cab in front, and we'll just follow her to find out where she goes – no doubt she's bound for some swell West End hotel. And that knowledge will be useful, for I may want to see her in the morning – to ask a question or two."

"Somewhat early for that, isn't it?" suggested Hetherwick. "Do we know enough?"

"Depends on what you call enough," replied Matherfield dryly. "What I know is this: that man Granett was poisoned. He had on him a brand new five-pound note. That note I've traced as far as Vivian's, where it was certainly paid to some customer in change on the very day before Granett and Hannaford's deaths: Vivian's is accordingly a place of interest. Now I hear of a mysterious man visiting Lady Riversreade – the man is tracked to Vivian's – I myself see Lady Riversreade emerging from Vivian's. I think I must ask Lady Riversreade what she knows about Vivian's and a certain Dr. Baseverie, and, incidentally, if she ever heard of a place called Sellithwaite and a police-superintendent named Hannaford? Eh! But we're leaving the region of the fashionable hotels."

Hetherwick looked out of the window, what he saw seemed unfamiliar.

"We're going up Edgware Road," said Matherfield. He leaned out of the cab and gave some further instructions to the driver. "I don't want to arouse any suspicion there in front," he remarked, dropping into his seat again. "The probability is that she's going to some private house, and I don't want her to get any idea that she's followed. Ah! – now we turn into Harrow Road."

The cab went away by Paddington Green, turned sharply at the Town Hall, and made up St. Mary's Terrace. Presently it slowed down; proceeded still more slowly; passed the other cab which had come to a standstill in front of a block of high buildings; a few yards farther on it stopped altogether. The driver got down from his seat and came to the door.

"That tall lady!" he said confidentially. "Her as got into the other cab. She's gone into St. Mary's Mansions – just below."

"Flats, aren't they?" asked Matherfield.

"That's it, sir," answered the driver. He looked down the street. "Cab's going off again, sir. Porter came out and paid."

"That looks as if she was going to stay here awhile," remarked Matherfield in an undertone. "Well, we'll get out, too, and take a look round." He paid and dismissed the driver, and crossing over to the opposite side of the roadway, pointed out to Hetherwick the block of flats into which Lady Riversreade had disappeared. "Big place," he muttered. "Regular rabbit-warren. However, no other entrance than this – the old burial ground's at the back, no way out there, I do know that! So she can't very well vanish that way."

"You're going to wait, then?" asked Hetherwick.

"I don't believe in starting out on any game unless I see it through," replied Matherfield. "Yes, I think we'll wait. But there's no necessity to hang around in the open street. I know this district – used to be at the police station round the corner. You see all these houses on this side, Mr. Hetherwick? They're all lodging-houses, and I know most of their keepers. Wait here a minute, and I'll soon get a room that we can watch from, without being seen ourselves."

He left Hetherwick standing under the shadow of a neighbouring high wall, and went a little way down the street. Hetherwick heard him open the gate of one of the little gardens and knock at a door. Then some little delay. Hetherwick passed the time in staring at the long rows of lighted windows in the flats opposite, wondering to which of them Lady Riversreade had gone and what she was doing there at all. It was clear to him that this was some adventure connected with the mysterious Baseverie and with Vivian's Night Club – but how, and of what nature?

Matherfield came back presently, cheerful and reassuring.

"Come along, Mr. Hetherwick!" he whispered. "There's a man here – lodging-house keeper – who knows me. We can have his front parlour window to watch from. Far better that than patrolling the street. We shall be comfortable there."

"You're intent on watching, then?" said Hetherwick as they moved off.

"I'm not coming all that way for nothing," replied Matherfield. "I'm going to follow her up till she settles for the night. That won't be here; she'll be off to some hotel or other before long."

But Matherfield's prediction proved to be faulty. Time dragged slowly by in the stuffy and shabby little room in which he and Hetherwick took up a position and from the window of which Matherfield kept a constant watch on the entrance of the flats, exactly opposite. Midnight came and went, but nothing happened. And at half-past twelve Hetherwick suggested that the game wasn't worth the candle, and that he should prefer to depart.

"You do as you like, Mr. Hetherwick," said Matherfield, stifling a suspicious yawn. "I'm sick enough of it, too. But here I stop till she comes out – whether it's this side of breakfast or the other side!"

"And what then?" asked Hetherwick, half derisively.

"Then we'll see – or I'll see, if you're going – where she goes next! Don't believe in half measures!" retorted Matherfield.

"Oh, I'll see it out!" said Hetherwick. "After all, it'll be daylight soon."

Daylight came over the house-tops at four o'clock. They had seen nothing up to then. But at twenty minutes to five Matherfield tugged his companion's arm. Lady Riversreade, in a big ulster travelling coat and carrying a small suitcase, was emerging alone from the opposite door.

# *ALIAS* MADAME LISTORELLE

The woman thus observed marched swiftly away down the deserted street in the direction of the Town Hall at the corner, and Matherfield, after one more searching look at her, dropped the slat of the Venetian blind through which he had been peeping, and turned on his companion. At the same instant he reached a hand for his overcoat and hat.

"Now, Mr. Hetherwick," he said sharply, "this has got to be a one-man job! There'll be nothing extraordinary in one man going along the streets to catch an early morning train, but it would look a bit suspicious if two men went together on the same errand and the same track! I'm off after her! I'll run her down! I'm used to that sort of thing. You go to your chambers and get some sleep. I'll look in later and tell you what news I have. Sharp's the word, now!"

He was out of the room and the house within the next few seconds, and Hetherwick, half vexed with himself for having lingered there on a job which Matherfield thus unceremoniously took into his own hands, prepared to follow. Presently he went out into the shabby hall; the man of the house was just coming downstairs, stifling a big yawn. He smiled knowingly when he saw Hetherwick.

"Matherfield gone, sir?" he inquired. "I heard the door close."

"He's gone," assented Hetherwick. "The person he wanted appeared suddenly, and he's gone in pursuit."

The man, a smug-faced, easy-going sort of person, smiled again.

"Rum doings these police have!" he remarked. "Queer job, watching all night through a window. I was just coming down to make you a cup of coffee," he continued. "I'll get you one in a few minutes, if you like. Or tea now? Perhaps you'd prefer tea?"

"It's very good of you," said Hetherwick. "But to tell you the truth I'd rather get home and to bed. Many thanks, all the same."

Then, out of sheer good nature, he slipped a treasury note into the man's hand, and, bidding him good morning, went away. He, too, walked down the street in the direction taken by Lady Riversreade and her pursuer. But when he came to the bottom and emerged into Harrow Road he saw nothing of them, either to left or right. The road, however, was not deserted; there were already workmen going to early morning tasks, and close by the corner of the Town Hall a roadman was busy with his broom. Hetherwick went up to him.

"Did you see a lady, and then a gentleman, come down here, from St. Mary's Terrace, just now?" he asked. "Tall people, both of them."

The man rested on his broom, half turned, and pointed towards Paddington Bridge.

"I see 'em, guv'nor," he answered. "Tall lady, carrying a little portmantle. Gone along over the bridge yonder. Paddington station way. And, after her, Matherfield."

"Oh, you know him, do you?" exclaimed Hetherwick, in surprise.

The man jerked a thumb in the direction of the adjacent police station.

"Used to be a sergeant here, did Matherfield," he replied. "I knows him, right enough! Once run me in – me an' a mate o' mine – for bein' a bit festive like. Five bob and costs that was. But I don't bear him no grudge, not me! Thank 'ee, guv'nor."

Hetherwick left another tip behind him and walked slowly off towards Edgware Road. The Tube trains were just beginning to run, and he caught a south-bound one and went down to Charing Cross and thence to the Temple. And at six o'clock he tumbled into bed, and slept soundly until, four hours later, he heard Mapperley moving about in the adjoining room.

Mapperley, whose job at Hetherwick's was a good deal of a sinecure, was leisurely reading the news when his master entered. He laid the paper aside, and gave Hetherwick a knowing glance.

"Got some more information last night," he said. "About that chap I tracked the other day."

"How did you get it?" asked Hetherwick.

"Put in a bit of time at Vivian's," answered Mapperley. "There's a fellow there that I know. Clerk to the secretary chap, named Flowers. That man Baseverie has a share in the place – sort of director, I think."

"What time were you at Vivian's?" inquired Hetherwick. "Late or early?"

"Early – for them," answered Mapperley.

"Did you see the man there?"

"I did. He was there all the time I was. In and about all the time. But at first he was in what seemed to be serious conversation with a tall, handsome woman. They sat talking in an alcove in the lounge there some time. Then she went off – alone."

"Oh, you saw that, did you?" said Hetherwick. "Well, I may as well tell you, since you know what you do, that the woman was Lady Riversreade!"

"Oh, I guessed that!" remarked Mapperley. "I figured in that at once.

But that wasn't all. I found out more. That dead man, Hannaford – from what I heard from Flowers – I've no doubt whatever that Hannaford was at Vivian's once, if not twice, during the two or three nights before his death. Anyway, Flowers recognised my description of him – which I'd got, of course, from you and the papers."

"Hannaford. There, eh?" exclaimed Hetherwick. "Alone?"

"No – came in with this Baseverie. They don't know him as Dr. Baseverie there, though. Plain Mister. I'm quite sure it was Hannaford who was with him."

"Did you get the exact dates – and times?" asked Hetherwick.

"I didn't. Flowers couldn't say that. But he remembered such a man."

"Well, that's something," said Hetherwick. He turned into another room and sat down to his breakfast, thinking. "Mapperley, come here!" he called presently. "Look here," he went on as the clerk came in. "Since you know this Vivian place, go there again tonight, and try to find out if that friend of yours knows anything of a tall man who corresponds to the description of the man whom Hannaford was seen to meet at Victoria. You read Ledbitter's account of that, given at the inquest?"

"Yes," replied Mapperley. "But of what value is it? None – for practical purposes! He couldn't even tell the shape of the man's nose, nor the colour of his eyes! All he could tell was that he saw a man muffled in such a fashion that he saw next to nothing of his face, and that he was tall and smartly dressed. There are a few tens of thousands – scores, perhaps – of tall, smartly-dressed men in London!"

"Never mind – inquire," said Hetherwick, "and particularly if such a man has ever been seen in Baseverie's company there."

He finished his breakfast, and then, instead of going down to the Central Criminal Court, after his usual habit, he hung about in his chambers, expecting Matherfield. But Matherfield did not come, and at noon Hetherwick, impelled by a new idea, left a message for him in case he called, and went out. In pursuance of the idea, he journeyed once more to the regions of Paddington and knocked at the door of the house wherein he and Matherfield had kept watch on the flats opposite.

The lodging-house keeper opened the door himself and grinned on seeing Hetherwick. Hetherwick stepped inside and nodded at the door of the room which he had left only a few hours before.

"I want a word or two with you," he said. "In private."

"Nobody in here, sir," replied the man. "Come in."

He closed the door on himself and his visitor, and offered Hetherwick a chair.

"I expected you'd be back during the day," he said, with a sly smile. "Either you or Matherfield, or both!"

"You haven't seen him again?" asked Hetherwick.

"No; he's not been here," replied the man.

"Well, I wanted to ask you a question," continued Hetherwick. "Perhaps two or three. To begin with, have you lived here long?"

74

"Been here since before these flats were built – and that's a good many years ago; I can't say exactly how many," said the other, glancing at the big block opposite his window. "Twenty-two or three, anyway."

"Then I dare say you know most of the people hereabouts?" suggested Hetherwick. "By sight, at any rate."

The lodging-house keeper smiled and shook his head.

"That would be a tall order, mister!" he answered. "There's a few thousand people packed into this bit of London. Of course, I do know a good many, close at hand. But if you're a Londoner you'll know that Londoners keep themselves to themselves. May seem queer, but it's a fact that I don't know the names of my next-door neighbours on either side – though to be sure they've only been here a few years in either case."

"What I was suggesting," said Hetherwick, "was that you probably knew by sight many of the people who live in the flats opposite your house."

"Oh, I know some of 'em by sight," assented the man. "They're a mixed lot over in those flats! A few old gentlemen – retired – two or three old ladies – and a fair lot of actresses – very popular with the stage is those flats. But, of course, it is only by sight – I don't know any of 'em by name. Just see them going in and coming out, you know."

"Do you happen to know by sight a tall, handsome woman who has a flat there?" asked Hetherwick. "A woman who's likely to be very well dressed?"

The lodging-house keeper, who was without his coat and had the sleeves of his shirt rolled up, scratched his elbows and looked thoughtful.

"I think I do know the lady you mean," he said at last. "Goes out with one o' those pesky little poms – a black 'un – on a lead? That her?"

"I don't know anything about a dog," replied Hetherwick. "The woman I mean is, as I said, tall, handsome, distinguished-looking, fair hair and a fresh complexion, and about forty or so."

"I dare say that's the one I'm thinking of," said the man. "I have seen such a lady now and then – not of late, though." Then he gave Hetherwick a shrewd, inquiring glance. "You and Matherfield after her?" he asked.

"Not exactly that," answered Hetherwick. "What I want to find out – now – is her name. The name she's known by here, anyway."

"I can soon settle that for you," said the lodging-house keeper with alacrity. "I know the caretaker of those flats well enough – often have a talk with him. He'll tell me anything – between ourselves. Now then, let's get it right – a tall, handsome lady, about forty, fair hair, fresh complexion, well dressed. That it, mister?"

"You've got it," said Hetherwick.

"Then you wait here a bit, and I'll slip across," said the man. "All on the strict between ourselves, you know. As I said, the caretaker and me's pals."

He left the room, and a moment later Hetherwick saw him cross the road and descend into the basement of the flats. Within a quarter of an hour he was back, and evidently primed with news.

"Soon settled that for you, mister!" he announced triumphantly. "He knew who you meant! The lady's name is Madame Listorelle. Here, I got him to write it down on a bit o' paper, not being used to foreign names. He thinks she's something to do with the stage. She's the tenant of flat twenty-six. But he says that of late she's seldom there – comes for a night or two, then away, maybe for months at a time. He saw her here yesterday, though; she hadn't been there, he says, for a good bit. But there, it don't signify to him whether she's there or away – always punctual with her money, and that's the main thing, ain't it?"

Hetherwick added to his largess of the early morning, and went away. He was now convinced that Lady Riversreade, for some purpose of her own, kept up a flat in Paddington, visited it occasionally, and was known there as Madame Listorelle. How much was there in that, and what bearing had it on the problem he was endeavouring to solve?

# WHO WAS SHE?

Late that night, when Hetherwick was thinking things over, a pounding on his stairs and a knock on his outer door heralded the entrance of Matherfield, who, with an expressive look, flung himself into the nearest easy chair.

"For heaven's sake, Mr. Hetherwick, give me a drop of that whisky!" he exclaimed. "I'm dead beat – and dead disappointed, too! Such a day as I've had after that woman! And what it all means the Lord only knows – I don't!"

Hetherwick helped his evidently far-spent visitor to a whisky and soda, and waited until he had taken a hearty pull at it. Then he resumed his own seat and took up his pipe.

"I gather that you haven't had a very successful day, Matherfield?" he suggested. "Hope it wasn't exactly a wild-goose chase?"

"That's just about what it comes to, then!" exclaimed Matherfield. "Anyway, after taking no end of trouble she got clear away, practically under my very nose! But I'll tell you all about it; that's what I dropped in for. When I went out of that house in St. Mary's Terrace, she was just turning the corner to the right, Bishop's Road way. Of course I followed. She went over the bridge – the big railway bridge – and at the end turned down to Paddington Station. I concluded then that she was going up by some early morning train. She entered the station by the first-class booking office; I was not so many yards in her rear then. But instead of stopping there and taking a ticket she went right through, crossed the station to the arrival platform and signalled to a taxi-cab. In another minute she was in it, and off. Very luckily there was another cab close by. I hailed that and told the driver to keep the first cab in sight and follow it to wherever it went. So off we went again, on another pursuit! And it ended at another terminus – Waterloo!"

"Going home, I suppose," remarked Hetherwick, as Matherfield paused to take up his glass. "You can get to Dorking from Waterloo."

"She wasn't going to any Dorking!" answered Matherfield. "I soon found that out. Early as it was, there were a lot of people at Waterloo, and when she went to the ticket office I contrived to be close behind her – close enough, at any rate, to overhear anything she said. She asked for a first single to Southampton."

"Southampton!" exclaimed Hetherwick. "Um!"

"Southampton!" repeated Matherfield. "First single for Southampton. She took the ticket and walked away, looking neither right nor left; she never glanced at me. Well, as I said yesterday, I don't believe in starting out on anything unless I go clean through with it. So after a minute's thought I booked for Southampton – third. Then I went out and looked at the notice board. Southampton, 5.40. It was then 5.25. So I went to the telephone office, rang up our head-quarters and told 'em I was after something and they needn't expect to see me all day. Then I bought a time-table and a newspaper or two at the bookstall, just opening, and went to the train. There were a lot of people travelling by it. The train hadn't come up to the platform then; when it came down a minute or two later I watched her get in; she was good to spot because of her tall figure. I got into a smoker, a bit lower down, and in due course off we went, me wondering, to tell you the truth, precisely why I was going! But I was going – wherever she went."

"Even out of the country?" asked Hetherwick, with a smile.

"Aye, I thought of that!" assented Matherfield. "She might be slinging her hook for anything I knew. That made me turn to the steamship news in the paper, and I saw then that the *Tartaric* was due to leave Southampton for New York about two o'clock that very afternoon. Well, there were more improbable things than that she meant to go by it, for reasons of her own, especially if she really is the Mrs. Whittingham of the Sellithwaite affair ten years ago. You see, I thought it out like this – granting she's Mrs. Whittingham, that was, she'll be astute enough to know that there's no time-limit to a criminal prosecution in this country, and that she's still liable to arrest, prosecution, and conviction; she'd probably know, too, that this Hannaford affair has somehow drawn fresh attention to her little matter, and that she's in danger. Again, I'd been working out an idea about her and this man Baseverie. How do we know that Baseverie wasn't an accomplice of hers in that Sellithwaite fraud? In most cases of that sort the woman has an accomplice somewhere in the background – Baseverie may have been mixed with her then. And now he may have information that has led him to warn her to make herself scarce, eh?"

"There's something in that, Matherfield," admitted Hetherwick. "Yes – decidedly something."

"There may be a good deal," affirmed Matherfield. "You see, we've let those newspaper chaps have a lot of information. I'm a believer in making use of the Press; it's a valuable aid sometimes, perhaps generally, but there are other times when you can do too much of it: it's a sort of giving valuable aid to the enemy. I don't know whether we haven't let those reporters know too much in this case. We've let 'em know, for instance, about the portrait found in Hannaford's pocket-book, and about the sealed packet in which, we believe, was the secret of his patent: all that's been in the papers, though, to be sure, they didn't make much copy out of it. Still, there was enough for anybody who followed the case closely. Now, supposing that Baseverie was Mrs. Whittingham's accomplice ten years ago, and that he'd read all this and seen the reproduction of the portrait, wouldn't he see that she was in some danger and warn her? I think it likely, and I wish we hadn't been quite so free with our news for those paper chaps. I'm glad, anyhow, that there's one thing I haven't told 'em of – that medicine bottle found at Granett's! There's nobody but me, you, and the medical men know of that, so far."

"You think this woman – Lady Riversreade as she is, Mrs. Whittingham as she used to be – was making off to Southampton, and possibly farther, on a hint from Baseverie?" said Hetherwick ruminatively.

"Put it this way," replied Matherfield. "Of course, you've got to assume a lot, but we can't do without assuming things in this business. Lady Riversreade was formerly Mrs. Whittingham. Mrs. Whittingham did a clever bit of fraud at Sellithwaite, and got away with the swag. Baseverie was her accomplice. Now then, ten years later Mrs. Whittingham has become my Lady Riversreade, a very wealthy woman. She's suddenly visited by Baseverie at Riversreade Court, and is obviously upset by his first visit. He comes again. Three nights later she's seen to come out of a club which he frequents. She spends most of the night in a flat in a quiet part of London, and next morning slopes off as early as five o'clock to a port – Southampton. What inference is to be drawn? That her visit to Southampton has certainly something to do with Baseverie's visits to her and her visit to Vivian's!"

"I think there's something in that, too," said Hetherwick, "But – we're on the way to Southampton. Go on!"

"Very good train, that," continued Matherfield. "We got to Southampton just before eight – a minute or two late. I was wanting something to eat and drink by that time, and I was glad to see my lady turn into the refreshment-room as soon as she left her carriage. So did I. I knew she'd never suspect a quiet, ordinary man like me; if she deigned to give me a glance – she's a very haughty-looking woman, I observed – she'd only take me for a commercial traveller. And we were not so far off each other in that room; she sat at a little table, having some tea and so on: I was at the counter. Of course, I never showed that I was taking any notice of her – but I got in two or three good, comprehensive inspections. Very good-looking, no doubt of it, Mr. Hetherwick – a woman that's worn well! But of course you've seen that for yourself."

"You must remember that I've only seen her twice," remarked Hetherwick, with a laugh. "Once at Victoria, when Miss Hannaford pointed her out; once night before last, when it was by a poorish gaslight. But I'll take your word, Matherfield. Well, and what happened next?"

"Oh, she took her time over her tea and toast," continued Matherfield. "Very leisured in all her movements, I assure you. At last she moved off – of course I followed, casually and carelessly. Now, as you may be aware, Southampton West, where the train set us down, is a bit out of the town, and I expected her to take a cab. But she didn't; she walked away from the station. So did I – twenty or thirty yards in the rear. She took her time; it seemed to me she was purposely loitering. It struck me at last why – she was waiting until the business offices were open. I was right in that: as soon as the town clocks struck nine she quickened her pace and made a beeline for her objective. And what do you think that was?"

"No idea," said Hetherwick.

"White Star offices!" answered Matherfield. "Went straight there, and walked straight in! Of course, I waited outside, where she wouldn't see me when she came out again. She was in there about twenty minutes. When she came out she turned to another part of the town. And near that old gateway, or bar, or whatever it is that stands across the street, I lost her – altogether!"

"Some exceptional reason, I should think, Matherfield," remarked Hetherwick. "How was it?"

"My own stupid fault!" growled Matherfield. "Took my eye off her in a particularly crowded part – the town was beginning to get very busy. I just happened to let my attention be diverted – and she was gone! At first I made certain she'd gone into some shop. I looked into several – risky as that was – but I couldn't find her. I hung about; no good. Then I came to the conclusion that she'd turned down one of the side streets or alleys or passages – there were several about there – and got clean away. And after hanging around a bit, and going up one street and down another – a poor job in our business at the best of times and all dependent on mere luck! – I decided to make a bold stroke and be sure of at any rate something."

"What? How?" asked Hetherwick.

"I thought I'd find out what she'd gone to the White Star offices for," replied Matherfield. "Of course, I didn't want to raise any suspicion against her under the circumstances. But I flatter myself I'm a bit of a diplomatist, and I laid my plans. I went in there, got hold of a clerk who was a likely looking chap for secret keeping, told him who I was and showed my credentials, and asked him for the information I wanted. I got it. As luck would have it, my man had attended to her himself and remembered her quite well. Of course, little more than an hour and a half had passed since she'd been in there."

"And – what had she been in for?" asked Hetherwick. "What did you hear?"

Matherfield nodded significantly.

"Just what I expected to hear," he answered. "She'd booked a second-class passage for New York in the *Tartaric*, sailing that afternoon, in the name of H. Cunningham. As soon as I found that out, I knew I should come across her again – there'd be no need to go raking the town for her. I ascertained that passengers would be allowed to go aboard from two o'clock; the boat would sail between five and six. So, having once more admonished the clerk to secrecy and given him plausible excuses for my inquisitiveness, I went off to relax a bit, and in due time sat down to an early and comfortable lunch – a man must take his ease now and then, you know, Mr. Hetherwick."

"Exactly, Matherfield – I quite agree," said Hetherwick. "But I dare say your brain was at work, all the same, while you ate and drank?"

"It was, sir," assented Matherfield. "Yes – I made my plans. I wasn't going to New York, of course; that was out of the question. But I was going to have speech with her. I decided that I'd watch for her coming aboard the *Tartaric* – being alone, she'd probably come early. I proposed to get her aside, accosting her, of course, as Lady Riversreade, tell her who I was and show my papers, and ask her if she would give me any information about a certain Dr. Cyprian Baseverie. I thought I'd see how she took that before asking anything further; if I saw that she was taken aback, confused, and especially if she gave me any prevaricating or elusive answer, I'd ask her straight out if before her marriage to the late Sir John Riversreade she was the Mrs. Whittingham who, some ten years ago, stayed for a time at the White Hart Hotel at Sellithwaite. And I practically made up my mind, too, that if she admitted that and I saw good cause for it, I'd detain her."

"You meant to go as far as that?" exclaimed Hetherwick.

"I did! I should have been justified," replied Matherfield. "However, that's neither here nor there, for I never saw her! I was down at the point of departure well before two, and I assured myself that nobody had gone aboard the *Tartaric* up to that time. I kept as sharp a look out as any man with only one pair of eyes could, right away from ten minutes to two until five-and-twenty past five, when the boat sailed, but she never turned up. Of course you'll say that she must have slipped on unobserved by me, but I'm positive she didn't. No, sir! It's my opinion that she thought better of it and didn't go – forfeiting her passage money, or a part of it, would be nothing to a woman of her means – or that she was frightened at the last minute of showing herself on that stage!"

"Frightened! Why?" asked Hetherwick.

Matherfield laughed significantly.

"There were two or three of our men from Scotland Yard about," he answered. "I'm not aware of what they were after; I didn't ask 'em. But I did ask them to give me a hand in looking out for a lady whom I fully described – which is why I'm dead certain she never went aboard. Now, it may have been that she came down there, knew – you never know! –

some of those chaps and – made herself scarce! Anyway – I never set eyes on her. Never, in fact, saw her again after I lost her in the morning. So – that's where I am!"

"You came back – defeated?" remarked Hetherwick.

"Well, if you like to call it so," admitted Matherfield. "Yes, I came back by the seven thirty-eight. Dog tired! But I'm not through with this yet, Mr. Hetherwick, and I want you to do something for me. This Miss Hannaford, now, is down at Riversreade Court. They'll be on the telephone there, of course. I want you to ring her up early tomorrow morning, and ask her if she can meet you on important private business in Dorking town at noon. Where shall we say?"

"'White Horse' would do," suggested Hetherwick.

"Very well – White Horse Hotel, at noon," agreed Matherfield. "We'll go down – for I'll go with you – by the 10.10 from Victoria. Now please be very careful about this, Mr. Hetherwick, when you telephone. Don't say anything of any reason for going down to Dorking. Don't on any account mention Lady Riversreade, in any way. Merely tell Miss Hannaford that you have urgent reasons for seeing her. And – fix it up!"

"Oh, I can fix it up all right," answered Hetherwick. "Miss Hannaford can easily drive down from Riversreade Court. But I don't know what you want her for."

"Wait till morning," replied Matherfield, with a knowing look. "You'll see. I'll meet you at Victoria at ten o'clock, sharp."

# IS IT BLACKMAIL?

Hetherwick was still in ignorance of the reason of Matherfield's desire to see Rhona when, just before noon next day, Matherfield and he walked up from Dorking Station into the High Street, and made for the "White Horse." Matherfield halted a few yards away from its door.

"Let's wait outside for her," he said. "Till I've asked her a question or two. I don't want to even run the risk of being overheard."

Rhona came along in a car a few minutes later, and seeing the two men advanced to meet them. Matherfield lost no time in getting to business.

"Miss Hannaford," he said, with a cautious look round, and in a low voice, "just tell me – is Lady Riversreade up there at the Court? She is!" he continued, as Rhona nodded. "When did she come back, then?"

"Very early yesterday morning," answered Rhona promptly. "By the 7.45 from Victoria. She was up at the Court by 9.30."

Matherfield turned an utterly perplexed face on Hetherwick. Then he stared at Rhona.

"Up at Riversreade Court at 9.30 yesterday – Tuesday – morning!" he exclaimed. "Impossible! I saw her at Southampton at 9.30 yesterday morning with my own eyes."

"I'm quite sure you didn't!" replied Rhona, with a satirical laugh. "You're under some queer mistaken impression, Mr. Matherfield. Lady Riversreade was in her own house, here, with me at 9.30 yesterday morning. That's a fact that I can vouch for!"

The two men looked at each other. Each seemed to be asking the other a silent question. But Matherfield suddenly voiced his, in tones full of wonder and of chagrin.

"Then who on earth is that woman that I followed to Southampton?"

Matherfield's question went without answer. Rhona, who had no idea of what he was talking about, turned a surprised and inquiring look on Hetherwick. And Hetherwick saw that the time had come for a lot of explanation.

"Look here!" he said. "We've got to do some talking, and we can't keep Miss Hannaford standing in the street. Come into the hotel – we'll get a private room for lunch, and then we can discuss matters all to ourselves. You're a bit puzzled by all this," he continued a few minutes later, turning to Rhona when all three were safely closeted together, and lunch had been ordered. "And no wonder! But I'd better tell you what Matherfield and I were after on Monday night, and what Matherfield was doing all yesterday. You see," he concluded, after giving Rhona an epitomised account of the recent proceedings, "I was absolutely certain that the woman whom we saw coming out of Vivian's on Monday night was the woman you pointed out to me on Sunday morning at Victoria as Lady Riversreade – she was dressed in just the same things, I'm positive! – in short I'm convinced it was Lady Riversreade. Then, Matherfield and I are both equally sure that that was the same woman we saw coming out of St. Mary's Mansions shortly before five o'clock yesterday morning, and whom Matherfield followed to Southampton, Up to now, we've never had a doubt that it was Lady Riversreade – not a doubt!"

"Well," said Rhona, with an incredulous laugh, "I can't say, of course, that you didn't see Lady Riversreade come out of Vivian's on Monday night. Lady Riversreade was certainly in town from Sunday noon to yesterday morning, and she may have gone to Vivian's on Monday night for purposes of her own. I know nothing about that. But I do know that she was not in Southampton yesterday, for, as I told you, she was back home at Riversreade Court, about half-past nine in the morning, and she's never left the house since. That's plain fact!"

"It's beyond me, then!" exclaimed Matherfield. "And I say again, if that wasn't Lady Riversreade that I tracked to Southampton, who was it? I'll say more – if that really was Lady Riversreade that we saw coming out of Vivian's, and followed to Paddington, and if she wasn't the woman who came out of those flats yesterday morning, and that I went after, well, then, Lady Riversreade has a double – who lives in St. Mary's Mansions! That's about it!"

"As regards that," remarked Hetherwick. "I didn't tell you last night, Matherfield, that I went back yesterday to that house from which we watched, and made some cautious inquiries about the tall, handsome woman who has a flat opposite. I got some information. The woman whom we followed there, and whom you were running after yesterday is known there as a Madame Listorelle. She's very little at her flat, though punctual with its rent. She's sometimes away altogether for long periods – in fact, she's rarely seen there. And she's believed to be connected with the stage. The caretaker who supplied this information saw her at the flat on Monday."

Matherfield smacked one hand on the open palm of the other.

"It's an alias!" he exclaimed. "Bet your stars she's Lady Riversreade! Away from her flat for long periods? Of course – because she's down here, at her big house. Keeps that flat up for some purpose of her own, and calls herself – what is it? – sounds French."

"But supposing that's so," remarked Hetherwick, with a sly glance at Rhona. "It's utterly impossible that Lady Riversreade could be at Riversreade Court yesterday, and in Southampton at the same time! Come, now!"

"Well, I tell you it beats me!" muttered Matherfield. "I know what I saw! If there's anything gone wrong, it's your fault, Mr. Hetherwick! I don't know this Lady Riversreade! All I know is that you said the woman we saw coming out of that club was Lady Riversreade. That, sir, is the woman I followed!"

"The woman I saw coming out of Vivian's was the woman pointed out to me by Miss Hannaford as Lady Riversreade," affirmed Hetherwick quietly. "That's certain! But—"

He was interrupted at this stage by the arrival of lunch. Nothing more was said until all three were seated, and the waiter had been sent away. Then Rhona looked at her companions and smiled.

"You both seem to have arrived at a very promising stage!" she said. "At first I thought it a regular impasse, but—"

"Isn't it?" asked Hetherwick. "At present I don't see any way through or over it."

"Oh, I think you're getting towards something!" she retorted. "All these things, puzzling as they are, are better than nothing. I've got some news, too – if you're sure there are no eavesdroppers about."

"Oh, we're all right!" said Hetherwick. "Good stout old doors, these – close-fitting. What next?"

Rhona leaned across the table a little, and lowered her voice.

"There was a sort of row at the Court; at least, at the Home, yesterday," she said. "With that man Baseverie!"

"Ah!" exclaimed Hetherwick. "That's interesting! Tell about it."

"Well, I told you that Lady Riversreade arrived from London yesterday morning about nine-thirty," continued Rhona. "Major Penteney arrived with her."

"Who's Major Penteney?" demanded Matherfield.

"He's a retired Army man who's greatly interested in Lady Riversreade's Home, and looks after its affairs in London," replied Hetherwick. "And Miss Hannaford thinks he's in love with the foundress. I've seen him – saw him with Lady Riversreade on Sunday. Yes," he added, turning to Rhona, "Major Penteney came back with her? Go on."

"As soon as they arrived – I saw them come, from my office window – they came across to the Home," continued Rhona. "It struck me that they both looked unusually grave and serious. They talked to me for a few minutes on business matters: then they went into Lady Riversreade's private office. They were there for some little time; then Lady Riversreade came out and went away; I saw her cross to the Court. Presently Major Penteney came to me, and told me that he wanted to have a little private talk with me. He said – as near as I can remember – 'Miss Featherstone—'"

Matherfield looked up quickly from his plate.

"Eh?" he said. "Miss – Featherstone?"

"That's the name Miss Hannaford's known by – there," said Hetherwick. "Her mother's name. I told you before, you know."

"True, true!" assented Matherfield, with a groan. "You did – I remember now. I'm muddled – with yesterday's affair."

"'Miss Featherstone,' Rhona went on – 'I believe you're aware that Lady Riversreade has lately been visited – twice – by a man who called himself Dr. Cyprian Baseverie?'

"'Yes,' I answered, 'I am, Major Penteney. I saw Dr. Baseverie on both occasions.' 'Well,' he said – 'I don't suppose you were at all impressed by him?' 'Not at all impressed, Major Penteney,' I replied, 'except very unfavourably.' 'Didn't like his looks, eh,' he asked with a smile. 'Do you?' I inquired. 'I've never seen the fellow,' he answered. 'But I expect to – this very morning. That's what I want to talk to you about. I believe he'll turn up about noon – as, I understand, he did before, wanting, of course, to see Lady Riversreade. I want you to tell the doorkeeper, Mitchell, to bring him straight in when he comes, and Mitchell is not to say that Lady Riversreade is not in – she won't be in – he's to admit him immediately; and you, if you please, are to show him straight into the private office. Instead of finding Lady Riversreade there, he'll find – me. Is that clear?' 'Perfectly clear, Major Penteney,' I replied. 'I'll see to it.' 'Well, there's something else,' he said. 'After I have had a little plain-spoken talk with this fellow, I shall ring the bell. I want you to come in, and to bring Mitchell with you. And – that's all, at present. You understand?' 'I understand, Major Penteney,' I answered. 'I'll see to it. But as you've never seen this man there's one thing I'd like to say to you – he's the sort of man who looks as if he might be dangerous.' He smiled at that. 'Thank you,' he said. 'I'm prepared for that, Miss Featherstone. You show him right in.'"

Rhona paused for a moment, to attend to the contents of her plate. But Hetherwick's knife and fork had become idle; so had Matherfield's; each man, it was plain, was becoming absorbed. And Matherfield suddenly brightened, and gave Hetherwick an unmistakable wink.

"Good! – good! – good!" he muttered, with something like a chuckle. "I'm beginning to see a bit of daylight! Excellent! – when you're ready, Miss Featherstone—"

"Well," continued Rhona, after a few minutes' pause, "about noon, Dr. Cyprian Baseverie drove up. I had already given Mitchell his instructions, and he brought Baseverie straight into my office. Baseverie was evidently in the very best of spirits – he bowed and grimaced at sight of me as if he expected to find me dying to see him. I made no answer to his flowery greetings; I just got up, ushered him to the door of the private room, and closed it after him as he stepped across the threshold. Then I laughed – he wouldn't see who was awaiting him until he got right into the room, and I'd already gathered from Major Penteney that his reception couldn't be exactly pleasant or agreeable."

Matherfield rubbed his hands together.

"Good! – good!" he chuckled. "Wish I'd been in that room!"

"It wasn't long before I was there, Mr. Matherfield," said Rhona. "I was, of course, tremendously curious to know what was going on there, but the door fits closely, and I heard nothing – no angry voices or anything. However, in less than ten minutes the bell rang sharply. I called Mitchell – he's a big, strapping, very determined-looking ex-Guardsman – and in we went. I took everything in at a glance, Major Penteney sat at Lady Riversreade's desk. On the blotting-pad, his right hand close to it, lay a revolver—"

"Hah!" exclaimed Matherfield. "To be sure! Just so! Fine!"

"Opposite the desk stood Baseverie, staring first at Major Penteney, then at us. It's difficult for me to describe how he looked. I think the principal expression on his face was one of intense surprise."

"Surprise?" ejaculated Hetherwick.

"Surprise! Astonishment! He looked like a man who had just heard something that he has believed it impossible to hear. But there was also such a look of anger and rage – well, if Major Penteney hadn't had that revolver close to his finger-ends, and if Mitchell hadn't been there, I should have screamed and run. However, it was not I who was to do the running. As soon as Mitchell and I entered, Major Penteney spoke – very quietly. He nodded at Baseverie. 'Miss Featherstone and you, Mitchell – you see this man? If ever he comes here again, you, Mitchell, will deny him entrance, and you, Miss Featherstone, on hearing from Mitchell that he's here, will telephone for the police and, if he hangs about, will give him in charge.' Then he turned to Baseverie. 'Now, my man!' he continued, pointing to the door. 'You get out – quick! Go!' Of course, I looked at Baseverie. He stood staring almost incredulously at Major Penteney. It seemed to me that he could scarcely believe his ears – he gave me the impression of being unable to credit that he could be so treated. But he was also livid with anger. His fingers worked; his eyes blazed; it was dreadful to see his lips. He got out some words at last—'"

"Give me the exact ones, if you can," interrupted Matherfield.

"I can – I'm not likely to forget them," said Rhona. "He said – 'What – you defy me, knowing what I know – knowing what I know!'"

"'Knowing what I know!'" muttered Matherfield. "Knowing what he knew! Um! – and then?"

"Then Major Penteney just pointed to the door. 'Get out, I tell you!' he said. 'And look in the papers tonight. Be off!'"

"'Look in the papers tonight,' eh?" said Matherfield. "Um – um! And then, I suppose, he went?"

"He went without another word then," assented Rhona. "Mitchell escorted him out and saw him off. Major Penteney looked at me when he'd gone. 'There, Miss Featherstone,' he said, 'you've seen one of the biggest scoundrels in London – or in Europe. Let's hope you'll never see him again, that that's the end of him here. I think he's had his lesson!' I made no answer, but I was jolly glad to see Baseverie's car scooting away down the drive!"

Matherfield picked up the tankard of ale at his side and took a hearty pull at its contents. He set the tankard down again with an emphatic bang.

"I know what this job is!" he exclaimed triumphantly. "Blackmail!"

"Just so!" agreed Hetherwick. "I've been thinking that for the last ten minutes. Baseverie has been endeavouring to blackmail Lady Riversreade. But that's not our affair, you know. What we're after is the solving of the mystery surrounding Hannaford's death. And – does this look likely to fit in anywhere?"

"I should say it decidedly does look likely!" answered Matherfield. "In my opinion it's all of a piece; at least, it's a piece out of a piece, one of many pieces, like a puzzle. The thing is to put these pieces together. And there are two things we can try to do at once. First, find out more about this man Baseverie; the other, get hold of more information about the lady in St. Mary's Mansions."

"What about approaching Lady Riversreade for information – or Major Penteney?" suggested Hetherwick.

"Yes – why don't you?" said Rhona, almost eagerly. "Do! I'm a bit tired of being there as Miss Featherstone. I want to tell Lady Riversreade the truth, and all the whys and wherefores of it."

But Matherfield shook his head. The time for that was not yet, he declared; let them wait awhile. And after more conversation he and Hetherwick returned to London.

# REVELATIONS

The late afternoon edition of the evening papers were just out when Hetherwick and Matherfield reached Victoria. Matherfield snatched one up; a moment later he thrust it before Hetherwick, pointing to some big black capitals.

"Good God!" he exclaimed. "Look at that!"

Hetherwick looked, and gasped his astonishment at what he read.

MURDER OF ROBERT HANNAFORD. FIVE THOUSAND POUNDS REWARD.

Hetherwick turned on his companion with a look that was both questioning and surprised.

"This is probably – no, certainly! – what Penteney referred to when he told Baseverie to look in the newspapers!" he said. "That was yesterday; it must have been in last night's papers, and this morning's. I saw neither."

"Wait!" said Matherfield. He hurried back to the bookstall and returned with an armful of papers, turning the topmost over as he came. "It's here – and here!" he continued. "Let's get a quiet corner somewhere and look this thing carefully over!"

"Come into a waiting-room, then," said Hetherwick. "Odd!" he muttered, as they turned away. "Who should offer a reward – like that, too! – who isn't concerned in the case?"

"How do we know who isn't concerned in the case?" exclaimed Matherfield. "Somebody evidently is! – somebody who can not only afford to offer five thousand pounds, but isn't afraid to spend no end in advertising. Look at that – and that – and that," he went on, turning over his purchases rapidly. "It's in every paper in London!"

"Let's read it carefully," said Hetherwick. He spread out one of the newspapers on the waiting-room table and muttered the wording of the advertisement while Matherfield looked over his shoulder. "Mysterious, very!" he concluded. "What's it mean?"

But Matherfield was re-reading the advertisement.

Whereas Robert Hannaford, formerly Superintendent of Police at Sellithwaite, Yorkshire, died suddenly in an Underground Railway train, near Charing Cross (Embankment) Station about 1.15 a.m. on March 19th last, and expert medical investigation has proved that he was poisoned, and there is evidence to warrant the belief that the poison was administered by some person or persons with intent to cause his death, this is to give notice that the above-mentioned sum of Five Thousand Pounds will be paid to anyone first giving information which will lead to the arrest and conviction of the person or persons concerned in administering the said poison and that such information should be given to the undersigned, who will pay the said reward in accordance with the above-stated conditions.

PENTENEY, BLENKINSOP & PENTENEY, Solicitors.
April 22nd, 1920. 853, Lincoln's Inn Fields, London, W.C.

Matherfield pointed to the names of the signatories.

"Penteney," he remarked. "That's the name of the man Miss Hannaford mentioned as having given Baseverie his dismissal."

"Of course – Major Penteney," said Hetherwick. "Probably a junior partner in the firm. I know their names, but not much about them."

"I thought he was a soldier," said Matherfield. "Major, she called him."

"Very likely a Territorial officer," replied Hetherwick. "Anyway, it's very plain what this is, Matherfield, considering all we know. This advertisement has been issued on behalf of Lady Riversreade. Penteney, Blenkinsop & Penteney are no doubt her solicitors. But – why?"

"Aye, why?" exclaimed Matherfield. "That's just what beats me! What interest has she in Hannaford's murder? Why should she want to bring his murderer to justice? If his granddaughter had offered, say, a hundred pounds for information, I could understand it – she's his flesh and blood. But Lady Riversreade! Why, if she's really the woman who was once Mrs. Whittingham, you'd have thought she'd have been rather glad that Hannaford was out of the way! And, after all, this mayn't come from her."

"I'm absolutely certain it does," asserted Hetherwick. "Putting everything together, what other conclusion can we come to? It comes from Lady Riversreade – and her adviser – Major Penteney, and it's something to do with that man Baseverie. But – what?"

"It ought to be looked into," muttered Matherfield. "They've never approached us on the matter. It's a purely voluntary offer on their part. They've left the police clean out."

"Well, I make a suggestion," said Hetherwick. "I think you and I had better call at Penteney's tomorrow morning. We can tell them something – perhaps they'll tell us something. Anyway, it's a foolish thing to divide forces; we'd far better unite in a common effort."

"Um!" replied Matherfield doubtfully. "But these lawyer chaps – they've generally got something up their sleeves – some card that they want to play at their own moment. However, we can try 'em."

"Meet me at the south-east corner of Lincoln's Inn Fields at half-past ten tomorrow morning," said Hetherwick. "Penteney's offices are close by. We'll go together – and ask them straight out what this advertisement means."

"All right – but if they won't tell?" suggested Matherfield.

"Then, in that case, we'll introduce Lady Riversreade's name, and ask them if Lady Riversreade of Riversreade Court and Mrs. Whittingham, formerly of Sellithwaite, are one and the same person," replied Hetherwick. "Come! I think we can show them that we already know a good deal."

"We have certainly a card or two to play," admitted Matherfield. "All right, Mr. Hetherwick! Tomorrow morning, then, as you suggest."

He was waiting at the appointed place when Hetherwick hurried up next morning. Hetherwick immediately turned him down the lower side of the Fields.

"I've found out something about these people we're going to see," he said. "My clerk, Mapperley, told me a bit; he's a sort of walking encyclopædia. Old, highly respectable firm this. Penteney, senior, is retired; the firm is now really Blenkinsop & Penteney, junior. And Penteney, junior, is the Major Penteney who takes such an interest in Lady Riversreade's Home – and in Lady Riversreade. As I suggested last night, he was a Territorial officer – so now he's back at his own job. Now then, Matherfield, let's arrange our plan of campaign. You, of course, have your official credentials – I'm a deeply interested person, the man who chanced to witness Hannaford's death. I think you'd better be spokesman."

"Well, you'll come in when wanted?" suggested Matherfield. "You're better used to lawyers than I am, being one yourself."

"I fear my acquaintance with solicitors is, so far, extremely limited, Matherfield," replied Hetherwick with a laugh. "I have seen a brief! – but only occasionally. However, here we are at 853, and a solid and sombre old house it is."

The two callers had to wait for some time before any apparent notice was taken of their cards by the persons to whom they had been sent in. Matherfield was beginning to chafe when, at last, an elderly clerk conducted them up to an inner room wherein one cold-eyed, immobile-faced man sat at a desk, while another, scarcely less stern in appearance, in whom Hetherwick immediately recognised the Major Penteney pointed out by Rhona, stood, hands in pockets, on the hearthrug. Each stared silently at the two callers; the man at the desk pointed to chairs on either side of his fortress. He looked at Matherfield.

"Yes?" he asked.

"Mr. Blenkinsop, I presume?" began Matherfield, with a polite bow to the desk. "And Mr. Penteney?" with another to the hearthrug.

"Just so," agreed Blenkinsop. "Precisely! Yes?"

"You have my card, gentlemen, and so you know who I am," continued Matherfield. "The police—"

"A moment," interrupted Blenkinsop. He picked up Hetherwick's card and glanced from it to its presenter. "Mr. Guy Hetherwick," he remarked. "Does Mr. Hetherwick also call on behalf of the police? Because," he added, with a dry smile, "I think I've seen Mr. Hetherwick in wig and gown."

"I am the man who was present at Robert Hannaford's death," said Hetherwick. "If you are conversant with the case—"

"Quite! – every detail!" said Blenkinsop.

"Then you know what I saw, and what evidence I gave at the inquest," continued Hetherwick. "I have followed up the case ever since – and that's why I am here."

"Not as *amicus curiæ*, then?" remarked Blenkinsop with a still dryer smile. "You're not a disinterested adviser. I see! And Mr. Matherfield – why is he here?"

"I was saying, Mr. Blenkinsop, that the police have seen the advertisement signed by your firm, offering five thousand pounds reward – *etcetera*," answered Matherfield. "Now, I have this Hannaford case in hand, and I can assure you I've done a lot of work at it. So, in his way, has Mr. Hetherwick. We're convinced that Hannaford was murdered by poison, and that whoever poisoned him also poisoned the man Granett at the same time. Now, as either you or some person – a client, I suppose – behind you is so much concerned in bringing Hannaford's murderer to justice as to offer a big sum for necessary information, we think you must know a great deal, and I suggest to you, gentlemen, that you ought to place your knowledge at our disposal. I hope my suggestion is welcome, gentlemen."

Blenkinsop drummed the blotting-pad before him with the tips of his fingers, and his face became more inscrutable than ever. As for Penteney, he maintained the same attitude which he had preserved ever since the visitors entered the room, lounging against the mantelpiece, hands in pockets, and his eyes alternately fixed on either Hetherwick or Matherfield. There was a brief silence; at last Blenkinsop spoke abruptly.

"I don't think we have anything to say," he said. "What we have to say has been said already in the advertisement. We shall pay the offered reward to the person who gives satisfactory information. I don't think that interferes with the police work."

"That doesn't help me much, Mr. Blenkinsop," protested Matherfield. "You, or your client, must know more than that! There must be good reasons why your client should offer such a big sum as reward. I think we ought to know – more."

"I am not prepared to tell you more," answered Blenkinsop. "Except that if we get the information which we think we shall get, we shall not be slow to hand it over to the police authorities."

"That might be too late," urged Matherfield. "This is an intricate case – there are a good many wheels within wheels." Then, interpreting a glance which he had just received from Hetherwick as a signal to go further, he added: "We know what a lot of wheels there are – no one better! For example, gentlemen, there is the curious fashion in which this affair is mixed up with Lady Riversreade!"

In spite of their evidently habitual practice of self-control, the two solicitors could not repress signs of astonishment. Blenkinsop's face fell; Penteney started out of his lounging attitude and stood upright. And for the first time he spoke.

"What do you know about Lady Riversreade?" he demanded.

"A good deal, sir, but not so much as I intend to know," answered Matherfield firmly. "But I do know this – that Hannaford, just previous to his sudden death, was in possession of a portrait of Lady Riversreade, and believed her to be identical with a certain Mrs. Whittingham who was through his hands on a charge of fraud, ten years ago, at Sellithwaite, in Yorkshire. I, too, believe that this Mrs. Whittingham is now Lady Riversreade, and I may tell you that I'm in full possession of all the facts relating to the Sellithwaite affair – an affair of obtaining a diamond necklace, worth about four thousand pounds, by means of a worthless cheque, and—"

Blenkinsop suddenly rose from his chair, holding up a hand.

"A moment, if you please!" he said. "Penteney," he continued, turning to his partner, "a word with you in your room."

Matherfield glanced triumphantly after the retreating pair, and laughed when a door had closed on them.

"That's got 'em, Mr. Hetherwick!" he exclaimed. "They see that we know more than they reckoned for. In some way or other, it strikes me, this advertisement is a piece of bluff!"

"Bluff!" said Hetherwick. "What do you mean?"

"What I say," answered Matherfield. "Bluff! Done to prevent somebody from bringing up that old Sellithwaite affair. Lay you a thousand to one it is. You'll see these two lawyers will be more communicative when they come back. Now they shall talk – and we'll listen!"

"If you have to do any more talking, Matherfield," said Hetherwick, "keep Miss Hannaford's name out of it. She's in a rather awkward position. She went there, of course, to find out what she could, and the result's been that she's taken a fancy to Lady Riversreade, got a genuine interest in the work there, and wants to stop. Bit of a bother, all that, and it'll need some straightening out. Anyway, keep her name out of it here."

"As I say, sir, when these chaps come back to us, they'll do the talking!" answered Matherfield, with a chuckle. "You'll see! If you want to keep Miss Hannaford's name out, so do they want to keep Lady Riversreade's name out – I know the signs!"

Blenkinsop and Penteney suddenly came back and seated themselves, Blenkinsop at his desk and Penteney close by. And Blenkinsop immediately turned to his callers. His manner had changed; he looked now like a man who is anxious to get a settlement of a difficult question.

"We have decided to talk freely to you," he said at once. "That means, to tell you everything we know about this matter. You, Mr. Matherfield, as representing the police, will, of course, treat our communication confidentially. I needn't ask you, Mr. Hetherwick, to regard all that's said here, as – you know! Now, to begin with – just get one fact, an absolutely irrefutable fact, into your minds at once. Lady Riversreade is not the woman who was known as Mrs. Whittingham at Sellithwaite ten years ago, nor did Hannaford believe that she was either!"

"What?" exclaimed Matherfield. "But—" he turned to Hetherwick. "You hear that?" he went on. "Why, we know—"

"Let Mr. Blenkinsop go on," said Hetherwick quietly. "He's explaining, I think."

"Just so," agreed Blenkinsop. "And I'm beginning by endeavouring to clear away a few mistaken ideas from your minds. Lady Riversreade is not Mrs. Whittingham. Hannaford did not think she was Mrs. Whittingham. It was not Lady Riversreade's portrait that Hannaford cut out of the paper."

Hetherwick could not repress a start at that.

"Whose was it, then?" he demanded. "For I certainly believed it was!"

Blenkinsop stooped and drew out a drawer from his desk. From a bundle of documents he produced a newspaper, carefully folded and labelled. Opening this, he laid it before the two visitors, pointing to a picture marked with blue pencil. And Hetherwick at once saw that here was a duplicate of the portrait in his own pocket-book. But there was this important difference – while Hannaford had cut away the lettering under his picture, it was there in the one which Blenkinsop exhibited. He started again as he read it – *Madame Anita Listorelle.*

"That's the picture which Hannaford cut out of the paper," said Blenkinsop. "It is not that of Lady Riversreade."

"Then it's that of a woman who's her double!" exclaimed Matherfield. "I'll lay anything that if you asked a hundred men who've seen Lady Riversreade if that's her picture, they'd swear it is!"

"I see," said Hetherwick, disregarding his companion's outburst, "that this purports to be a portrait of a Madame Listorelle, who is described in the accompanying letterpress as a famous connoisseur of precious stones. Now, in relation to what we're discussing, may I ask a plain question? Who is Madame Listorelle?"

Blenkinsop smiled – oracularly.

"Madame Listorelle," he replied, "is the twin sister of Lady Riversreade!"

# STILL MORE

Blenkinsop's sudden announcement, not altogether unexpected by Hetherwick as a result of the last few minutes' proceedings, seemed to strike Matherfield with all the force of a lightning-like illumination. His mouth opened; his eyes widened; he turned on Hetherwick as if, having been lost for a while in a baffling maze, he had suddenly seen a way pointed out to him.

"Oh, that's it, is it?" he exclaimed. "A twin sister, eh? Then – but go on, Mr. Blenkinsop; I'm beginning to see things."

"The matter is doubtless puzzling – to outsiders," responded Blenkinsop. "To clear it up, I shall have to go into some family history. Lady Riversreade and Madame Listorelle are, I repeat, twin sisters. They are the daughters of a man who in his time was captain of various merchant ships – the old sailing ships – and who knocked about the world a good deal. He married an American woman, and his two daughters were born in Galveston, Texas. They were educated in America – but there's no need to go into the particulars of their early lives—"

"There's a certain particular that I should like to have some information about, if you please," interrupted Hetherwick. "The Mrs. Whittingham who was at Sellithwaite ten years ago had the figure of a snake tattooed round a wrist, in various colours. She wore a black velvet band to cover it. Now—"

Blenkinsop turned to his partner with a smile.

"I thought that would come up," he said. "Well Mr. Hetherwick, if you want to know about that matter, both sisters are tattooed in the same fashion. That was a bit of work of the old sea-dog, their father – a fancy, and a very foolish one, of his. He had the children tattooed in that way when they were quite young, much to their disgust when they grew older. Each lady wears a covering velvet armlet – as I know."

"Proceed, if you please," said Hetherwick. "That's cleared up!"

"I gather that you've been making inquiries on your own account," observed Blenkinsop. "Well, since we're determined to tell you everything, we'll be as good as our word. So let's come to the Sellithwaite affair. You've probably heard only one version – you may have got it from Hannaford; you may have got it from old newspapers; you may have got it on the spot – it's immaterial to us. But you haven't heard the version of the lady who was then Mrs. Whittingham. That puts a rather different complexion on things. For reasons of her own, with which we've nothing to do, Mrs. Whittingham – her proper and legal name at that time – stayed at Sellithwaite for a while. She had various transactions with a jeweller there; eventually she bought from him a diamond necklace at a price – three thousand nine hundred pounds. She gave him a cheque for the amount, fully expecting that by the time it reached her bankers in Manchester certain funds for her credit would have reached them from America. There was a hitch – the funds didn't arrive – the cheque was returned. The jeweller approached the police – Hannaford, their superintendent there, got out a warrant and tracked down Mrs. Whittingham. He arrested her, and she got away from him, left England, and returned to America. For some time she was in financial straits. But she did not forget her liabilities, and eventually she sent the Sellithwaite jeweller the agreed price of the diamond necklace, and eight years' interest at five per cent. On the amount. She holds his formal receipt for the money she sent him. So much for that episode – whether Hannaford ever knew of the payment or not, I don't know. We are rather inclined to believe that he didn't. But – the necklace was paid for, and paid for handsomely."

"I may as well say that I'm aware of that," remarked Hetherwick. "I have been informed of the fact at first hand."

"Very good. I see you have been at Sellithwaite," said Blenkinsop with another of his shrewd smiles. "Now then, we come to what is far more pertinent – recent events. The situation as regards Lady Riversreade and Madame Listorelle some little time ago – say, when Hannaford came to town – was this: Lady Riversreade, widow of Sir John Riversreade, had inherited his considerable fortune, was settled at Riversreade Court in Surrey, and had founded a Home for wounded officers close by, of which my friend and partner, Major Penteney there, is London representative. Her sister, Madame Listorelle, had a flat at Paddington and another in New York. She was chiefly in New York, but she was sometimes in London and sometimes in Paris. As a matter of fact, Madame Listorelle is an expert in precious stones, and a dealer in them. But she has recently become engaged to be married to a well-known peer, an elderly, very wealthy man – which possibly has a good deal to do with what I am going to tell you."

"Probably, I think, Blenkinsop – not possibly," suggested Penteney. "Probably! – decidedly."

"Probably, then – probably!" assented Blenkinsop. He leaned forward across his desk towards the two listeners. "Now, gentlemen, your closest attention, for I'm coming to the really important points of this matter – those that affect the police particularly. About a fortnight ago Lady Riversreade, being in her private office at her home, close by Riversreade Court, was waited upon by a man who sent in a card bearing the name of Dr. Cyprian Baseverie. Lady Riversreade thought that the presenter of this card was some medical man who wished to inspect the Home, and he was admitted to see her. She soon found out that he had come on no such errand as she had imagined. He told her a strange tale. He let her know, to begin with, that he was fully conversant with that episode in her sister's life which related to Sellithwaite and the diamond necklace. Lady Riversreade, who knew all about it, felt that the man's information had been gained at first hand. He also let her know that Madame Listorelle's whereabouts and engagement were familiar to him; in short, he showed that he was well up in the present family history, both as regards Lady Riversreade and her sister. Then he let his hand be seen more plainly. He told Lady Riversreade that a certain gang of men in London had become acquainted with the facts of the Sellithwaite matter, the warrant, the arrest, the escape, and that they were also aware of Madame Listorelle's engagement to Lord – we will leave his name out at present, or refer to him as Lord X – and that they wanted a price for their silence. In other words, they were determined on blackmail. If they were not paid their price, they were going to Lord X, with all the facts, to tell him that he was engaged to a woman who, as they would put it, was still liable by the law of the land to arrest and prosecution for fraud."

"Isn't she?" asked Matherfield suddenly. "No time-limit in these sort of cases, I think, Mr. Blenkinsop. Liable ten or twenty or thirty years after – I think!"

"I've already said that the Sellithwaite affair was one of account," replied Blenkinsop. "There was no intent to defraud, and the full amount and interest on it was duly paid. But that's not the point – we're dealing with the presentment of this to Lady Riversreade by the man Baseverie. Of course, Lady Riversreade didn't know how the law might be, and she was alarmed on her sister's account. She asked Baseverie what he wanted. He told her plainly then that he could settle these men – if she would find the money. He had, he said, a certain hold over them which he could use to advantage. Lady Riversreade wanted to know what that hold was; he wouldn't tell her. She then wanted to know how much the men wanted; he wouldn't say. What he did say was that if she would be prepared to find the money to silence them, he, during the next week, would exert pressure on them to accept a reasonable amount, and would call on her on the following Friday and tell her what they would take. She made that appointment with him."

"And, I hope, took advice in the meantime," muttered Matherfield. "Ought to have handed him over there and then!"

"No – she took no advice in the meantime," continued Blenkinsop. "Madame Listorelle was in Paris – Major Penteney was away on business in the country. Lady Riversreade awaited Baseverie's next coming. When he came he told her what his gang wanted – thirty thousand pounds. He specified, too, the way in which it was to be paid – in a fashion which would have prevented the payment being traced to the people who received it. But now Lady Riversreade was more prepared – she had had time to think. She expected Major Penteney next day; she also knew that her sister would return from Paris on the following Monday. So she told Baseverie that she would give him an answer on Monday evening if he would make an appointment to meet her at some place in London. Eventually they made an appointment at Vivian's, in Candlestick Passage. Baseverie went away; next day Lady Riversreade told Major Penteney all that had happened. As a result, he went with her to Vivian's on Monday evening. They waited an hour beyond the fixed time. Baseverie made no appearance—"

"Just so!" muttered Matherfield. "He wouldn't – the Major being there!"

"Perhaps," assented Blenkinsop. "Anyway, he didn't materialise. So Lady Riversreade went away, leaving Major Penteney behind her. I may say that he stopped there for some further time, keeping a sharp look-out for the man whom Lady Riversreade had described in detail – a remarkable man in appearance, I understand. But he never saw him."

"No!" exclaimed Matherfield cynically. "Of course he didn't! But she would ha' done – if she'd gone alone!"

"Well, there it was," continued Blenkinsop. "Now for Lady Riversreade. She drove to her sister's flat in Paddington, and found Madame Listorelle just returned from Paris. She told her all that had happened. Madame Listorelle determined to go to New York at once and get certain papers from her flat there which would definitely establish her absolute innocence in the Sellithwaite affair. Leaving Lady Riversreade in the flat, Madame Listorelle set off for Southampton before five o'clock next morning – yes?"

Matherfield, uttering a deep groan, smote his forehead.

"Aye!" he muttered. "Just so! To be sure! But go on! – go on, sir."

"You seem to be highly surprised," said Blenkinsop. "However – at Southampton she booked a passage in a name she always used when travelling – her maiden name – by the *Tartaric*, sailing that afternoon. That done, she went to a hotel for lunch. Then she began to think things over more calmly. And in the end, instead of sailing for New York, she went back, cancelled her booking, and set off by train to Lord X's country seat in Wiltshire, and told him the whole story. She wired to her sister as to what she had done, and in the evening wrote to her. Meanwhile, Lady Riversreade had returned, early in the morning, to Riversreade Court. Major Penteney went with her. He was confident that Baseverie would turn up. He did turn up! But he did not see Lady Riversreade. He saw Major Penteney – alone. And Major Penteney, after a little plain talk to him, metaphorically kicked him out, and told him to do his worst. He went – warned that if ever he showed himself there again he would be handed over to the police."

Matherfield groaned again, but the reason of his distress was obviously of a different nature.

"A mistake, sir – a great mistake!" he exclaimed, shaking his head at Penteney. "You shouldn't have let that fellow go like that! You should have handed him over there and then. Go? You don't know where he may be!"

"Oh, well, we're not quite such fools as we seem, Matherfield," he replied. "When I went down to Dorking with Lady Riversreade on Tuesday morning I had with me a smart man whom I can trust. He saw Baseverie arrive; he saw Baseverie leave. I think we shall be able to put our fingers on Baseverie at any moment. Our man won't lose sight of him!"

"Oh, well, that's better, sir, that's much better!" said Matherfield. "That's all right! A chap like that should be watched night and day. But now, gentlemen, about this reward! Your notion of offering it sprang, of course, from this Baseverie business. But – how, exactly? Did he mention Hannaford to Lady Riversreade?"

"No!" replied Blenkinsop. "I'll tell you how we came to issue the advertisement. All Sunday afternoon and evening, and for some time on Monday morning, Lady Riversreade, Major Penteney, and myself were in close consultation about this affair. I'll tell you at once how and why we connected it with the poisoning of Hannaford, of which, of course, all of us had read in the newspapers."

"Aye! – how, now?" asked Matherfield.

"Because of this," answered Blenkinsop. He tapped his desk to emphasise his words, watching Matherfield keenly as he spoke. "Because of this: Baseverie told Lady Riversreade that the gang of blackmailers had in their possession the original warrant for Mrs. Whittingham's arrest!"

Hetherwick felt himself impelled to jump in his chair, to exclaim loudly. He repressed the inclination, but Matherfield was less reserved.

"Ah!" he exclaimed sharply. "Ah!"

"Baseverie made a false step there," continued Blenkinsop. "He should never have told that. But he did – no doubt he thought a rich woman easy prey. Now, of course, when we came to consult, we knew all about the Sellithwaite affair; we knew, too, that Hannaford was superintendent at the time and that he had the warrant; it was not at all improbable that he had preserved it in his pocket-book, and had it on him when he came to London. What, then, was the obvious conclusion – that the men who now held that warrant had got it, probably by foul means, from Hannaford, and were concerned in his murder? And – more than that – did the gang of which Baseverie spoke really exist? Wasn't it likely that the gang was – Baseverie?"

"Aye!" muttered Matherfield. "I've been thinking of that!"

"Yet," said Blenkinsop, "it was on the cards that there might be a gang. We searched all the newspapers' accounts thoroughly. We found that next to no information could be got as to Hannaford's movements between the time of his arrival in London and the night of his death. The one man who might have given more information about Hannaford's doings on the evening preceding his death – Granett – was dead, evidently poisoned, as Hannaford was poisoned. These were circumstances – they've probably occurred to both of you – which led us to believe that Hannaford had formed the acquaintance of folk here in town who were of a shady sort. And one thing was absolutely certain – if the gang, or if Baseverie, had really got that warrant, they had got it from Hannaford! Eh?"

"That may be taken as certain," assented Hetherwick. "Either directly or indirectly, it must have been from him."

"We think they, or he, got it directly from him," said Blenkinsop. "Our theory is that if there is a gang Baseverie is an active, perhaps the leading, member; that Hannaford was previously acquainted with him or some other member; that Hannaford was with him or them on the evening preceding his death; that he jokingly told them that he had discovered the identity of Madame Listorelle with Mrs. Whittingham; and that they poisoned him – and Granett, as being present – in order to keep the secret to themselves and to blackmail Madame Listorelle and her sister, Lady Riversreade. That's our general idea – and that's why, on Monday noon, we issued the advertisement. We meant to keep things to ourselves at first, and if substantial evidence came, to pass it over to the police. Now you know everything. It may be, if there is a gang, that one member will turn traitor for the sake of five thousand pounds and if he can exculpate himself satisfactorily; it may be, too, that matters will develop until we're in a position to fasten things on Baseverie—"

"I still wish that either Lady Riversreade or Major Penteney had handed him over to custody!" said Matherfield. "You see—"

"You've got to remember that Baseverie never demanded anything for himself," interrupted Penteney. "He represented himself as a go-between. But our man's safe enough – a retired detective, and—"

Just then a clerk opened the door and entered with a telegram. Blenkinsop tore open the envelope, glanced hurriedly at the message and flung the form on his desk with an exclamation of annoyance.

"This is from our man!" he said. "Sent from Dover. Followed Baseverie down there – and Baseverie's slipped him!"

# THE TORN LABELS

Penteney strode forward and picked up the telegram; a moment later he passed it over to Hetherwick.

"That's most unfortunate!" he exclaimed. "And unexpected, too! Of course, the fellow's slipped off to the Continent."

Matherfield looked over Hetherwick's shoulder and read the message.

*"Followed him down here last night. Put up at same hotel, but he slipped me and got clear away early this morning. Returning now."*

"You should have employed two men, gentlemen," said Matherfield. "One's not enough – in a case of that sort. But it's as I said before – this man should have been given into custody at once. However—"

He got up from his chair, as if there was no more to be said, and moved towards the door. But half-way across the room he paused.

"You'll let me know if anybody comes forward about that reward?" he suggested. "It's more of a police matter, you know."

The two partners, who were obviously much annoyed by the telegram, nodded.

"We shall let you know – at once," answered Blenkinsop. "Of course, you'll regard all we've told you as strictly confidential?"

"Oh, to be sure, sir," replied Matherfield. "It's not the only private and confidential feature of this affair, I assure you."

Outside he turned to Hetherwick.

"Well!" he said. "We've cleared up a few things, Mr. Hetherwick – or, rather, those two have cleared them up for us. But are we any nearer answering the question that we want answering – who poisoned Robert Hannaford?"

"I think we are!" replied Hetherwick. "I am, anyhow! Either Baseverie poisoned him – or he knows who did!"

"Knows who did!" repeated Matherfield. "Ah! – that's more like it. I don't think he did it – he wouldn't be so ready about showing himself

102

forward."

"I'm not so sure of that," remarked Hetherwick. "From what we've heard of him, he seems to be a bold and daring sort of scamp. Probably he thought he'd have a very easy prey in Lady Riversreade; probably, too, he believed that a woman who's got all that money would make little to do about parting with thirty thousand pounds. One thing's sure, however – Baseverie knows what we want to know. And – he's gone!"

"Perhaps – perhaps!" said Matherfield. "And perhaps not. This man of Penteney's no doubt tracked him to Dover, and there he lost him, but that isn't saying that Baseverie's gone on the Continent. If Baseverie's the cute customer that he seems to be, he'd put two and two together when Major Penteney warned him off Riversreade Court. He'd probably suspect Penteney of setting a watch on him; he may have spotted the very man who was watching. Then, if he'd any sense, he'd lead that man a bit of a dance, and eventually double on him. No! – I should say Baseverie's back here in town! That's about it, Mr. Hetherwick. But what's this? Here's one of my men coming to meet us. I left word where I should be found."

Hetherwick looked up and saw a man, who was obviously a policeman in plain clothes, coming towards them. He was a quiet-looking, stodgy-faced man, but he had news written all over his plain face.

"Well, Marler?" inquired Matherfield as they met. "Got something?"

There was nobody about in that quiet corner of Lincoln's Inn Fields, yet the man looked round as if anxious to escape observation, and he spoke in a whisper.

"I believe I've got that chemist!" he answered. "Leastways, it's like this. There's a chemist I tried this morning – name of Macpherson, in Maiden Lane. I showed him the facsimiles of the lost labels on the medicine bottles, and asked him if he could give me any information. He's a very cautious sort of man, I think; he examined the facsimiles a long time, saying nothing. Then he said he supposed I was a policeman, and so on, and of course I had to tell him a bit – only a bit. Then he said, all of a sudden, 'Look here, my friend,' he said, 'you'd better tell me, straight out – has this to do with that Hannaford poisoning case?' So, of course, I said that, between ourselves, it had. 'Isn't Matherfield in charge of that?' he said. Of course, I said you were. 'Very well' he said. 'You send Matherfield to me. I'm not going to say anything to you,' he said. 'What I've got to say I'll say to Matherfield.' So I went back to head-quarters, and they told me you'd gone to Lincoln's Inn Fields."

"All right, my lad!" said Matherfield. "If you've found the right man, I'll remember you. What's his name – Macpherson, Maiden Lane? Very good – then I'll just step along and see him. Not a word to anybody, Marler!" he added, as the man turned away. "Keep close. Now, this is a bit of all right, Mr. Hetherwick!" he continued, chuckling and rubbing his hands. "This beats all we heard at Penteney's! Only let me get the name and address of the man for whom that bottle of medicine was made up, and I think I shall have taken a long stride! But come along – we'll see the chemist together."

The shop in Maiden Lane before which they presently paused was a small, narrow-fronted, old-fashioned establishment, with little in its windows beyond the usual coloured bottles and over the front no more than the name "Macpherson" in faded gilt letters on a time-stained signboard. It was dark and stuffy within the shop, and Hetherwick had to strain his eyes to see a tall, thin, elderly, spectacled man, very precise and trim in appearance, who stood behind the single counter, silently regarding him and Matherfield.

"Mr. Macpherson?" inquired Matherfield. "Just so! Good morning, sir. My name is Matherfield – Inspector Matherfield. One of my men tells me—"

"One moment!" interrupted the chemist. He stepped behind a screen at the rear of his shop and presently returned with a young man, to whom he whispered a word or two. Then he beckoned to his two visitors, and opening a door at the further corner, ushered them into a private parlour. "We shall be to ourselves here, Mr. Matherfield," he said. "And I've no doubt your business is of a highly confidential nature."

"Something of that sort, Mr. Macpherson," assented Matherfield, as he and Hetherwick took chairs at a centre table. "But my man'll have prepared you a bit, no doubt. He tells me he showed you the photographed facsimiles of certain torn labels that are on a medicine bottle which figures in the Hannaford case, and that in consequence of your seeing them you asked to see me. Well, sir, here I am!"

"Aye, just so, Mr. Matherfield, just so, precisely," replied the chemist, turning up the gas-jet which hung above the table. "Aye, to be sure!" He, too, sat down at the table, and folded his thin long fingers together. "Aye, and you'll be thinking, Mr. Matherfield, that yon bottle has something to do with the poisoning of Hannaford?"

"I'll be candid with you, Mr. Macpherson," answered Matherfield. "But first let me ask you something. Have you read the newspaper accounts of this affair?"

"I've done that, Mr. Matherfield – yes, all I could lay hands on."

"Then you'll be aware that there was another man poisoned as well as Hannaford – a man named Granett, who was in Hannaford's company on the night when it all happened? This gentleman here is the one that was in the Underground train and saw Hannaford die, and Granett make off, as he said, to fetch a doctor."

"That'll be Mr. Hetherwick, I'm thinking," said the chemist, with a polite bow. "Aye, just so!"

"I see you've read the reports of the inquest," remarked Matherfield, with a smile. "Very well, as I say, Granett was found dead later. I discovered a medicine bottle and a glass at his bedside. There'd been whisky in both, but according to the medical experts there had also been poison – the traces, they say, were indisputable. Now, on that medicine bottle were two torn labels – on the upper one, as you see from the facsimile photograph, there's been a name written – all that's left is the initial C. and the first letter of a surname, A. All the rest's gone. And what I want to know is – are you the chemist that made up the medicine or the tonic, or whatever it was, that was in that bottle, and, if so, who is the customer for whom you made it, and whose Christian name begins with C. and surname with A.? Do you comprehend me?"

"Aye, aye, Mr. Matherfield!" answered the chemist eagerly. "I'm appreciating every word you're saying, and very lucid it all is. And I'm willing to give you all the information in my power, but first I'd just like to have a bit myself on a highly pertinent matter. Now, you'll be aware, Mr. Matherfield, if you've seen the newspapers of this last day or two, that there's a firm of solicitors in Lincoln's Inn Fields that's offering a reward of five thousand pounds—"

"I'm well enough aware of it, Mr. Macpherson," interrupted Matherfield with a laugh and a sly glance at Hetherwick. "Mr. Hetherwick and myself have just come straight from their office, and what you want to know is – if you give me information will it be the same thing as giving it to them? You want to make sure about the reward?"

"Precisely, Mr. Matherfield, precisely!" assented the chemist eagerly. "You've hit my meaning exactly. For, of course, when there's a reward like yon—"

"If you give us information, Mr. Macpherson, that'll lead to the arrest and conviction of the guilty party, you can rest assured you'll get that reward," said Matherfield. "And Mr. Hetherwick'll support me in that, I'm sure."

"I'm satisfied – I'm satisfied, gentlemen!" exclaimed Macpherson, as Hetherwick murmured his confirmation. "Well, it's a strange, black business, and I'd no idea that I would come to be associated with it until that man of yours called in this morning, Mr. Matherfield. But then I knew! And I'll shorten matters by telling you, at once – I made up the tonic that was in that bottle!"

Matherfield rubbed his hands.

"Good!" he said quietly. "Good! And now, then – the critical question! For whom?"

"For a Dr. Charles Ambrose, from a prescription of his own," replied Macpherson. "It's a sort of pick-me-up tonic. I first made it up for him two years ago; I've made it up for him several times since. The last occasion was about six weeks ago. I have all the dates, though, in my books; I can show you them."

"Wait a bit," said Matherfield. "That's of no great importance – yet. Dr. Charles Ambrose, eh? Have you his address?"

"Aye, to be sure!" answered the chemist. "His address is 38, Number

59, John Street."

"Adelphi!" suggested Matherfield.

"Adelphi, precisely – 33, Number 59, John Street, Adelphi," repeated Macpherson. "That's in the books, too."

Matherfield suddenly became silent, staring at the floor. When he looked up again it was at Hetherwick.

"Didn't Granett exclaim that he knew of a doctor, close by, when he rushed out of that train at Charing Cross Underground?" he asked. "Gave the impression that he knew of one close by, anyway?"

"He said distinctly close by," answered Hetherwick. "Why, are you thinking—"

Matherfield interrupted him with a wave of the hand, and turned again to the chemist. "You've seen this Dr. Charles Ambrose?" he asked abruptly.

"Oh, I have, Mr. Matherfield, many a time and often," replied Macpherson. "But now I come to think of it, not lately."

"When – last?" demanded Matherfield.

"I should think last when he called in and told me to make him another bottle of his tonic," answered Macpherson, after some thought. "As I said just now, perhaps about six weeks ago. But the books—"

"Never mind the books yet. What's this Dr. Charles Ambrose like?"

"A tall, handsome man, distinguished-looking – I should say about forty years of age. A dark man – hair, eyes, beard. He wears his moustache and beard in – well, a sort of foreign fashion; in fact, he's more like a Spaniard than an Englishman."

"But – is he an Englishman?"

"He was always taken by me for an Englishman; he speaks like one – that is, like an Englishman of the upper classes. He once told me he was an Oxford man – we'd been talking about universities."

"Well-dressed man?"

"Aye, he was that! A smart, fine man."

"Did you ever see him in a big, dark overcoat, with a large white silk muffler about his neck and the lower part of his face?"

"Aye, I've seen him like that! On chilly evenings. Indeed, that's another thing he told me – he was subject to bronchial attacks."

"Muffled himself well up, eh?" suggested Matherfield.

"Aye, just so! He's been in here like that."

Matherfield turned to Hetherwick with a significant glance.

"That's the man who met Hannaford at Victoria Station that night! – the man that Ledbitter saw, and that nobody's seen since!" he exclaimed. "A million to one on it! Now then, who is he?"

"You know his name and his address," remarked Hetherwick.

"Yes – and I know, too, that Mr. Macpherson here hasn't seen him lately!" retorted Matherfield dryly. "How often, now, Mr. Macpherson, did you use to see him? I mean, did you use to see him at other times than when he came into your shop?"

"Oh, yes! I've seen him in the street, outside," replied the chemist. "I've seen him, too, going in and out of Rule's, and in and out of Romano's."

"In other words," remarked Matherfield, "he was pretty well known about this end of the Strand. I'm not sure, now, that I don't remember such a man myself – black, silky, carefully-trimmed beard, always a big swell. But – Mr. Macpherson hasn't seen him lately! Hm! Do you know if he was in practice, Mr. Macpherson?"

"I could not say as to that, Mr. Matherfield. Seeing that he called himself Dr. Ambrose, I supposed he was a medical practitioner, but I don't know what his degrees or qualifications were at all."

Matherfield glanced at a row of books which stood over a desk at the side of the parlour.

"Have you got an up-to-date medical directory?" he asked. "Good! Let's look the man up. You turn up his name, Mr. Hetherwick," he went on as the chemist handed down a volume; "you're more used to books than I am. Find out if there's anything about him."

Hetherwick turned over the pages of the directory, and presently shook his head.

"There's no Charles Ambrose here," he said. "Look for yourselves."

Matherfield glanced at the place indicated and said nothing. Macpherson made an exclamation of surprise.

"Aye, well, he may be a foreigner, after all," he observed. "But I shouldn't have considered him one, and he certainly told me he was an Oxford graduate."

"Foreigner or Oxforder, I'm going to know more about him!" declared Matherfield, rising and grasping his stick with an air of determination. "Well, Mr. Macpherson, we're obliged to you, and if this results in anything – you know! But for the moment – a bit of that caution that you Scotsmen are famous for – eh?"

Outside, Matherfield laid his hand on Hetherwick's elbow.

"Mr. Hetherwick," he said solemnly, "we're on the track – at last! Sure as my name's Matherfield, we've hit the trail! Now we're going to John Street, Adelphi – and I'll lay you anything you like that the man's vanished!"

# THE TELEGRAM

Hetherwick followed his companion across the Strand, into the Adelphi, and to the house they wanted – an old Adams mansion, now divided into flats. Matherfield did not take the trouble to ascend to the upper regions; he sought and found a caretaker and put a question to him. The man shook his head.

"Dr. Ambrose, sir?" he replied. "Oh, yes, Dr. Ambrose lives here – 38. But he ain't in, sir – ain't at home, in fact. He's been away three weeks or so – don't know where he is."

With a meaning look at Hetherwick, Matherfield drew the caretaker aside and talked to him for a few moments; the man presently turned and went downstairs to the basement from which they had summoned him.

"That's all right," remarked Matherfield, with a wink. "He's going to let us into Ambrose's flat. Didn't I tell you we shouldn't find Ambrose here? Not he! I should say he's off!"

"Supposing he returns – while we're here?" asked Hetherwick.

"Wish he would!" chuckled Matherfield. "Nobody I want to see more! If he did, why, I should just ask him to take a little walk with me – to explain a few matters. But he won't! Here's the man. We'll go up."

The caretaker reappeared with a bunch of keys and led the way to a flat at the top of the old house. He unlocked a door and stood aside.

"You needn't wait," said Matherfield. "I'll shut the place up again when we leave and let you know. All right."

He walked in, with Hetherwick at his heels, as soon as the caretaker had gone, and, once inside, closed the door carefully upon himself and his companion. But Hetherwick, after a first glance at the sitting-room into which they had entered, a somewhat untidy, shabbily furnished place, went straight to the hearth and pointed to a framed photograph, time-stained and faded, which hung over the mantelpiece.

"There's a striking and significant piece of evidence – at once!" he exclaimed. "Do you know what that is, Matherfield?"

Matherfield looked in the direction indicated, and shook his head.

"Not the slightest idea!" he answered. "I see it's a photograph of some old church or other – that's all."

"That's the famous Parish Church of Sellithwaite!" said Hetherwick. "One of the very finest in England! I had a look at it – only a mere look – when I was down there. Now then, what's this man doing with a picture of Sellithwaite Parish Church in his rooms? Hannaford came from Sellithwaite!"

"That's a mighty significant thing, anyway," agreed Matherfield. "We're getting at something this morning!" He looked more carefully at the photograph. "Grand old building, as you say," he continued. "Of course, the mere fact of his having it put up there shows that he's some interest in it. Sellithwaite man, likely. But we'll find all that out. Now let's look round."

There was little to see, Hetherwick thought. The flat consisted of a sitting-room and bedroom and a small bathroom. The furniture was plain, old, rather shabby; the whole place suggested that its occupant was not over well-to-do; the only signs of affluence to be seen were manifested in the toilet articles on the dressing-table, in a luxurious, if well-worn, dressing-gown which hung on the rail of the bed, and in the presence of carefully folded and pressed garments laid out in the bedroom. There were a few books, chiefly medical treatises, in shelves in the sitting-room; a few personal pictures, mainly of college and school groups, on the walls; and a desk in the centre, littered with more books, writing materials, and papers. Matherfield began to turn them over.

"See that?" he exclaimed suddenly, pointing to a movable calendar which stood on the top ledge of the desk. "Notice the date? March 18th! That's the day on which Hannaford got his quietus. At least, strictly speaking, it was the day before. Hannaford actually died on the nineteenth – about – what was it? – very early in the morning, anyway. What's one to gather from this? – that Ambrose hasn't been here since the eighteenth. So – hallo!"

Turning over the loose papers that lay about the blotting-pad, he had suddenly lighted upon a telegram; just as suddenly he thrust it into Hetherwick's hands.

"Look at that!" he exclaimed. "Now, that is a find! Biggest we've ever had – so far!"

Hetherwick read the apparently innocent message.

*"All right. Will meet you Victoria bookstall this evening as suggested.*
"Hannaford."

"See the date?" said Matherfield excitedly. "March 18th! Now we've got at it! Ambrose was the man that met Hannaford at Victoria, the tall, muffled-up man that Ledbitter saw! That's – certain!"

109

"Seems so," agreed Hetherwick. He was still studying the telegram. "Sent off from Fleet Street twelve-fifteen that day," he muttered. "Yes – there doesn't seem much doubt about this. I wonder who this man Ambrose is?"

"We'll soon get to know something about that, Mr. Hetherwick!" exclaimed Matherfield briskly. "Now, I'm just going to put that wire in my pocket, lock up this flat again, have another word or two with that caretaker chap, and go in search of the information you refer to. Come with me! Later, I shall get a search warrant, and make a thorough examination of this flat. Let's be moving."

Downstairs again, Matherfield called up the caretaker.

"You say Dr. Ambrose has been away for a bit?" he asked. "Is there anything unusual in that?"

"Well, not so very," answered the man. "Ever since he came here, two or three years ago, he's been used to going away for a while. I believe he used to go over to Paris. But I never remember him being away more than a week at a time before."

"Evidently he's a doctor," suggested Matherfield. "Did he ever have patients come to see him here?"

The caretaker shook his head.

"No," he replied. "He never had anybody much come to see him here – never remember anybody, unless it was somebody he brought in at night for a smoke, you know. He generally went out early in a morning, and came home late – very late."

"What about his meals?" asked Matherfield.

"He'd no meals here – unless he made himself a cup of coffee or so in a morning," said the caretaker. "All his meals out – breakfast, too. Sundays as well as weekdays. We saw very little of him."

"Who does up his rooms – makes the bed and so on?" inquired Matherfield.

"My wife," answered the caretaker. "She does all that."

"And she hasn't had anything to do for – how long?"

"Well, it'll be three weeks, I'm sure. He never used to say anything at any time when he went off – just went. He'd call downstairs when he came back and let us know he was back, d'ye see? But we never thought he'd be as long away as this, this time. It was only this morning, just before you came, that my missus said to me that it seemed queer."

"Why queer?"

"Because he's taken nothing with him. However short a time he might be away before, he always took a suitcase, clean linen, shaving things, so on – he was a very particular gentleman about his appearance – always dressed like a swell and had a clean shirt every day; used to have a nice heavy washing-bill, anyhow!"

"Did he seem to be pretty well supplied with money?" asked Matherfield. "Or – the opposite?"

"Couldn't rightly say," replied the caretaker. "Always paid his rent, and us, and the washing regular, but as for anything else, why, we'd no means of knowing. Of course, as I tell you, he always looked the gentleman."

"I see!" said Matherfield. "All right – you'll see me again this afternoon."

He strode away towards the Strand, and there ushered Hetherwick into the first empty taxi-cab they met.

"Where now?" asked Hetherwick as Matherfield followed him into the cab after a word to its driver.

"We're going now, sir, to Hallam Street, to the offices of the General Medical Council," answered Matherfield promptly. "I've had experience of inquiring into the antecedents of medical men before, and I know where to find out all about any of 'em. I'm going to find out all about this Dr. Charles Ambrose – that is, of course, if he's an English doctor."

"Probably he isn't," remarked Hetherwick, "any more than Baseverie is."

"Ah, Baseverie!" exclaimed Matherfield. "I'd forgotten that man for the time being! Well, while we're about it, we'll see if we can unearth a bit of information concerning him. We've done a bit of good work this morning, ye know, Mr. Hetherwick!" he went on, rubbing his hands with satisfaction. "We've practically made certain that Ambrose was the man who met Hannaford at Victoria, and we're sure he's the man to whom Macpherson supplied the bottle in which the poison was discovered at Granett's room. And now we'll hope for a bit more illumination in the darkness!"

Hetherwick presently found himself closeted with Matherfield and a grave official who, after seeing Matherfield's credentials and listening to his reasons for his visit of inquiry, began to consult various books of reference. Presently he left the room and was away some time; when he returned he brought with him two slips of paper, which he handed to Matherfield.

"I have had the particulars you require written out for you," he said, "so you can examine them at your leisure. I – " here he smiled frostily – "I gather that you are somewhat anxious to get in touch with these men?"

"I think it's extremely probable, sir, that before the day's over I shall be exceedingly anxious to get in touch with both!" answered Matherfield, with something very like a wink. "More than anxious!"

The grave official nodded and smiled again, and Matherfield and Hetherwick went away. Outside Matherfield looked right and left.

"Mr. Hetherwick," he said, "it's well past twelve, and I'd my breakfast before eight – I'm hungry! Let's turn into the first decent place we see and get a bite and a sup! And we'll examine these papers."

He presently led Hetherwick into the saloon bar of a tavern, and remarking that he had a taste for ale and bread and cheese at that time of day, provided himself with these matters and retreated to a snug corner, whither Hetherwick followed him with a whisky and soda.

"Here's success to our endeavours, Mr. Hetherwick!" said Matherfield, lifting his tankard. "I'm now firmly under the impression that we're adding link after link to the chain! But let's see what we've got here in this crabbed writing."

He laid the slips of paper on the table at which they sat; both bent over them. There were not many words on either, but to Hetherwick they were significant enough in their plain straightforwardness.

*Charles Ambrose, M.B. (Oxon). Medical Officer of Health, Crayport, Lanes, 1903-4; in practice Whiteburn, Lanes, 1904-9; police surgeon, Sellithwaite, W.R., Yorks, 1909-12; in practice Brondesbury, London, 1912-18. Struck off Register by General Medical Council for unprofessional conduct, 1918.*

"So much for him!" muttered Matherfield, his cheek bulging with bread and cheese. "I thought it would turn out to be something of that sort! Now t'other!"

*Cyprian Baseverie, L.R.C.P., L.R.C.S. In practice Birmingham, 1897-1902; at Wyborough, Northants, 1902-11; at Dalston, N., 1911-17, Convicted of fraud at Central Criminal Court, 1917, and struck off Register by General Medical Council, 1918.*

"Ho-ho!" exclaimed Matherfield. "Been in the dock already, has he? Well, well, Mr. Hetherwick, we continue to learn, sir! We know still more. Baseverie's a convicted criminal. Both have been struck off the register. Ambrose was certainly at Sellithwaite – and he'd be there, according to these dates, at the time of the Whittingham affair. A promising pair – for our purpose! What do you think?"

"I'm wondering if the two men know each other," answered Hetherwick.

"Shouldn't wonder," said Matherfield. "Probably they do. Probably they're mixed up together in this affair. Probably they're actual partners in it – accessories to each other. But now that I know this much about them, I can find out more, especially about Ambrose, as he was a police surgeon. I can find out, too, what Baseverie's particular crime was. Defrauding a patient, I should imagine. But I'll put one or two men on to working up particulars and records of both Baseverie and Ambrose this afternoon, and, of course, I shall go back and thoroughly examine that flat in John Street."

"And, I suppose, in view of the evidence supplied by Macpherson, set up a search for Ambrose?" suggested Hetherwick.

"To be sure! We'll get out a 'tracked by the police' notice, describing him to the best of our power," replied Matherfield. "But I'll tell you – in my opinion it'll be a stiff job getting hold of him. If you want my opinion, as a private individual, he's probably got that secret invention of Hannaford's and gone off across the Atlantic with it – to turn it into money."

"That's very likely," assented Hetherwick. "But what about Baseverie?"

"I'm not so much concerned about him now," said Matherfield. "Ambrose seems to be the man I want – first, anyway. But I shall do what I can to get hold of Baseverie. If these Penteney and Blenkinsop people had only come to us instead of laying plans of their own, some good would have been done. I shouldn't have let the man got away!"

"My belief," observed Hetherwick, "is that Baseverie and Ambrose are partners in this affair. And – how do we know that they didn't meet at Dover, and that they haven't gone off together?"

Still wondering about this, Hetherwick next morning went round to Lincoln's Inn Fields and asked to see one of the partners. He was shown into the room in which he and Matherfield had had their interview on the previous day. But he found Major Penteney alone. Blenkinsop, remarked the junior partner, had business in the Courts that morning.

"I called," explained Hetherwick, "to ask if you had any more information about Baseverie's disappearance at Dover."

Penteney made a wry face.

"More vexed than ever about that!" he answered. "Most inexcusably stupid conduct on the part of our man – man we've always found so reliable previously. He came back yesterday afternoon, crestfallen, told us all about it, and got a jolly good wigging. He'd done well at first. Tracked his man from Riversreade Court to Dorking, and thence to Redhill, and thence to Dover, after one or two changes. Baseverie put up at some hotel – I forget which – near the harbour; our man, certain that Baseverie was quite unconscious that he was being followed, put up there, too. Nothing happened. He saw Baseverie at dinner that night, saw him in the smoking-room after; in fact, he had a game of billiards with him, and saw him retire to bed; their rooms were adjacent. He felt sure of seeing him at breakfast, but when he went down he found that the bird had flown – flown, said the night porter, before six o'clock; he didn't know where. Nor could our man trace him at station or pier, or anywhere."

"Careless sort of watching," said Hetherwick.

"Worse than careless!" agreed Penteney. "As I said, he caught it hot. But now—"

The telephone bell on Blenkinsop's desk rang. With a word of excuse Penteney turned to it. A moment later a smothered ejaculation of surprise came from him, followed by a sharp interrogation on his part. Suddenly he turned on Hetherwick.

"Good heavens!" he exclaimed. "What's all this? This is Lady Riversreade speaking. She says her sister, who came yesterday, and Miss Featherstone have been kidnapped! Kidnapped – this morning!"

Hetherwick leapt to his feet with a sharp exclamation – half amazed, half incredulous. But already his thoughts were with Rhona; he saw the dangers of the situation for her as Penteney could not see them.

"Impossible!" he said. "Kidnapped! In broad daylight? And – from there?"

But Penteney was still busy at the telephone, giving and receiving rapid answers.

"Yes, yes!" he was saying. "To be sure! – police – yes! I'm coming straight there now – car – tell the police to get busy."

He turned sharply to Hetherwick as he laid down the instrument.

"Fear there's no impossibility about it!" he said. "Lady Riversreade says they were carried off as they crossed from the Court to the Home – she's heard something of a big car with strange men in it. I'm going down there at once – there's more in this affair than one sees at first."

"I'll come with you," said Hetherwick. "Where can we get a car – a fast one?"

"Garage close by, in Kingsway," answered Penteney, hurriedly seizing on one of several greatcoats that hung in a recess. "Here! – get into one of these – you're about my height, and the air's still nippy, motoring. Now come on – we'll be there in under the hour. You know," he continued, as they left the office and hastened towards Kingsway, "I think I see through something of this already, Hetherwick. These fellows probably believed they were kidnapping Lady Riversreade! – and got her sister in mistake for her. Ransom, you know! The blackmailing dodge failed – now they're trying this. A desperate and dare-devil lot, evidently!"

Hetherwick nodded a silent assent. He was wondering whether or not to tell Penteney that the Miss Featherstone of whom he had just spoken was in reality the granddaughter of the man whose mysterious murder appeared to be the starting-point of the more recent, equally mysterious events. That fact, it seemed to him, would have to come out sooner or later – and there might be possible complications, perhaps unpleasantness, when Lady Riversreade discovered that Rhona had gone to her as a spy. Might it not be well to take Penteney into his confidence and explain matters? But, on reflection, he decided to wait until they knew the exact situation at Riversreade Court; so far, in spite of Lady Riversreade's news he felt it difficult to believe that two women, one of them, to his knowledge, a girl of character and resource, and the other a woman of the world, used to travelling and to adventure, could be carried off in broad daylight in immediate prospect of two large houses – the thing seemed impossible.

# THE LONDON ROAD

Some fifty minutes later, the big, powerful car, which Penteney had commissioned in Kingsway, dashed up to Riversreade Court. Hetherwick found that there had been no exaggeration in Lady Riversreade's telephone message. She herself came hurrying out to meet them; there were men standing about the terrace outside and others visible in the park; a couple of uniformed policemen followed Lady Riversreade from her study, where Hetherwick supposed her to have been in consultation with them. And her first glance was directed on Hetherwick himself; she addressed him before Penteney could go through any hurried introduction.

"I've seen you before!" she exclaimed abruptly. "You were with my secretary, Miss Featherstone, at Victoria, Sunday morning. Are you engaged to her?"

"No!" replied Hetherwick. "But we are close friends."

"Well, Miss Featherstone's been run away with – and so has my sister, Madame Listorelle," continued Lady Riversreade. "That's the long and short of it! You seemed almost incredulous when I rang you up," she continued, turning to Penteney, "but there's no doubt about it – they've been kidnapped, under my very windows. And we haven't a single clue, a trace of any sort."

"So far, you mean," answered Penteney coolly. "But come – but let me hear all about it. What are the details?"

"Details!" exclaimed Lady Riversreade. "We don't know any details! All I know is this – my sister came here from Hampshire yesterday evening, to stay a few days. This morning, after we had breakfasted, she and Miss Featherstone set out across the park for the Home, leaving me here – I meant to follow in a few minutes. I did follow! – I wasn't ten minutes behind them. But when I got to the Home, they weren't there, and Mitchell, the man at the door, said they hadn't come. They didn't come! Eventually, I came back here, to find out if something had happened and they'd returned by some other way. But they weren't here. Then I began to make some inquiry. One of the housemaids, who'd

115

been looking out of a top window, said she'd seen a car go at a great rate down the middle drive in the direction of the high road soon after Madame Listorelle and Miss Featherstone left the house. And of course there's no doubt about it – they've been carried off in that! This is more work of that man Baseverie's!"

"You said something over the 'phone about strange men being seen in the car," remarked Penteney.

"Oh, that? – yes, the same girl said she thought she could see two men sitting in the car," answered Lady Riversreade. "Of course they'd be strange."

Penteney turned to the policemen, at the same time tapping Hetherwick's arm. "I think we'd better go across the park and see for ourselves if there are any signs of a struggle at any particular place," he said. "I don't think either Madame Listorelle or Miss Featherstone likely persons to be carried off without making a fight for it. Have you been across the grounds yet?" he added, to the elder of the two men. "I mean by the path they took?"

"Not yet, sir; we've only just arrived," answered the man.

"Come along, then," said Penteney. He lingered a moment as Hetherwick and the policemen left the hall, and said a few words to Lady Riversreade; then he hurried out and headed his party. "This way," he continued, leading Hetherwick along the terrace, "I know the usual route to the Home – plain sailing from here to there, except at one spot, and there, I conclude, whatever has happened did happen!"

Hetherwick paid particular attention to the route along which Penteney led his party. The path went straight across the park, from the end of the terrace at the Court to near the front entrance of the Home, and from the Court itself it looked as if there was no break in it. But about half-way between the two houses there was an important break which could not be seen until pedestrians were close upon it. Transecting the park from its southern to its northern boundaries was a sunken roadway – the middle drive to which Lady Riversreade had referred – gained from the park above, on each side, by ornamental steps. Whatever happened in that roadway, Hetherwick saw at once, could not have been seen from the higher ground above, save by anyone close to its edge. But two or three hundred yards or so from the steps, which made a continuation of the path, the embankments of the sunken road flattened out into the lower stretches of the park, and there the road itself could be seen from the top windows of the Court, and from those of the Home also.

Penteney paused at the top of the ornamental steps.

"If these two ladies have been carried off, as they certainly seem to have been," he said, turning to his companions, "this is the spot! Now, just let me explain the lie of the land. The main road edges the park at the northern end, as you all know. But there is a good road at the southern extremity, and the sunken road runs down from it. A car could come down from there, be pulled up here, and kept waiting until the two ladies came along. They would have to descend these steps, cross the road, and ascend the steps on the other bank to get to the other half of the park. Now suppose they're forced into a car at the foot of the steps – the car goes off for the main road and gets clear away within a minute or two of the kidnapping taking place! There's the difficulty! The thing would be easy to do – granted force. Probably, the two captives were forced into the car at the point of revolvers."

"That's about it, sir!" agreed the elder of the policemen. "No choice in the matter, poor things! And, as you say, they'd be in and off – miles off – before they fairly knew what had happened."

"Come down and let's see the roadway," said Penteney.

But there was nothing to see at the foot of the steps. The road, like all roads and paths on the Riversreade Court property, was in a perfect state of repair, and there was scarcely a grain of dust on its spick-and-span, artificially treated and smoothed surface; certainly there were no signs of any struggle.

"That's how it's been, you may depend upon it," observed Penteney to Hetherwick as they looked about. "The men were waiting here with revolvers. They'd force them into the car and get in after them; a third man, an accomplice, would drive off. If only we had some more definite information about the car and its occupants!"

"There's an old chap coming down the road who seems to have his eye on us," remarked Hetherwick, looking round. "He may have something to tell. After all, some of the people hereabouts must have seen the car!"

The old man, evidently a labourer, came nearer, looking inquiringly from one to the other. He had the air of one who can tell something on occasion.

"Be you gentlemen a-enquirin' about a moty-car what was round here this mornin'?" he asked, as he came up. "I hear there was somebody a-askin' questions that way, so I just come down-along, like."

"We are," answered Penteney. "Do you know anything?"

The old man pointed up the sunken road to a part of the park where it was lost amongst trees and coppices.

"Lives up there, I do," he said. "My cottage, it be just behind they trees, t'other side o' the road what this here runs into; my garden, it runs down to the edge o' that road. And when I was a-gardenin' this morning – mebbe 'bout half-past-nine o'clock, that was – I sees a moty-car what come along from your way, and turns into this here sunken road. Mebbe that's what you're a-talkin' 'bout?"

"No doubt," agreed Penteney. "And we're much obliged to you. Now what sort of a car was it? Closed, or open?"

"Oh, 'twas closed up, same as one o' they old cabs what us don't see no more now," said the old man. "But I see inside it, for all that. Two gentlemen."

"Two gentlemen, eh?" repeated Penteney. "Just so. And a driver outside, of course."

"Oh, aye; there was a driver outside, to be sure. In livery, he was – like a gentleman's servant. Smart feller!"

"Could you describe the gentlemen?"

"No, surely – two gentlemen, though; a-sitting back, I sees 'em! And sees the moty-car, too, turn down this here very road."

"What sort of car was it?" inquired Penteney. "What colour was it painted?"

"Well, now, you beats me! It med be a sort o' greyish colour – or again, it med be a sort o' yaller, lightish yaller, or it med be drabbish – I couldn' 'zac'ly go to for say what it was, proper. But a lightish colour."

"Lightish – grey, yellow, or drab – something of that sort?"

"Surely! Her wasn't a dark 'un, anyhow. But the feller what drove, now he were in a dark livery – I took partic'lar notice of he, 'cause he was so smart as never was. Green! That was his colour, and gold lace. Looked like a duke, he did! And I thought, hearin' as there was them in the park as was inquirin', like, as 'ow I'd come and tell 'ee."

Penteney rewarded the informant with some silver, and turned to his companions with a shake of the head.

"A light-coloured car with two men in it, driven by a man who wore a dark-green livery with gold lace on it!" he remarked. "That's about all we're likely to get. And – if this has been a carefully-planned affair, the chauffeur would change his livery before they'd gone far – slip another coat on! However—"

They went back to the Court, consulting together; obviously, there was nothing to do but to send out inquiries in the surrounding country. Penteney was sceptical about the success of these.

"When one considers the thousands of cars to be seen in any given area during one morning," he said, "how can one expect that anybody, even rustics, should give special attention to any particular one? There's no doubt about it – they've got clean away!"

It seemed as if nothing could be done but to give the kidnapping full publicity through the police and the press. In the neighbourhood of the Court nobody beyond the housemaid and the old cottager appeared to have seen the car and its occupants. But during the afternoon, as Hetherwick and Penteney were about to set out for London, a man came to the house and asked to see Lady Riversreade. Lady Riversreade went out to him; the two men accompanied her, and found at the hall door an elderly, respectable-looking fellow who had driven up in a light cart. He had heard, he said, of what had happened at Riversreade Court that morning, and he believed he could tell something, for he was sure that he had seen a car, such as that the police were inquiring after, pass his house.

"And where is that?" asked Lady Riversreade.

"About two miles the other side of Dorking, my lady, on the London

Road. I'm a market gardener – name of Thomas Chillam. And I was outside my garden gate this morning, about, as near as I can reckon, ten o'clock, when I saw a car, light-coloured, coming from Dorking, at a particularly high speed – a good deal faster than it had any right to do! I watched it careful, my lady. But just as it got near to my place, there was a man drove some sheep out of a by-lane, a few yards past my garden and the car was obliged to slow down. And so I saw the folks in it."

"Yes?" said Lady Riversreade. "And – who was in it?"

"There was a couple of men, my lady, on the front seat, and a couple of ladies in the back. Of course, it was a closed car, but I saw 'em, plain enough, all four. It seemed to me as if they were all either quarrelling or having high words – they were all talking together, anyway. But though the car had slowed down 'cause of the sheep, it was still moving at a fair pace, and, of course, they were past and gone, London way, in a minute, as it were. All the same, I saw 'em clearly enough to see that one of the men inside was a man I've seen before."

"About here?" exclaimed Lady Riversreade.

"No, my lady," answered Chillam. "In London. It's this way, my lady – me and my missis, we've a grown-up daughter what's in service in London – Grosvenor Gardens. Now and again we go up to see her, and stop a night or two close by. And of course we take a look round. Now I've seen that man two or three times about Victoria Station way – I knew him at once when I saw him this morning, and—"

"Just tell us what he's like, will you?" interrupted Penteney. "As near as you can."

"Well, sir, I ain't good at that, but he's a tall, good-looking, smart-dressed gentleman, with a beard and moustache – taller nor what you and that other gentleman is, sir. I seen him in Victoria Street – mebbe it was his height made me notice him."

"And you're sure that was the man you saw in the car this morning?"

"Make no doubt on it, sir! I'm as certain as that I see yourself. Oh, yes!"

Hetherwick put in a question.

"The second man in the car? Did you notice him? Can you remember him?"

Chillam reflected for awhile.

"I remember that he was a white-faced chap," he said at last. "Wore a top-hat, silk."

When Chillam had gone away, Hetherwick turned to his companions.

"That sounds like Ambrose, for one man, and Baseverie for the other," he said. "What devilry are they up to now? Penteney – we must get back to London!"

# CONVERGING TRACKS

It was an hour later when they pulled up at Matherfield's head-quarters and went in to find him. Matherfield, brought to them after some search, rubbed his hands at sight of them.

"Come at the right moment!" he exclaimed, "I've got news – of Ambrose!"

Matherfield evidently expected his visitors to show deep interest, if not passive enthusiasm, in respect of this announcement, and he stared wonderingly on seeing that their faces showed nothing but gloom and concern.

"But you – you look as if you'd had bad news!" he exclaimed. "Something gone wrong?"

"I forgot that we might have telephoned you from Riversreade Court," replied Hetherwick, suddenly realising that Matherfield seemed to know nothing of the day's happening. "But I thought the Dorking police would do that. Gone wrong! – yes, and it may have to do with Ambrose – we've heard news that seems to fit in with him. But it's this," he went on to give Matherfield a brief account of the day's events. "There you are!" he concluded. "I've no doubt whatever that Baseverie and Ambrose are in at this – kidnapping in broad daylight. Matherfield, you've got to find them!"

Matherfield had listened with close attention to Hetherwick's story, and now he looked from him to Penteney; from Penteney to a printed bill which lay on his desk at his side. "I think I see what all this is about," he remarked, after a pause. "Those chaps think they've got – or they thought they got – Lady Riversreade! To hold for ransom, of course. They took Miss Hannaford because she chanced to be there. What they really kidnapped – and there's more of that done than you gentlemen might think, I can tell you! – was Lady Riversreade's sister. But now, however sisters – twin sisters – may closely resemble each other, there comes a time when difference of identity's bound to come out. By this time – perhaps long before – those men must have discovered that they laid hands on the wrong woman! And the question is – what would they do then?"

"It seems to me that the more immediate question is – where are the two women?" exclaimed Hetherwick. "Think of their danger!"

"Oh, well, Mr. Hetherwick, I don't suppose they're in any personal danger," answered Matherfield. "They're in the hands of brigands, no doubt, but I don't think there'll be any maltreatment of them – set your mind at rest about that. They don't do that sort of thing nowadays; it's all done politely and with every consideration, I believe. As to where they are? Why, somewhere in London! And there are over seven millions of other people in London, and hundreds upon hundreds of thousands of inhabited houses – a lot of needles in that bundle of hay, gentlemen!"

"They've got to be found!" repeated Hetherwick doggedly. "You'll have to set all your machinery to work! This can't—"

"Wait a bit, Hetherwick," interrupted Penteney. He turned to Matherfield. "You said you had news of this man Ambrose? What news?"

Matherfield tapped the printed bill which lay on his desk.

"I had that circulated broadcast this morning," he answered. "And then, of course, the newspapers have helped. Well, not so very long before you came in, I was called to the telephone by a man named Killiner, who told me he was the landlord of the Green Archer Tavern, in Wood Street, Westminster—"

"Westminster again!" exclaimed Hetherwick. "That seems to be the centre point!"

"And a very good thing to have a centre-point, Mr. Hetherwick," said Matherfield. "When things begin to narrow down, one gets some chance. Well, I was saying – this man rang me up to say that if I'd go down there he thought he could give me some information relative to the bill about the missing man. What he'd got to say, he said, was too long for a telephone talk. I answered that I'd be with him shortly, and I was just setting off when you arrived. Of course, I don't know what he can tell – it may be nothing, it may be something. Perhaps you gentlemen would like to go with me and hear what it is?"

"I would, but I mustn't," replied Penteney. "I must go to my office and hear if Lady Riversreade or the local police have had any fresh news. Keep in touch with me, though, Matherfield – let me know what you hear."

"I'll go with you," said Hetherwick. "Westminster!" he muttered again, when Penteney had gone. "It looks as if this man Ambrose was known in that district."

"Likely!" assented Matherfield. "But you know, Mr. Hetherwick, there are some queer spots in that quarter! People who know the purely ornamental parts of Westminster, such as the Abbey, and the Houses of Parliament, and Victoria Street, and so on, don't know that there are some fine old slums behind 'em! But I'll show you when we get down there. We shall go through one or two savoury slices."

He was putting on his overcoat as he spoke, in readiness for setting out, but before he had buttoned it a constable entered with a card.

"Wants to see you particularly, and at once," he said. "Waiting outside."

"Bring him in – straight!" answered Matherfield. He pushed the card along his desk in Hetherwick's direction. "Lord Morradale!" he exclaimed. "Who's he?"

"The man who's engaged to Madame Listorelle," replied Hetherwick, in an undertone. "Hampshire magnate."

Matherfield turned expectantly to the open door. A shortish, stoutish person, who looked more like a typical City man, prosperous and satisfied, came hustling in and gave Hetherwick and his companion a sharp, inquiring glance which finally settled on Matherfield.

"Mr. Matherfield?" he asked. "Just so! I'm Lord Morradale – oh, of course, I sent in my card – just so! Well, Mr. Matherfield, I've had an extraordinary communication from Lady Riversreade. She telephoned to my house in Hill Street this morning, but I was down in the City, and didn't hear of her message till late this afternoon. She says her sister, Madame Listorelle, has been kidnapped! Kidnapped – preposterous!"

"I'm afraid it's neither preposterous nor improbable, my lord," answered Matherfield. "I'm quite sure Madame Listorelle has been kidnapped, and Lady Riversreade's secretary, Miss Featherstone, with her. I've been down at Riversreade Court most of the day, and there's no doubt about it – the two ladies were carried off from there by three men in a fast car, which was driven towards London. That's a fact!"

"God bless my soul!" exclaimed Lord Morradale. "In broad daylight! Twentieth century, too! And is there no clue?"

"None so far, my lord. Of course, we've noised the affair as much as possible, and all our people are on the look out. But it's a difficult case," continued Matherfield. "The probability is that the ladies have been rushed to some house in London and that they're there in captivity. Of course, one theory is that the kidnappers took Madame Listorelle for her sister. They meant to get Lady Riversreade and hold her to ransom."

Lord Morradale pursed his lips. Then he rubbed his chin. Then he shook his head. Finally he gave Hetherwick a shrewd glance, eyeing him from head to foot.

"Um!" he said. "Ah! This gentleman? Not one of your people, I think, Matherfield?"

"No, my lord. This gentleman is Mr. Hetherwick, of the Middle Temple, who is interested very deeply in certain matters connected with the affair. Mr. Hetherwick has been down to Riversreade with me, and your lordship can speak freely before him."

Lord Morradale gave Hetherwick a friendly, knowing nod. Then he glanced at the door, and Matherfield made haste to close it.

"Thank 'ee," said Lord Morradale. "Just as well to be in private. 'Um!

– I think I'd better tell you something, Matherfield. I dare say that's a reasonable supposition of yours – that these villains took Madame Listorelle for her sister. But I don't think they did. I think they knew very well whom they were seizing. Mind you – they'd have seized Lady Riversreade too if she'd happened to be there. But it was madame they were after!"

"If your lordship would explain—" suggested Matherfield.

"I'm going to – it's what I come here for! I think I can just put you on the right scent. You may have heard that Madame Listorelle and I are about to marry? Very well, I accordingly knew a good deal about her affairs. Now, I don't know whether you know or not that Madame Listorelle is actively concerned – or has been – in buying and selling jewels on commission? That's her speciality."

"Heard something of it, my lord," replied Matherfield.

"Very well. Now, quite recently Madame Listorelle bought up in Paris a magnificent set of stones which had been at one time the property of a member of the Russian Imperial family. She brought them here to London, meaning, shortly, either to send or take them personally to America to her customer. This deal, unfortunately, got into the papers. Now, it's my belief that these fellows have kidnapped madame in order to get hold of these jewels. Do you see?"

"Ah!" exclaimed Matherfield. "I see, my lord! That puts a new aspect on the case. But – surely Madame Listorelle wouldn't have the stones on her?"

Lord Morradale winked – deliberately – at both his hearers.

"No!" he said. "No – she wouldn't. But the scoundrels would figure on this – that when she was fairly in their power they would be in a position to make her give them up – to force her, in short, to disclose their whereabouts. If they're desperate villains, not likely to stick at anything, I think they'll have forced madame to compliance – and in doing so give you a chance to lay hands on them!"

"How, my lord?" asked Matherfield eagerly.

Lord Morradale gave the two men a confidential glance.

"This way," he replied. "The jewels were deposited, for safety, by Madame Listorelle at the Imperial Safe Deposit. She rents a safe there. Now, don't you see what I'm suggesting? These men may force her to give them the necessary key and a signed order to the safe people to let the bearer open madame's safe and take away a certain case in which the jewels are packed. That's what I think will be done. And what you ought to do is to see the Imperial Safe Deposit officials at once, warn them of what I suggest may happen, and take your own means of watching for such a messenger arriving, and for tracking him when he departs. Eh?"

"Or arresting him there and then," said Matherfield.

"No, I shouldn't!" declared Lord Morradale. "I'm not a policeman, you know, but I can give a hint to one. Instead of arresting the man –

who, you must remember, will be sure to have madame's written authority on him – that is if things turn out as I suggest – I should carefully follow him. For – he'll probably go back to where madame and the young lady, Miss What's-her-name, are detained! Eh?"

Matherfield shook his head.

"I should doubt that, my lord!" he answered. "If things work out as you suggest, – and it's a highly probable theory – that's about the last thing he would do! Once the jewels were in his possession—"

"You forget this," interrupted Lord Morradale. "They may use a catspaw! Eh?"

"Well, there's that in it, certainly," assented Matherfield. "However, I'll see that the Imperial Safe Deposit people are warned and that this entrance is carefully watched tomorrow morning. But – the thing may have been done already! There's been plenty of time since the ladies were carried off."

"No!" said Lord Morradale. "Nothing's happened so far. I called in at the Imperial Safe Deposit as I came here; they had neither seen Madame Listorelle nor had any communication from her today. And now the place is closed for the night."

"Did you warn them, then?" inquired Matherfield.

"I didn't. I thought it best to see you first," replied Lord Morradale. "The warning and the rest of it will come best from you."

"Very good, my lord. Much obliged to your lordship for looking in," said Matherfield. "We'll keep you posted up in anything that happens – at Hill Street. Now," he continued, when Lord Morradale had left the office, "we'll get along to Westminster, Mr. Hetherwick, to the 'Green Archer' and its landlord, Killiner."

The "Green Archer" proved to be a respectable tavern which boasted a saloon bar. Behind the glass screens of this they found a middle-aged, sharp-eyed man, who at the sight of his visitors immediately opened the door of a parlour in the rear and ushered them into privacy. He pointed silently to a copy of the bill asking for news of Ambrose.

"Aye!" said Matherfield. "Just so. I had your message. You think you know this man?"

"From this description of him in that bill, yes," replied the landlord. "I think he's a man – gentleman, by all appearances – who used to come into my saloon bar pretty regularly during this last six months. Since the end of last summer, I should say, up to about three weeks or so ago."

"Not since then, eh?" asked Matherfield. "Three weeks?"

"About that. No – he hasn't been in for quite that. But up to then he'd been in, well, four or five days a week. Handsome, fine man – in fact, you've described him exactly there. I never knew who he was – used to pass the time o' day with him, you know, but that was all. He always came in about the same time – one to one-thirty. He'd have sometimes a glass of bitter ale and a sandwich or two; sometimes a whisky and soda and two or three biscuits. Stood and had his snack and went away. Never talked much. I took him for some gentleman that had business hereabouts, and just wanted a bite and a sup in the middle of the day, and turned in here for it. But I don't know what business he could be concerned in round here. He hadn't the tradesman's look on him, you understand. I should have said he was a professional man of some sort. Always very well dressed, you know – smart. However, I did notice one peculiar thing about him."

"What now?" asked Matherfield. "It all helps!"

"Well," said the landlord, "I noticed that his hands and fingers were stained – all sorts of colours. Sometimes it was more noticeable than at others. But there it was."

"Um!" remarked Matherfield. He exchanged a knowing glance with Hetherwick. And when, a few minutes later, they left the tavern, he turned to him with an air of assurance. "I'm beginning to feel the end!" he said. "Feel it, if I don't see it. Stained fingers, eh? We've heard of them before, Mr. Hetherwick. And I'll tell ye what it is. Somewhere about this very spot there's some place where men are dabbling – secretly, I should think – with chemicals, and Ambrose is one of 'em, and perhaps Baseverie another, and it was there that Hannaford and that man Grannet had been that night, and where they were poisoned – and there, too, no doubt, these two ladies are at this minute! Well – come to my place first thing in the morning."

Hetherwick, at a loss what to do further that night, went away and dined, and, that done, strolled home to his chambers. There was a light in his parlour, and when he opened the door he found Mapperley, evidently awaiting him, and with Mapperley a curly-headed, big-nosed, beady-eyed young Jew.

# THE ORDER IN WRITING

Hetherwick realised at once that Mapperley had news, and was waiting there to communicate it. But he looked not so much at Mapperley as at Mapperley's companion. Mapperley, as Hetherwick had remarked to more than one person in the course of those proceedings, concealed his sharpness under an unusually commonplace exterior; he looked, as a rule, like a young man whose ideas rarely soared above a low level. But the Jew was of a different aspect – Hetherwick was not quite sure whether he was rat or ferret. There was subtlety and craft written all over him, from his bright beady eyes to his long, thin, dirty fingers, and before Mapperley spoke his employer felt sure that in this son of Israel the clerk had found a valuable associate.

"Hullo, Mapperley!" exclaimed Hetherwick. "Waiting for me? You've some news, I suppose?"

Mapperley, grave and formal, pointed a finger at the Jew.

"Mr. Isidore Goldmark, sir," he said. "Friend of mine. I got him to give me a bit of assistance in this Baseverie and Vivian affair. The fact is, sir, he knows Vivian's – don't you, Issy?"

"Thome!" replied Mr. Goldmark, with a grin.

"And he knows Baseverie, too," continued Mapperley. "By sight, anyhow. So I got him – for a consideration – to watch for Baseverie's next appearance on that scene, and then, when he did come, to keep an eye on him – trick him, in fact. And Issy's seen him tonight, Mr. Hetherwick, and followed him. Then Issy came to me, and I brought him here."

"Good!" said Hetherwick. "Sit down, both of you, and I'll hear about it." He dropped into his own easy chair and again regarding the Jew decided that he was probably a creditable witness. "What do you do at Vivian's?" he asked. "Employed there?"

Mr. Goldmark glanced at Mapperley and smiled knowingly. Mapperley nodded.

"All confidential, Issy," he said reassuringly. "Going no further."

"Of course this is all confidential – and secret," remarked

Hetherwick. "I only want to know the precise connection between Vivian's and Mr. Goldmark."

"It'th a thort of themi-official, mithter," answered the Jew. "The fact ith, I do a bit o' commith'on work for Vivian'th cuthtomerth, turf you know. Tho' – I'm in and out of an evening. Thee?"

"I see," said Hetherwick. "All right! And you know Baseverie?"

"Ath well ath I know my own nothe," replied Mr. Goldmark.

"How long have you known him?"

"Thome time."

"Do you know what he is?"

"Aint an idea, mithter – and noboody elthe that I knowth of! Liv'th on hith wit'th, I should thay, if you athk me. Wrong 'un!"

"Nor where he lives?"

"No, mithter! All I knowth ith that he come'th to Vivian'th – now and then."

"And you saw him tonight?"

"I did, mithter – tonight ath ever wath!"

"What time was that?"

"About eight o'clock, mithter – near ath I can fix it."

"Well, what happened?"

"Thith, mithter. He came in about eight, ath I thay. I wath there, doing a bit o' bithneth with another cuthmur. Batheverie, he didn't thtop. He wathn't in the plathe three minuteth, and while he wath in he theemed – to me – to be a bit fidgety – thuthpithious, like. Looked round and about – cautiouth. Then he went – and I followed him. According to inthructionth from Mapperley there."

"Where did he go?"

"Well, mithter, I'll give you the particularth – in full: when I theth out on a job o' that thort I do it proper. He turned out o' Candlethtick Pathage into the Lane, and he had a drink at a bar there. Then he went to Trafalgar Square Tube. I wath clothe behind him when he booked—"

"A moment. Does he know you?"

"May jutht know me by thite, mithter, but not enough to exthite any thuthpithion in hith mind if he thaw me there behind him. I never had no truck with him – never thpoke to him."

"Well, go on. Where did he book to?"

"Warwick Avenue, mithter. Tho did I – of courth. When we got there, I followed him out – at a thafe dithtance. He turned down to the Canal, crothed the bridge, and went down to Thant Mary'th Manthion'th. And there he went in."

Hetherwick glanced at Mapperley. Mapperley permitted himself to wink at his employer – respectfully, but knowingly.

"Went into St. Mary's Mansions, eh?" said Hetherwick. "Walked straight in?"

"Straight in, mithter – front entranth. I thee him, from acroth the road, talking to the man in livery – porter or whatever he hith. I could thee through the glath doorth. Then I thee both of 'em go up in the lift. Tho I waited about a bit, jutht to thee if he'd come out. He did."

"Soon?" asked Hetherwick.

"He wath inthide about ten minuteth. Then he came out. Alone. Thith time he went in t'other direction. I followed him acroth Paddington Green to Edgware Road Tube, and there – well, to tell you the truth, mithter, there I lotht him! There wath a lot o' people about, and I made thure he'd be going thouth. But he mutht ha' gone wetht. Anyway, I lotht him altogether."

"Well – I think you saw enough to be of help," said Hetherwick. "Now – just keep this to yourself, Goldmark." He motioned Mapperley into another room, gave him money for his assistant, and waited until the Jew had gone, shown out by the clerk. "Eleven o'clock!" he remarked, glancing at his watch as Mapperley came back. "Mapperley! we're going out – to St. Mary's Mansions. And after we've been there, and made a call, you'd better come back here with me and take a shake-down for the night – I shall want you in the morning, unless I'm mistaken."

It was one of Mapperley's chief virtues that he was always ready to go anywhere and do anything, and he at once accompanied Hetherwick to the top of Middle Temple Lane, found a taxi-cab within five minutes, and proposed himself to sit up and shakedown that night and the next, if necessary.

"Scent's getting hot, I think, sir," he remarked as they drove off, after bidding the driver carry them to Paddington Green. "Things seem to be coming to a head."

"Yes – but I don't think you know everything," answered Hetherwick. He proceeded to give the clerk an epitomised account of the day's doings as they had related to himself, concluding with Matherfield's theory as expressed after leaving the Green Archer. "You're a smart chap, Mapperley," he added. "What do you think?"

"I see Matherfield's point," answered Mapperley. "I can follow his line. He thinks like this: Hannaford, when he came to London, wanted to get rid, advantageously, of that formula of his about a new ink. He got into touch with Ambrose, whom, of course, he'd known before at Sellithwaite. Ambrose introduced him to some men who deal or dabble in chemicals, of whom one, no doubt, is Baseverie, and who seem to have a laboratory or something of that sort somewhere in the Westminster district. On the night of the murder Ambrose met Hannaford, by appointment, at Victoria, and took him there. Probably, Hannaford left the sealed packet – opened by that time – with these fellows. Probably, too, while there he told them – jokingly, very likely – what he'd discovered, from the picture in the papers, about the identity of Mrs. Whittingham and Madame Listorelle. And now comes in – Granett!"

Hetherwick gave an exclamation that denoted two or three things –

surprise, for one.

"Ah!" he said. "Granett! To be sure! I'd forgotten Granett!"

"I hadn't," remarked Mapperley with a cynical laugh. "Granett – and his murder – is an essential factor. What I think is this: We know that Hannaford met Ambrose at Victoria Station that all-important evening. Ambrose, without doubt, took him to the place I hinted at just now – the exact location of which is a mystery. I think Hannaford stopped there until late in the evening. But – I also think he went back again! With – Granett!"

"Ah!" exclaimed Hetherwick. "I see!"

"We know," continued Mapperley, "that Granett went that evening to see the chemist who gave information about him; we know, too, that he and the chemist went and had a drink together, and parted at about closing time, Granett then, according to the chemist, going towards Victoria Street. Now I think that Granett then met Hannaford – accidentally. They'd known each other in Sellithwaite. They talked – Granett told Hannaford he was down on his luck. Hannaford, evidently, was a kind-hearted man, and I think he did two things out of kindness for Granett. He gave him that five-pound note—"

"That was got at Vivian's!" interrupted Hetherwick quickly.

"To be sure!" assented Mapperley. "But we know that Hannaford had been at Vivian's – with Baseverie – undoubtedly. Taken there by Baseverie, which makes me certain that for two or three days before his death he'd been in touch with both Baseverie and Ambrose. Hannaford got that fiver in change at Vivian's. And he gave it to Granett, on hearing his story. But he did something else – something that was far more important – that is far more important – to us!"

"What?" asked Hetherwick.

"He turned back to the place he'd just left, and took Granett with him!" answered Mapperley with confidence. "He knew Granett was a trained and qualified chemist; he thought he could get him a job with these men who, presumably, were going to take up his own invention. It would be little more than half-past ten then. Where else than at this place are Hannaford and Granett likely to have been between that time and the time at which they got into your carriage at St. James's Park? Of course they were there – with Ambrose and Baseverie."

"As you put it – highly probable," said Hetherwick. "Two and a half hours – doing what?"

"Ah, now we come to the real thing!" exclaimed Mapperley. "My own belief is that Hannaford was fatally poisoned when he left those two men the first time! They'd two objects in poisoning him – or, to put it another way, he'd entrusted them with two secrets – one about Madame Listorelle; the other about his invention. They wanted to keep both to themselves and to profit by both. The invention, no doubt, has considerable value – Hannaford believed it had, anyway. They thought they could blackmail Madame and her sister, Lady Riversreade. So, before Hannaford left them the first time, they poisoned him – cleverly, subtly, devilishly – knowing that so many hours would elapse before the poison worked, and that by that time he'd be safe in bed at his hotel and would die in his sleep. But – he went back to them again, and took another man with him! So – that man had to die, too!"

Hetherwick thought awhile in silence.

"All very good theory, Mapperley," he said at last. "But – it may be nothing but theory. Why did Granett run off at Charing Cross?"

"Because Granett knew that Ambrose lived in John Street, close by," replied Mapperley with promptitude. "He may have known it before; he may not have known it until that evening. But – he knew it! Most likely he thought that Ambrose had returned home from the place in Westminster: Ambrose may have left there before Hannaford and Granett did. Anyway, we may be reasonably certain that when Granett left you with the dying or dead man, he ran off to Ambrose's flat – a few minutes away."

"Why didn't he come back?" demanded Hetherwick. "I'm only wanting to get at probabilities."

"I've thought of that, too," replied Mapperley. "I think he found Ambrose out. But by that time he'd had time to reflect. He knew something was wrong. He knew that if he went back, he'd find the police there, and would be questioned. He might be suspected. And so – he went home, with the bottle in which Ambrose had given him a drop of whisky for himself. And – died in his sleep, as they thought Hannaford would."

"Why should Ambrose have that bottle down at Westminster?" asked Hetherwick.

"Why shouldn't he?" retorted Mapperley. "A man who's taking a tonic takes it at least three times a day – regularly. He'd have his bottle with him. Probably there are several similar empty bottles there at that place."

"Where is that place?" exclaimed Hetherwick. "Where?"

"Got to be found," said Mapperley, as the cab came to a stand. "But – here's this!"

Hetherwick led his companion across Paddington Green and to the house from which he and Matherfield had watched the flats opposite. Late as it was, the lodging-house keeper was up, and lent a willing ear to Hetherwick's request that he should go with him to his friend the caretaker of the Mansions. That functionary was at supper. He continued to sup as Hetherwick, morally supported by the lodging-house man, explained matters to him, but at last he allowed his cheek to bulge with unswallowed food and turned a surprised and knowing eye on his principal visitor.

"Blamed if I didn't wonder whether it was all O.K. With that chap!" he exclaimed, banging the table with the haft of his knife. "For all he was quite the gentleman, I somehow suspicioned him! And yet, he'd a straight tale to tell: come here on Madame's behalf, to get something for her out of her rooms, had her keys, and give me a note from her saying as how I was to allow the bearer to go up to her flat! What more could I expect – and what could I do – under the circs? I asks yer!"

"Oh, he had a note, had he?" inquired Hetherwick. "In Madame's writing?"

The caretaker laid down his knife, and thrusting his hand in his breast-pocket, drew forth an envelope and silently handed it over. It was an azure-tinted envelope, of a very good quality of paper, such as is only sold in high-class stationery shops, and the sheet inside matched it in tint and quality. But Hetherwick at once noticed something about that sheet; so, too, did Mapperley, peering at it from behind his elbow. About an inch and a half had been rather roughly cut off at the top; obviously some address had been engraved, or embossed, or printed on the missing portion. As for what was written on the sheet, it was little – a simple order that the caretaker should allow bearer to go into Madame Listorelle's flat.

"You recognised that as Madame's handwriting?" suggested Hetherwick.

"Oh, that's her fist, right enough, that is!" replied the caretaker. "I knew it at once. And no wonder! I ain't no scholard, not me! – but I knows enough to know that it 'ud puzzle one o' them here forgers as ye reads about to imitate that there sort o' writing – more like as if it had been done with a wooden skewer than a Christian pen! Oh, that's hers."

Hetherwick handed the letter and envelope to Mapperley, who was holding out a hand.

"Well," he said. "I wish ye'd just let me have a look into Madame's flat. There's something seriously wrong, and—"

"Oh, you can do that – 'long as I'm with you," said the caretaker readily. He rose and led the way to the left, and presently ushered them into a smart flat and turned on the electric light. "Don't see nothing wrong here," he observed. "The chap wasn't here ten minutes, and he carried nothing heavy away, whatever he had in his pockets."

Hetherwick and Mapperley looked round. Everything seemed correct and in order – the surroundings were those of a refined and artistic woman, obviously one who loved order and system. But on a desk that stood in the centre of the sitting-room a drawer had been pulled open, and in front of it lay scattered a few sheets of Madame Listorelle's private notepaper, with her engraved address and crest. Near by lay some envelopes, similarly marked. And with a sudden idea in his mind, Hetherwick picked up a sheet or two of the paper and a couple of envelopes and put them in his pocket.

A few minutes later, once more in the cab which they had kept waiting, and on the way to Hill Street, whither Hetherwick had bidden the driver go next, Mapperley turned to his employer with a sly laugh, and held up something in the light of a street lamp by which they were passing.

"What's that?" asked Hetherwick.

"The order written by Madame Listorelle," answered Mapperley, chuckling. "The caretaker didn't notice that I carried it off, envelope and all, under his very eyes! But I did – and here it is!"

"What do you want to do with it?" demanded Hetherwick. "What's your notion?"

But Mapperley only chuckled again and without giving any answer restored the azure-tinted envelope and its contents to his pocket.

# THE HIGHLY-RESPECTABLE SOLICITOR

Lord Morradale, who kept up honest, country-squire habits even in London, had gone to bed when Hetherwick and Mapperley arrived at his house, but he lost little time in making an appearance, in pyjamas and dressing-gown, and listened eagerly to Hetherwick's account of the recent transactions.

"Force!" he muttered, nodding his head at each point of the story. "Force! Got it out of her by force. That is, if the order's genuine."

Mapperley produced the sheet of paper, which he had filched under the caretaker's eyes, and silently handed it over.

"Oh, that's Madame Listorelle's handwriting!" exclaimed Lord Morradale. "Hers, without doubt. Difficult to imitate, of course. Oh, yes – hers! Well, that proves what I've just said, Mr. Hetherwick – force! She's in their power – with the young lady, Miss – Miss – Featherstone, to be sure – and they've made her write that. Next, they'll make her write an order on the Imperial Safe Deposit. We must be beforehand with them there. Early – early as possible in the morning. Meet me at Matherfield's – I think he's pretty keen. Bless me! What a pack of villains! Now I wonder where, in all London, these unfortunate ladies are?"

"That's precisely what all this ought to help us to find out," remarked Hetherwick. "I'm not so much concerned about the valuables these men are after as about the safety of—"

Lord Morradale gave him a quick, understanding glance.

"Of Miss Featherstone, eh?" he said. "I see – I see! And I'm concerned, too, about Madame Listorelle. Well, this, as you say, ought to help. But look here – we must be cautious – very cautious! We mustn't let Matherfield – you know what the police are – we mustn't let him be too precipitate. Probably – if a man comes to the safe place, he'll go away from it to where these scoundrels are. We must follow – follow!"

"I agree," said Hetherwick.

"Nine o'clock, then, at Matherfield's," concluded his lordship. "And

133

may we have a strong scent, a rousing one, and a successful kill!"

With this bit of sporting phraseology in their ears, Hetherwick and Mapperley returned to the Middle Temple and retired for the rest of the night, one to bed, the other to a shake-down on the sitting-room sofa. But when Hetherwick's alarm clock awoke him at seven-thirty and he put his head into the next room to rouse the clerk, he found that Mapperley had vanished. The cushions, rugs, and blankets with which he had made himself comfortable for the night were all neatly folded and arranged – on the topmost was pinned a sheet of brief-paper, with a message scrawled in blue pencil.

*You won't want me this morning; off on an important notion of my own. Look out for message from me about noon.*
*M.*

Muttering to himself that he hadn't the least idea as to what his clerk was about, Hetherwick made a hurried toilet, and an equally hurried breakfast, and hastened away to meet Matherfield and Lord Morradale. He found these two together, and with them a quiet, solemn-faced individual, clad in unusually sombre garments, whom Matherfield introduced as Detective-Sergeant Quigman. Matherfield went straight to business.

"His lordship's just told me of your adventure last night, Mr. Hetherwick," he said, "and I'm beginning to get a sort of forecast of what's likely to happen. It was, of course, Baseverie who went to madame's flat last night – that's settled. But what do you suppose he went for?"

"Can't say that I've worked that out," answered Hetherwick, with a glance at the others. "But I imagine that he went there to get, say, certain keys – having forced Madame Listorelle to tell him where they were. The keys of her safe at the Deposit place, I should think."

"No!" replied Matherfield, shaking his head knowingly, and with a sly smile at Quigman. "No, not that. I'll tell you what he went for – a very simple thing. He went to get some of Madame's private notepaper! He knew well enough that if he was to take an order on that Safe Deposit to allow the bearer access to Madame's safe it would have to be what the French, I believe, call *en régle* – eh? Written on her own notepaper in her own handwriting, and so on. See?"

"I think you're right, and I think he got it," said Hetherwick. "A drawer in her desk containing boxes of stationery had been pulled out, and some of its contents lay about the desk. As a matter of fact, though I scarcely know why I did it, I put some paper and some envelopes in my pocket – here they are! I had a faint idea that they might be useful – somehow."

"Well, that's the notion, depend on it," asserted Matherfield, glancing at the paper which Hetherwick produced. "I've no doubt that somebody, representing Madame Listorelle, and bearing an authorization from her, written on her notepaper in her own writing, will present himself at the Imperial Safe Deposit this morning. But – it won't be Baseverie! And it won't be Ambrose!"

"A stranger, eh?" suggested Hetherwick.

"We shall see. Now," continued Matherfield, glancing at the clock, "we'll be off to the scene of operations. This Imperial Safe Deposit is in Kingsway – Holborn end – and very fortunately situated for our job, being close to the Tube station; there'll be lots of people about there, and we shan't attract attention. And this is the way of it – his lordship and myself will go into the Safe Deposit, see the people in charge, explain matters, and get them to tell us at once if and when the expected ambassador arrives. We shall let him—"

"Or her," interrupted Quigman solemnly.

"Just so, my lad – it might be a she," assented Matherfield. "Quite likely! We shall let him or her get what is wanted from the safe and go away, closely followed by all four of us. While Lord Morradale and I are inside, you and Quigman, Mr. Hetherwick, will be outside, talking, casually. When we come out – and you'll both keep a sharp watch on the entrance hall – I'll give you the office as to the particular person we're following, and wherever that person goes, you two will go. But don't come near us – we'll keep one side of the street, you the other. If the person takes to a cab or a bus – well, we'll have to do the same. But I've reasons for thinking he or she will stick to his feet!"

"How do we go? – all together?" asked Hetherwick. "Because – it's a mere idea – how do you know, Matherfield, that these people – there would appear to be more than one concerned – aren't keeping an eye on you?"

"I've thought of that," answered Matherfield. "No – we're all going separately. It's now nine-fifteen. That Imperial Safe Deposit doesn't open its doors till ten – nobody can get in there until that time, anyway. We all four go out of this office on our own hook. Each takes his own method of getting to the top of Kingsway. As soon as I get there, I go straight in and ask for the manager. As soon as Lord Morradale gets there, he follows suit – he and I forgather in the manager's room. As for you two, go how you like – fly, if it suits you – or wander round the side streets. But – you meet right opposite the Safe Deposit entrance at precisely ten o'clock, and under pretence of casual meeting and conversation keep your eyes on it, noticing everybody who goes in and comes out. That clear? Then we all clear out – one by one."

Outside, and left to his own devices, Hetherwick walked a little way and then hailed a taxi-cab. He gave his driver a confidential smile.

"You can just help me to employ forty minutes," he said, as he got in. "Drive round – anywhere you like – up and down – as long as you put me down at the corner of the Holborn Restaurant at precisely two minutes to ten. Got that?"

The driver comprehended, and began a leisurely journey round certain principal streets and thoroughfares. Two minutes before ten he pulled up at the Holborn-Kingsway corner and gave his fare a grin.

"Done it to the second, sir," he announced, nodding at an adjacent clock.

"Good man!" said Hetherwick, handing out something over the registered fare. Then an idea struck him. "Look here!" he continued confidentially. "I – and another man – may have to follow somebody from here, presently. Just drive down the street here, keep your flag down, and wait – if I want you, I shall be close at hand."

The driver showed his understanding by a nod and a wink and moved a little distance off to the kerbstone. Hetherwick walked slowly down the west side of Kingsway. And precisely as the clock struck ten he saw Lord Morradale come from one direction and enter the formidable-looking and just opened door of the Safe Deposit, and Matherfield appear from the other: looking round again he was aware of the solemn-faced Quigman who sauntered round the corner of Parker Street and came towards him. Hetherwick went on to meet him.

"There you are!" he said, doing a little acting in case any inimical eyes were on him. "To the minute! We'd better appear to be doing a bit of talk, eh? The others have just gone in."

"I saw 'em, sir," replied Quigman, coming to a halt on the kerb, and affecting an interest in anything rather than on what he was really working. "Ah! But the question is – when will they come out? Might be in a few minutes – so to speak. Mightn't be for hours – as it were!"

"You seem to be a melancholy chap," observed Hetherwick.

"Melancholy job!" muttered Quigman. "Watching isn't my line. But Matherfield – he particularly wanted me to be in at this."

"Why?" asked Hetherwick.

"Peculiar knowledge of solicitors and their clerks in this part o' London," replied Quigman. "My line. Matherfield, he's an idea that the order to open this safe'll be presented by a solicitor."

"Good Lord! – has he?" exclaimed Hetherwick. "I wonder! But – "

"Big help to these chaps, don't you see, if they can make a solicitor do the cat's-paw work," suggested Quigman. "Who'd suspect a solicitor of the High Court? And as I know pretty nearly all of 'em – there's one I know now coming up t'other side of the street," he continued suddenly. "That tallish, thin, pale-faced chap – see him? Look at him without seeming to look. Now I wonder if he's the party we want?"

Hetherwick looked in the direction indicated. He saw a youngish, spectacled man in a silk hat, morning coat, and the corresponding additions of professional attire, who was walking rapidly along from South to north. He was a very mild, gentle-looking person, not at all the sort to be concerned in dark plots and mysterious aims, and Hetherwick said so.

"Aye, well, you never know!" remarked Quigman lugubriously. "But, as I say, I know him. Mr. Garrowell – Mr. Octavius Garrowell – solicitor, of St. Martin's Lane, that is. Been in practice for himself about four years or so. Nice young feller! – quiet. And he is going in there – see?"

Hetherwick saw. There were several people, men and women, entering the Safe Deposit just then, but Mr. Garrowell's silk hat and sloping shoulders made him easily identifiable.

"I dessay it's him!" observed Quigman, with a sigh. "Just the sort to be took in, he is! Innocent, unsuspecting sort o' gentleman. However – it mayn't be. Deal o' people use these Safe Deposits nowadays."

Mr. Garrowell disappeared. The two watchers waited. Five, ten, fifteen, twenty minutes went by; then Mr. Garrowell came out. He came out just as any man would come out after transacting his business, quietly. Nobody followed him: nobody seemed to be watching him – from the Safe Deposit. But Hetherwick noticed at once that whereas he had entered carrying nothing but an umbrella, he now carried a small, square, leather-covered box. With this in his left hand he crossed the roadway, and advanced straight towards Hetherwick and Quigman.

"No need to move, sir," whispered the detective. "Take no notice – spot him, though."

Mr. Garrowell, seen at close quarters, looked to be a somewhat absent-minded gentleman. But, chancing to look up as he stepped on the pavement, his eyes encountered Quigman, who touched his hat.

"Morning, Mr. Garrowell," said the detective. "Nice morning, sir."

"Morning, Quigman," responded Mr. Garrowell. "A very nice morning!"

He nodded smilingly and went on his way, and round the corner into Parker Street. Quigman glanced at Hetherwick and shook his head.

"Not him!" he said. "Matherfield's not following. And, as I said, we may have to wait – hours!"

But at the end of another ten minutes Matherfield and Lord Morradale came together out of the entrance hall opposite. An official, smiling and talking, accompanied them to the threshold; when they left him they came straight across the road. And it was obvious to Hetherwick that each was in a state of surprise – possibly, of perplexity. Matherfield hailed them as soon as he was within speaking distance.

"Here's a queer business!" he said. "Did you see a professional-looking chap come away just now who carried a small leather box?"

"We saw Mr. Garrowell, solicitor, St. Martin's Lane," answered Quigman. "I know him. Gone down Parker Street."

"It was Garrowell," assented Matherfield. "I know him, too. Well," he turned to Hetherwick, "it's a queer business. They knew Garrowell across there – he's been to Madame Listorelle's safe for her before. He came there just now, with the usual authorisation, on her notepaper, went to the safe, got that small box, and went. Garrowell – a highly respectable legal practitioner!"

"Why didn't you stop him and ask him questions?" inquired Hetherwick.

Matherfield exchanged a glance with Lord Morradale.

"Not there!" he said. "It – well, it looks as if Madame really had sent him! Her business."

"Of course she'd sent him!" exclaimed Hetherwick. "Sent him under compulsion! The whole thing's a clever plant! These fellows probably know that she's employed Garrowell now and then, and they forced her to write a letter to him, authorising him to come here again, and enclosing an order on the Safe Deposit people! Don't you see?"

"By Gad, there's something in that, Matherfield!" said Lord Morradale. "Didn't strike me, though! 'Pon my honour, I really thought he had come direct from her. Couldn't think why, exactly, but then, as Matherfield says, a highly-respectable solicitor – eh?"

"We'll soon settle it!" exclaimed Matherfield suddenly. "We'll go to Garrowell's office. Better discuss it there than have tackled him here. Anyway, he'll have the square box. Quigman, call a taxi!"

"There's a man here waiting for me," said Hetherwick. He signalled to his former driver who quickly came alongside. "For anything we know," he continued, as all four took their seats, and were driven off, "Garrowell may have gone straight away somewhere to hand that box over! We ought to have followed."

"I don't think so," replied Matherfield. "The whole thing's queer, and not at all what I expected. Lord Morradale says that he never heard of madame employing Garrowell, and yet the Safe people say he's been here two or three times on her business. But we'll soon have it out of him."

# THE LANDLADY OF
# LITTLE SMITH STREET

Garrowell's office proved to be up two flights of stairs in St. Martin's Lane. They were dark and dingy stairs, and none of the four men clambering up them noticed that an office-boy, rushing unceremoniously downward carried a small parcel with which he fled out of the door and away down the street. They were, indeed, thinking of Garrowell – and within five minutes they were all in his private room. For another five minutes Matherfield was explaining matters – explaining to an obviously startled and much astonished listener.

"That's how it stands," concluded Matherfield. "You've evidently got the explanation, Mr. Garrowell. Now—"

"But you surprise me!" broke in the solicitor. "I've acted for Madame Listorelle in two or three matters – I've got things from her safe for her before, once or twice. And I saw nothing unusual in the letter she sent me this morning. Here it is! You can see it. Her usual notepaper – certainly her handwriting – nobody, I think, could imitate that successfully. You see what she says – I was to give the enclosed authorisation to the Safe people, take out a small, square, brown-leather-covered box from the safe, pack it up, and send it off to Mr. C. Basing, Post Office, Southampton, at once, by express delivery. Nothing unusual in all that, I think. Of course, I carried out her wishes. But look at the letter."

All four men were looking at the letter. It was as Garrowell described, and whether it had been written under duress or not, the writing was bold and firm. But Matherfield seized on the envelope, and after a glance at it, pointed to the postmark.

"See that!" he exclaimed. "Posted in the S.W. District late last night. If madame had been at home in Paddington the postmark would have been different. Well – but the square box, Mr. Garrowell! You've got it, of course? Do you know that that box probably contains jewels worth—"

"The box?" ejaculated Garrowell. "Got it? Of course not! It's gone! The boy went off to the post office with it – oh, just before you came."

"Gad!" muttered Lord Morradale. "Well – the post office, at once, Matherfield!"

But Matherfield suddenly laughed, throwing up both hands as if with a sudden inspiration.

"No, my lord, no!" he said. "No! The box is safe enough in the post. It's off to Mr. C. Basing, Post Office, Southampton. And when Mr. Basing calls to collect it – he'll find me!"

There was triumphant conviction in Matherfield's tone: there was the impulse to immediate action in the way in which he pulled out a railway guide from his pocket, and rapidly turned its pages. But Hetherwick and Lord Morradale looked at each other. And each saw that the other was dubious.

"Yes," said Lord Morradale slowly. "Um – no doubt, Matherfield. But I say, you know – those jewels are worth no end! Safe enough, perhaps, in the hands of the postal authorities, now they are there, but – there's many a slip, you know, and—"

"You might take the postal authorities into your confidence," suggested Hetherwick. "These people are up to all sorts of wily tricks—"

Matherfield laughed quietly. It was the laugh of a man who knows his own business thoroughly, and is a little impatient of outside criticism.

"I know what I'm doing, gentlemen," he answered. "Leave it to me as to what I do with the post office people. I've as good as got the handcuffs on Baseverie or on Ambrose – perhaps on both! This is how I figure the thing," he went on, with a final glance at the time-table. "These two men have got Madame Listorelle and the young lady-secretary in their power, safe somewhere in London. They forced madame, last night, to write that letter to Mr. Garrowell here – we know what they made her write. Mr. Garrowell got the small box containing the jewels, and he's sent it off, already, by express delivery, to Southampton. It will be there early this evening, and one or other of the men will be there to meet it. If Baseverie calls for it, Ambrose will be round the corner. If Ambrose calls for it, Baseverie will be close at hand. Probably they're already in Southampton – they'd go this morning, to be on the spot. As soon as the box is in their hands they'll be off – probably to the Continent, by Southampton and Havre. They won't try the Atlantic – the five days' voyage would be too risky. They'll make for France. But they won't get to France – they'll find themselves in the lock-up at Southampton before bed-time! You see if that doesn't come off, gentlemen, as sure as my name's what it is. Now, Quigman, you come with me. We've just nice time to catch the one-thirty, and to get in touch with the Southampton police, and lay our plans and make our arrangements. Some time tonight, gentlemen, you'll hear from me!"

Then Matherfield hurried Quigman away, and the three men left behind looked at each other. Mr. Garrowell was obviously much concerned, and his hands, thin and nervous, trembled as he began to arrange the papers on his desk.

"This is a most distressing business, gentlemen," he said. "It is very painful to me to think that I have been made an instrument in a crime of this sort, however innocent a one! But how could I tell that this letter was forced out of Madame Listorelle? On the face of it—"

"Oh, there's no blame attaching to you, Mr. Garrowell!" interrupted Lord Morradale. "On the face of it, the letter's genuine enough. But I wanted to ask you a question: How much do you know of Madame Listorelle? I mean, how often has she employed you?"

"Two or three times only," replied Garrowell. "She came to me first about an agreement which I had had to send her on behalf of another client. She seemed very friendly, and was kind enough to say that next time she had any legal business she would remember me as she hadn't any regular solicitor of her own. I think," he added with a deprecating smile, "she probably saw that I was beginning, and hadn't much to do."

"I see," said Lord Morradale, looking round at the somewhat humble appointments of the office. "And you've been to that Safe Deposit place on her behalf – how often?"

"Twice. On each occasion Madame Listorelle wrote her instructions from abroad. Once she was in Paris. The other time she was at Nice. The instructions were similar on both occasions: I was to go to the Safe Deposit, get a certain parcel or article and post it to an address given. The first time I sent a small parcel to Amsterdam – I have the exact address and name; the second, to New York. So that, of course, when I got Madame's letter this morning, I saw nothing unusual in it."

"Just so!" agreed Lord Morradale. "You wouldn't. Well, I hope Matherfield will clap the irons on the men who forced her to write it! Eh, Hetherwick?"

"With all my heart!" responded Hetherwick "But I, too, want to ask Mr. Garrowell a question. How long," he continued, "have you been here, in St. Martin's Lane?"

"Oh, four or five years," replied Garrowell.

"Then you know this district pretty well, of course. Have you ever come across a man whom I'll try to describe to you?" He went on to give an accurate, if concise, description of Baseverie. "That man," he concluded, "is sometimes seen around here."

Garrowell nodded.

"I know him!" he said. "In fact, he's been in this very room – to see me. But I don't know his name, nor anything much about him. He was brought here by another man and he only stayed a few minutes."

"How much do you know about him – however little?" asked Hetherwick.

"This much. You know that people who have invented things come to solicitors for legal advice, and sometimes to get information as to how they can best dispose of their inventions? Well, about nine months ago a man came to me who claimed to have invented a drop-bottle – that is, a bottle from which you could only drop one drop of stuff at a time. He said such a thing was badly wanted, and that there ought to be a pile of money in it. He wanted to know how best to get it on the market. I didn't know, but I mentioned the matter to one or two people, and a man I know – or knew at that time, for he's since dead, unfortunately – said that he knew a man who was a sort of commission agent for inventions – took up a good idea, don't you see, and introduced it – and he promised to bring him to see me. He brought him; the man he brought was, without doubt, the man you describe. His name was not mentioned, but I am sure he was that man. I don't know what your man is, but I felt sure that the man I am talking about either was or had been a medical man."

"Ah!" exclaimed Hetherwick. "What made you think that?"

"From his conversation – from the remarks he made about the bottle. He didn't take it up; he said my client was too late and was wrongly informed into the bargain: there was such a thing, and a superior one, already on the market. He went away then, and, as I say, I never heard his name, and I've never seen him since."

"That's the man we want!" said Hetherwick. "If Matherfield can only lay hands on him! But we shall know more by midnight."

Outside, he turned to Lord Morradale with a shake of the head.

"We're no nearer to any knowledge of where the two women are!" he exclaimed.

"Oh, I don't know!" responded Lord Morradale. "I think we are, you know. You see, if Matherfield nabs those chaps, or even one of them, he or they will see that the game's up, and will give in and say where their captives are. Odd business, Hetherwick, that people can be kidnapped and imprisoned in broad daylight in London!"

"I don't think anything's impossible or odd – in London," answered Hetherwick dryly. "If one had only the least idea as to which quarter of the town that car was driven, one might be doing something!"

"Lots of sub-sections in every quarter, and sub-sections again in each of those," replied Lord Morradale with equal dryness. "Take some time to comb through this town! No! I think we must trust to Matherfield. Nothing else to trust to, in fact."

But Hetherwick suddenly thought of Mapperley. He began to wonder what the clerk was after, what his notion had been. Then he remembered Mapperley's admonition to look out for a message about that time, and excusing himself from Lord Morradale, he jumped on a bus and went along to the Temple. There, in the letter-box, he found a telegram:

"*Meet me Victoria three o'clock. Mapperley.*"

Hetherwick set off for Victoria there and then. But it was only a quarter-past two when he got there, and as he had had no lunch, he turned into the restaurant. There, when he was half-way through a chop, Mapperley found him, and slipped into a chair close by before Hetherwick noticed his presence.

"Thought I might find you in here, sir," said Mapperley. They were alone in a quiet corner, but the clerk lowered his voice to a whisper. "Well," he continued, bending across the table, "I've done a bit, anyhow."

"In what way?" asked Hetherwick.

Mapperley produced from his breast pocket some papers, and from amongst them selected an envelope – the azure-tinted envelope which he had picked up from the caretaker's supper table at St. Mary's Mansions.

"You recognise this?" he said, with a sly smile. "You know where I got it. This is the envelope which Baseverie took to the caretaker, with the order to enter Madame Listorelle's flat. You knew that I carried it off, from under the man's nose, last night. But you didn't know why. I only laughed when you asked me."

"Well, why, then?" inquired Hetherwick.

"This reason," replied Mapperley. "We both noticed that the sheet of paper on which the order had been written by Madame had been shortened – there was no doubt that a printed or embossed address had been trimmed off, rather roughly, too. We noticed that, I say, both of us. But I don't think you noticed something far more important – far, far more important – for our purposes."

"No," admitted Hetherwick. "I didn't. What?"

"This," said Mapperley, turning back the broken flap of the envelope. "You didn't notice that here, on the envelope, is the name and address of the stationer who supplied this stuff! There you are – W. H. Calkin, 85, Broadway, Westminster. You never saw that, Mr. Hetherwick. But I did!"

Hetherwick began to comprehend. He smiled – gratefully.

"Smart of you, Mapperley!" he exclaimed. "I see! And – you've been there?"

"I've been there," answered Mapperley. "I saw a chance of tracking these men down. I couldn't get hold of Calkin till nearly noon, but I got on like a house afire when I did get him. You see," he went on, "that paper is, to start with, of an unusual tint, in colour. Secondly, it's of very superior quality, though very thin – intended chiefly for foreign correspondence. Thirdly, it's expensive. Now, I felt certain its use would be limited, and what I wanted to find out from the stationer was – to whom he'd supplied it. That was easy. He recognised the paper and envelope at once. Of the handwriting on the paper, he knew nothing whatever – Madame's writing, you know – that he'd never seen before. But he said at once that he'd only supplied that particular make of paper and envelopes to three people, and for each person he'd prepared a die, to emboss the addresses. The embossing had been done at his shop, and he showed me specimens of each. One was for the Dowager Lady Markentree, 120, Grosvenor Gardens. That was no use. The second was for Miss Chelandry, 87, Ebury Street. That was out of count, too. But the third was what I wanted. It was just the address, 56, Little Smith Street, S.W.1. As soon as I saw it, I knew I'd got on the right track."

"Go on!" said Hetherwick.

"The stationer, Calkin, didn't know the name of the man who ordered this paper and gave this address," continued Mapperley. "He knew him well enough as a customer, though, and described him. Baseverie, without a doubt! Calkin says that Baseverie, during the last few months, bought various items of stationery from him – notebooks, duplicating paper, office requisites, and so on. He never knew his name, but as he always carried away his own purchases, and paid spot cash for them, that didn't matter. Calkin supplied him with ten quires of this paper and envelopes to match, a couple of months ago. So – there you are! And there I was – sure at last that Baseverie's mysterious hiding-place was 56, Little Smith Street!"

"Good – good!" said Hetherwick. "What next?"

"Well, I thought we could do with a bit of help," replied Mapperley, smiling. "So I left Calkin – bound to secrecy, of course – and telephoned to Issy Goldmark. Issy is just the sort of chap for games of this sort! Issy came – and he and I took a stroll round. Do you know Little Smith Street?"

"Not I!" answered Hetherwick. "Never heard of it!"

"Oh, well, but it is a street," said Mapperley. "It lies between Great Smith Street and Tufton Street, back o' the Church House – not so far from the Abbey. Bit slummy down those quarters, round about – sort of district that's seen decidedly better days. Still, there's good, solid houses here and there – 56 is one of 'em. From outside, it looks the sort of house you can't get into – dark, silent, heavily-curtained windows – sort of place in which you could murder anybody on the quiet. Very substantial front door, painted dark green, with an old-fashioned brass knocker – that sort of house. We took a good look at it."

"See anything?" asked Hetherwick.

"Nothing but what I've told you – lifeless sort o' place," answered Mapperley. "However, having once seen it, I wasn't going to leave it unwatched, so I posted Issy there, in the window of a convenient public-house, and came away to telegraph to you. And there Issy is – either in his pub, or loafing round. And now we ought to go and hear if he's anything to report. And if he hasn't – what then?"

"Just so," said Hetherwick. "That's it – what then? But before we do anything at all, Mapperley, I'd better post you up as to what's happened elsewhere this morning. You see," he continued, when he had finished his story, "if Matherfield's theory is correct, and Baseverie has already gone to Southampton to collect that parcel on its arrival, and if Ambrose has gone with him, we shan't find Baseverie at this address. But – we might inquire if he's known there."

Mapperley reflected a while. Then an idea seemed to suggest itself.

"Pay your bill, sir, and let's get out to a Post Office Directory somewhere," he said. "We'll get the name of the occupier of 56, Little Smith Street."

Ten minutes later they were looking down the long columns of names in a directory; Mapperley suddenly pointed to what they wanted.

"There we are!" he said. "Mrs. Hannah Mallett – boarding-house proprietor."

"Come along!" said Hetherwick. "We'll see Mrs. Mallett, anyhow."

But on arrival at Little Smith Street, Mapperley looked round first, for his friend, Mr. Goldmark. Mr. Goldmark materialised suddenly – apparently from nowhere – and smiled.

"Afternoon, mithter!" he said politely to Hetherwick. "Lovely weather, ithn't it? Ain't theen nothing, Mapperley, old bean! Ain't been a thoul in or out o' that houth, thinth you hopped it! Theemth to me it'th locked up."

"We'll see about that," remarked Hetherwick. "Come with me, Mapperley. You stay here. Goldmark, and keep your eyes as open as before."

He advanced boldly, with the clerk at his heels, to the door of number 56, and knocked loudly on the stout panel, supplementing this with a ring at the bell. This dual summons was twice repeated – with no result.

"Somebody coming!" whispered Mapperley, suddenly. "Bolted – inside – as well as locked!"

Hetherwick distinctly heard the sound of a stout bolt being withdrawn, then of a key being turned. The door was opened – only a little, but sufficiently to show them the face and figure of an unusually big woman, an Amazon in appearance, hard of eye and lip, who glared at them suspiciously, and as soon as she saw that there were two of them, narrowed the space through which she inspected her callers. But Hetherwick got a hand on the door and a foot across the threshold.

"Mrs. Mallett?" he inquired in a purposely loud voice. "Just so! Is Doctor Baseverie in?"

Both men were watching the woman keenly, and they saw that she started a little, involuntarily. But her head shook a ready negative.

"Nobody of that name here!" she answered.

She would have shut the door, but for Hetherwick's foot – he advanced it further, giving Mrs. Mallett a keen, searching glance.

"Perhaps you know Dr. Baseverie by another name?" he suggested. "So – is Mr. Basing in?"

But the ready shake of the head came again, and the hard eyes grew harder and more suspicious.

"Nobody of that name here, either!" she said. "Don't know anybody of those names."

"I think you do," persisted Hetherwick sternly. He turned to Mapperley, purposely. "We shall have to get the police—"

"Look out, sir!" exclaimed Mapperley, snatching at Hetherwick's arm. "Your fingers!"

The woman suddenly banged the door to, narrowly missing Hetherwick's hand, which he had closed on the edge; a second later they heard the bolt slipped and the key turned. And Hetherwick, as with a swift illumination, comprehended things, and turned sharply on his clerk.

"Mapperley!" he exclaimed. "Sure as fate! Those ladies are in there! Trapped!"

"Shouldn't wonder, sir," agreed Mapperley. "And as you say – the police—"

"Come back to Goldmark," said Hetherwick.

Going lower down the street and retreating into the shelter of a doorway, the three men held a rapid consultation, suddenly interrupted by an exclamation from the Jew, who still kept his eyes on the house:

"Th'elp me if the woman ain't leavin' that houth!" he said. "Thee! The – thee ith! Lockin' the door behind her, too! Goin' up the thtreet!"

Hetherwick looked and saw, and pushed Goldmark out of the doorway.

"Follow!" he said. "And for God's sake, don't miss her!"

# THE HOUSE IN THE YARD

The Jew silently and promptly set out in the wake of the hurrying woman; presently she and her pursuer disappeared round a corner.

"That's the result of our call, Mapperley!" said Hetherwick. "She's gone somewhere – to tell somebody!"

"Likely!" assented Mapperley. "But wherever she's gone, Issy Goldmark'll spot her. He's the eyes of a lynx."

"He let Baseverie slip him, the other night, though," remarked Hetherwick.

"Well, there was some excuse for that," said Mapperley, "to begin with, he was only instructed to find out where Baseverie went, and to end with he had found out! He'll not let this woman slip him. She's good to follow – plenty of her."

"I wish we knew what she'd left in that house," said Hetherwick. "We'll have to find out, somehow!"

"That's a police job," replied Mapperley. "Can't walk into people's houses without a warrant. And you say Matherfield's on the other track? However, I should say that this woman's gone off now to find somebody who's principally concerned – she looked afraid, in my opinion, when she saw me."

"She's in it, somehow," muttered Hetherwick.

"That house looks mysterious enough for anything. We'll keep a close watch on it, anyway, until Goldmark comes back, however long that may be."

But the Jew was back within twenty minutes. So was the woman. She came first, hurrying up the street quicker than when she had left it. As far as the watchers could make out from their vantage point, twenty yards away from her door, she looked flustered, distressed, upset. After her, on the opposite pavement, came Mr. Issy Goldmark, his hands in his pockets.

The woman re-entered the house; they heard the door bang. A moment later the Jew turned into the entry in which Hetherwick and Mapperley stood, half hidden from the street. He smiled, inscrutably.

"Thee her go back to her houth?" he asked. "Well, I followed. I thaw where thee'th been, too."

"Where, then?" demanded Hetherwick, impatiently.

Goldmark jerked his head in the direction from whence he had come.

"Round that corner," he said, "you get into a regular thlum. Little thtreeth, alleyth, pathageth, and tho on. In one of 'em, a narrow plathe, where there'th a thort of open-air market, there'th a good thithed pieth of blank wall, with an iron-fathen'd door in it. Well, the woman went in there – let herthelf in with a key that thee took from her pocket. Ath thoon ath thee'd gone in, I took a clother look. The door'th fathen'd with iron, or thteel, ath I thaid – jolly thtrong. There ain't no name on it, and no keyhole that you can look through. The wall'th a good nine or ten feet high, and it'th covered with broken glath at the top. Not a nithe plathe to get into, nohow!"

"Well?" inquired Hetherwick. "She went in?"

"Went in, ath I thay, mithter, and the door clothed on her. After I'd taken a glimpth at the door I got a potht behind one of the thtalls in the thtreet and watched. She came out again in about ten minitth – looked to me, too, ath if thee hadn't had a very plethant time inthide. Upthet! And thee thet off back here, fathter than vhat thee came. Now thee'th gone into her houth again – ath you no doubt thaw. And that'th all. But if I wath you, mithter," concluded Issy, "I should jutht find out vhat there ith behind that door and the wall it'th thet in – I thhould tho!"

"That's a police job," said Mapperley once more. "If we'd only got Matherfield with us, we could—" Hetherwick paused – thinking. "Look here, Mapperley," he continued, with a sudden inspiration. "I know what we'll do! You get a taxi-cab, as quickly as possible. Drive to the police station where I usually meet Matherfield. There's another man there whom I know, and who's pretty well up in this business – Detective-Sergeant Robmore. Ask for him. Tell him what we've discovered, and ask him to come back with you and to bring another man if he thinks it necessary. Now then, Goldmark! Tell Mapperley exactly where this place is."

The Jew pointed along the street to its first corner.

"Round that corner," he said. "Firtht turning to the right; then firtht to the left; then firtht to the right – that'th the thpot. Lot'th o' little thtallth in it – a bithy, crowded plathe."

"Didn't ye notice the name?" demanded Mapperley, half scoldingly.

"To be thure I did!" grinned Goldmark. "Pencove Thtreet. But it'th better to dethcribe it than to name it. And don't you go tellin' no tackthy-driver to drive you in there! – cauth' there ain't room!"

Mapperley gave no answer to this piece of advice; he shot off in the direction of Victoria Street, and Hetherwick turned to the Jew.

"We'll go and have another look at this place, Goldmark," he said. "But we'll go separately – as long as we're in this street, anyway. You stroll off to that first corner, and I'll join you."

He crossed the street when the Jew had lounged away, and once more took a narrow look at the house into which the big woman had vanished. It was as close barred and curtained as ever; a veritable place of mystery. For a moment Hetherwick doubted whether he ought to leave it unwatched. But the descriptions of the wall and door in Pencove Street had excited his imagination, and he went on, turned the corner, and rejoined Goldmark. Goldmark at once went in front, piloting him into a maze of unusually dirty and crowded streets, and finally into one, narrower than the rest, on each side of which were tent-like stalls whereon all manner of cheap wares were being offered for sale by raucous-voiced vendors. He saw at once that this was one of those open-air markets of which there are many in the poorer neighbourhoods of London, and wherein you can buy a sixpenny frying-pan as readily as a paper of fried fish, and a gay neckerchief alongside a damaged orange.

Threading his way behind Issy, and between the thronged stalls and the miserable shops that lined the pavement, Hetherwick presently came to the piece of blank wall of which the Jew had told him. The houses and shops round about were old and dilapidated, but the wall was either modern or had been rebuilt and strengthened. It stretched between two low houses, one used as a grocer's, the other as a hardware shop. In length, it was some thirty feet; in height, quite ten; its coping, as Goldmark had said, was liberally embattled with broken glass. The door, set flush with the adjoining masonry, was a solid affair, faced with metal, newly painted, and the lock was evidently a patent one. A significant fact struck Hetherwick at once – there was no sign of a bell and none of a knocker.

"You say the woman let herself in here?" he asked, as he and Issy paused.

"That'th it, mithter Hetherwick – let herthelf in," replied Issy. "I thee her take the key from her pocket."

Hetherwick glanced at the top of the wall.

"I wonder what's behind?" he muttered. "Building of some sort, of course." He turned to a man whose stall stood just in front of the mysterious door, and who at that moment had no trade. "Do you know anything about this place?" he asked. "Do you know what's behind this wall? What building it is?"

The stall-keeper eyed Hetherwick over, silently and carefully. Deciding that he was an innocent person and not a policeman in plain clothes, he found his tongue.

"I don't, guv'nor!" he answered. "'Aint a bloomin' notion! I been comin' here, or hereabouts, this three year or more, but I 'aint never seen behind that wall, nor in at that there doorway. S'elp me!"

"But I suppose you've seen people go in and come out of the door?" suggested Hetherwick. "It must be used for something!"

"I reckon it is, guv'nor, but I don't call nobody to mind, though, to be sure, I see a woman come out of it a while ago – big, heavy-jawed woman, she was. But queer as it may seem, I don't call to mind ever seeing anybody else. You see, guv'nor, I comes here at about ten o'clock of a morning, and I packs up and 'ops it at five – if there's folks comes in and out o' that spot, it must be early in a morning and late at night, and so I shouldn't see 'em. But it's my belief this 'ere wall and door is back premises to something – the front o' the place'll be on the other side."

"That's a good idea," said Hetherwick, with a glance at Goldmark. "Let's go round."

But there was no going round. Although they tried various alleys and passages and streets that ought to have been parallel to Pencove Street, they failed to find any place that could be a frontage to the mysterious wall and its close-set door. But the Jew's alert faculties asserted themselves.

"We can thee vhat'th behind that vail, mithter, eathy enough if we get one o' them thop-keeperth oppothit to let uth go upthtairth to hith firtht floor," he said. "Look right acroth the thtreet there, thtallth and all, into vhatever there ith. Try that one," he went on, pointing to a greengrocer's establishment which faced the close-set door. "Tell him we're doin' a bit o' land thurveyin' – which ith thtrue!"

Hetherwick made his request – the greengrocer's lady showed him and Goldmark upstairs into a bow-windowed parlour, one of those dismal apartments which are only used on Sundays, for the purpose of adding more gloom to a gloomy day. She observed that there was a nice view both ways of the street, but Hetherwick confined his inspection to the front. He saw across the wall easily enough, now. There was little to see. The wall bounded a yard, bounded on its left and right sides by the walls of the adjoining houses, and at its further extremity by a low, squat building of red brick, erected against the rear of a high, windowless wall beyond. From its mere aspect, it was impossible to tell what this squat, flat-roofed structure was used for. Its door – closed – was visible; visible, too, were the windows on either side. But it was easy to see that they were obscured, as to their lower halves, by coats of dark paint. There was no sign over the building; no outward indication of its purpose. In the yard, however, were crates, boxes, and carboys in wicker cases; a curiously-shaped chimney, projecting from the roof above, suggested the presence of a furnace or forge beneath. And Hetherwick, after another look, felt no doubt that he was gazing at the place to which Hannaford had been taken, and where he had been skilfully poisoned.

Goldmark suddenly nudged his arm, and nodded at the crowded street below.

"Mapperley!" he whispered. "And two men with him!"

Hetherwick, glancing in the direction indicated, saw Robmore and another man, both in plain clothes, making their way down the street, between the stalls and the shops. With them, and in close conversation, was a uniformed constable. He turned to leave the room, but Goldmark again touched his elbow.

"Before we go, mithter," he said, "jutht take another glanth at that plathe oppothite, and it'ths thurroundin'th. I thee where we can get in! D'ye thee, mithter Hetherwick, the wall between that yard and the next houth – the right-hand thide one – 'ith fairly low at the far end. Now, if the man in that houth would let uth go through to hith back-yard – vhat?"

"I see!" agreed Hetherwick. "We'll try it. But Robmore first – come along."

He slipped some silver into the hand of the green-grocer's lady, and went down to the street. A few brief explanations to the two detectives supplemented the information already given them by Mapperley, and then Robmore nodded at the constable who stood by, eagerly interested.

"We've been talking to him, Mr. Hetherwick," he said. "He's sometimes on day duty here, and sometimes he's on night. He says he's often wondered about this place, and it's a very queer thing that though he's known this district more than a year, he's never seen a soul go in or out of that door, and hasn't the least notion of what business, if it is a business, is carried on there!"

"Never seen anything or anybody!" corroborated the constable. "At any time – day or night. When I first came on this beat, maybe fifteen months ago, that door had been newly set and painted, and the glass had just been stuck a-top of the wall. But it's a fact – I've never seen anybody go in or come out!"

"I propose to go in," said Hetherwick. "I think we've abundant cause, knowing what we do. It may be that the two missing ladies are there. I've been having a look into the yard, and we could get into it easily by going through the grocer's shop there, on the right, and climbing the wall from his back premises. What do you say, Robmore?"

"Oh, I think so!" agreed Robmore. "Now we're on the job, we'll carry it through. Better let me tackle the grocer, Mr. Hetherwick – I'll see him first and then call you in."

The other waited while Robmore entered the shop and spoke with its owner. They saw him engaged in conversation for several minutes; then he came to the door and beckoned the rest to approach.

"That's all right," he said in an aside to Hetherwick. "We can go through to his back-yard, and he'll lend us a stepladder to get over the wall. But he's told me a bit – he knows the two men who have this place in the next yard, and there's no doubt at all, from his description of them, that one's Ambrose and the other Baseverie. He says they've had the place almost eighteen months, and he thinks they use it as a laboratory – chemicals, or something of that sort. But he says they're rarely seen – sometimes he's never seen them for days and even weeks together. Usually they're there of a night – he's seen lights in the place at all hours of the night. Well – come on!"

The posse of investigators filed through the dark little shop to a yard at its rear, the grocer's apprentice going in front with a step-ladder, which he planted against the intervening wall at its lowest point. One by one, the uniformed constable going first, the six men climbed and dropped over. But for their own presence, the place seemed deserted and lifeless. As Hetherwick had observed from the greengrocer's parlour the windows were obscured by thick coats of paint; nevertheless, two or three of the men approached and tried to find places from which the paint had been scratched, in an effort to see what lay inside. But the constable, bolder and more direct, went straight to the entrance.

"Door's open!" he exclaimed. "Not even shut!" He pushed the door wide, and went into the building, the rest crowding after him. "Hullo!" he shouted. "Hullo!"

No answer came to the summons. The constable crossed the lobby in which they were all standing, and opened an inner door. And Hetherwick saw at once that the grocer's surmise as to the purpose to which the place was put had been correct – this was a chemical laboratory, well equipped, too, with modern apparatus. But there was not a sign of life in it.

"Nobody here, apparently," murmured one of the men. "Flown!"

Robmore went forward to another door, and opening it, revealed a room furnished as an office. There was a roll-top desk in it, and papers and documents lying there; he and Hetherwick began to finger and examine them. And Hetherwick suddenly saw something that made a link between this mysterious place and the house he had called at earlier in the afternoon. There, before his eyes, lay some of the azure-tinted notepaper which Mapperley had traced with the embossed address on it of which the stationer had told.

"There's no doubt we've hit on the place at last, Robmore," he said. "I wish we'd had Matherfield here. But—"

Before he could say more, a sudden shout came from Goldmark, who, while the others were investigating the lower regions, had courageously, and alone, gone up the low staircase to the upper rooms.

"Mithter!" he called. "Mithter Hetherwick! Come up here – come up, all of you. Here'th a man here, a-thittin' in a chair – and th'elp me if I don't believe he'th a thtiff 'un – dead!"

# DEAD!

The rest of the searchers, hearing that startled cry from the Jew, with one accord made for the upper part of the building. Robmore and Hetherwick reached him first; he was standing at the half-opened door of a room, into which he was staring with eager eyes. They pushed by him and entered.

Hetherwick took in the general aspect and contents of that room at a glance. It had been fitted up – recently, he thought, from certain small evidences – as a bed-sitting-room. A camp-bed stood in one corner; there was a washstand, a dressing table, a chest of drawers, two or three pictures, a shelf of books, a small square of carpet in the centre of the floor, the outer edges of which had been roughly and newly stained. On the bed lay, open, a suitcase, already packed with clothes and linen; by it lay an overcoat, hat, gloves, umbrella; it was evident that the man to whom it belonged had completed his preparations for a departure, and had nothing to do but to close and lock the suitcase, put on his overcoat and hat, pick up the other things and go away.

But the man himself? There was a big, old-fashioned easy chair at the side of the bed – a roomy, comfortable affair. A man lay, rather than sat, in it, in an attitude which suggested that he had dropped there as with a sudden weariness, laid his head back against the padded cushion, and – gone to sleep. But the men knew, all of them, as they crowded into that room, that it was no sleep that they had broken in upon – it was death. This, as the Jew had been quick to see, was a dead man – dead!

Hetherwick took him in as quickly as he had taken in his surroundings. His head lay quietly against the padding of the chair, a little inclined to his left shoulder: the face was fully visible. It was – to Hetherwick – the face of a stranger; in all his and Matherfield's investigations it had not been described to them. Yet he was certain that he was looking on the man known to them by repute as Ambrose. Disguised, of course – he had shaved off the dark beard and moustache of which they had heard, and he could see at once that the loss of them had made a remarkable difference in his appearance. But nothing could disguise his height and general build. This, without doubt, was the man Matherfield and he had hunted for, the man who had met Hannaford at Victoria, who had disappeared from his flat in the Adelphi – the man who was associated with Baseverie, and who—

"Dead as a doornail!" muttered Robmore, bending close to the still figure. "And – he's been dead a good bit, too! – some hours, anyway. Stiff! Do ye know him, Mr. Hetherwick?"

Hetherwick said what he thought. Robmore pointed to the things on the bed.

"Looks as if he'd been taken with a seizure just as he was about to set off somewhere," he remarked. "Well, if this is the Dr. Ambrose we've been seeking – but let's see if he's got anything on him to prove his identity."

While the rest of the men stood by watching, he put his hand into the dead man's inside breast pocket – he was wearing a smart, brand-new grey tweed suit, Hetherwick, later on, remembered how its newness struck him as being incongruously out of place, somehow – and drew out a pocket-book. Touching Hetherwick's elbow and motioning him to follow him, he went over to the window, leaving the others still staring wonderingly at the dead man.

"This is a queer business, Mr. Hetherwick," he whispered as they drew apart. "You think this is the Dr. Ambrose we were after?"

"Sure of it!" answered Hetherwick. "He's shaved off his beard and moustache, and that's no doubt made a big difference in his appearance, but you may depend on it, this is the man! But what's caused his sudden death?"

Then a keen, vivid recollection flashed up in him, and he turned sharply, glancing at the rigid figure in the background.

"What is it?" asked Robmore curiously. "Something strikes you?"

Hetherwick pointed to the dead man's attitude.

"That's – that's just how Hannaford looked when he died in the railway carriage!" he whispered. "After the first signs – you know – he laid back and – died. Just like that – as if he'd dropped quietly asleep. Can – can it be that—"

"I know what you're thinking," muttered Robmore. "Poisoned! Well – what about – eh – the other man?"

"Baseverie!" exclaimed Hetherwick.

"Why not? – to rid himself of an accomplice! But – this pocket-book," said Robmore. "Let's see what's in it. Doesn't seem to be anything very much, by the thinness."

From one flap of the pocket-book he drew out a wad of carefully-folded bank notes, and rapidly turned them over.

"Hundred and fifty pounds there," he remarked. "And what's this paper – a draft on a New York bank for two hundred. New York, eh? So that's where he was bound? And this," he went on, turning out the other

THE CHARING CROSS MYSTERY

flap. "Ah! See this, Mr. Hetherwick? He'd got his passage booked by the *Maratic*, sailing tonight. Um! And Matherfield's gone to Southampton, after Baseverie. I'm beginning to see a bit into this, I think."

"What do you see?" asked Hetherwick.

"Well, it looks to me as if Baseverie had gone ahead to collect that box containing the jewels, and that Ambrose was to follow later, join him there, when Baseverie had secured the loot, and that they were then to be off with their harvest! But – do you notice this – the name under which the passage is booked? Not Ambrose – Charles Andrews, Esquire. Andrews! And Baseverie is Basing. Basing and Andrews. Now I wonder if they carried on business here under these names?"

"That's an unimportant detail," said Hetherwick. "The important thing, surely, is – that! How did that man come by his death?"

"Well, but I don't think that is very important – just now," replied Robmore. "After all, he is dead, and whether he died as the result of a sudden seizure, or whether Baseverie cleverly poisoned him before he left, is a question we'll have to settle later. But I'll tell you what, Mr. Hetherwick – I'll lay anything he didn't poison himself! Look round – there isn't a sign of anything he's been drinking out of. No, sir – the other man's done this. And if Matherfield has the luck to lay hands on him tonight – ah! But now, what was this your clerk, Mapperley, told us as we came along about the Little Smith Street landlady coming here this afternoon?"

"She was followed here by Goldmark," replied Hetherwick. "Goldmark saw her admit herself by a key which she took from her pocket. She stayed inside a few minutes, came out looking much upset, and hurried away to her own house."

"And now you and I'll just hurry after her," said Robmore. "After all, she's living, and we'll make her find her tongue. Of course, she came in here expecting to find this man, and to tell him somebody was on the look-out. And – she found him dead! Come round there with me, Mr. Hetherwick, at once."

He turned to the other detective and the constable, and after giving them some whispered instructions, left the room, Hetherwick, after a word or two with Mapperley, following him. But before they had reached the outer door, they heard steps in the yard, and suddenly two men appeared in the doorway.

If Hetherwick and his companion looked questioningly at these two men, they, on their part, looked questioningly at Robmore and Hetherwick. They were youngish men – Hetherwick set them down as respectably-dressed artisans. That they were surprised to find anyone confronting them at the door whereat all four now stood, was evident; their surprise, indeed, was so great that they came to a sudden halt, staring silently. But Robmore spoke. "Wanting somebody?" he asked sharply.

The two strangers exchanged a glance, and the apparently elder one replied:

"Well, no!" he said. "Not that we know of. But might we ask if you are? And how you got in here? Because this place happens to be ours!"

"Yours!" exclaimed Robmore. "Your property?

"Well, if buying it, paying for it, and taking a receipt and papers makes it so!" answered the man. "Bought it this morning – and settled up for it, too, anyway."

Robmore produced and handed over a professional card, and the faces of the two men fell as they read it. The elder looked up quickly.

"I hope there's nothing wrong?" he said anxiously. "Detectives, eh? We've laid out a nice bit on this – savings, too, and—"

"I don't suppose there's anything wrong that way," replied Robmore reassuringly. "But there's something uncommonly wrong in other ways. Now look here, who are you two, and from whom did you buy this place?"

"My name's Marshall, his is Wilkinson," answered the leader. "We're just starting business for ourselves as electrical engineers. We advertised for a likely place hereabouts, and Mr. Andrews came to us about this – said he and his partner, Mr. Basing, were leaving, and wanted to sell it, just as it stood. We came to look at it, and as it's just the place we need to start with, we agreed to buy it. They said it was their own property, and to save law expenses we carried out the purchase between ourselves. And we paid over the purchase money this morning, and got the papers and the key."

"What time was that?" asked Robmore.

"Ten o'clock or thereabouts," replied Marshall. "By appointment, here."

"Did ye see both men – Basing and Andrews?"

"Both! In that little room to the right. We settled the business – paid them in cash – and settled all up. It was soon done, then they stood us a drink and a cigar, and we went."

"Stood you a drink, eh?" said Robmore suddenly. "Where?"

"Here! Basing, he pulled out a big bottle of champagne and a cigar-box, and said we'd wet the bargain. We'd a glass apiece, Wilkinson and me, then we left 'em to finish the bottle: we were in a hurry. But – is anything wrong?"

"What is wrong, my lad, is that the man you know as Andrews is lying dead upstairs!" replied Robmore. "Poisoned, most likely, by his partner. But, as I said just now, I don't suppose there's anything wrong about your buying the property, providing you can show a title to it; you say you've got the necessary papers?"

Marshall clapped a hand on the pocket of his coat.

"Got 'em all here, now," he said. "But – did you say Andrews was dead – poisoned? Why, he was as alive as I am when we left the two of 'em together. They were finishing the bottle—"

"Look here," interrupted Robmore. "Wait awhile until we come back

– we've some important work close by. There are people of ours upstairs – tell them I said you were to wait a bit. Now, Mr. Hetherwick."

Outside the yard and in the crowded street, Robmore turned to his companion with a cynical laugh.

"Champagne – to wet the bargain!" he said. "Left them to finish it, eh? And no doubt what finished Ambrose was in that champagne – slipped in by Baseverie when his back was turned. I'll tell you what it is, Mr. Hetherwick, that chap's a thorough-paced 'un – he goes the whole hog! I only hope he won't be too deep for Matherfield at Southampton! I shall be anxious till I hear."

"Is it possible for him to escape Matherfield?" exclaimed Hetherwick. "How can he? I look on him as being as good as in custody already! He's bound to call at the post office for that box."

"Is he, though?" interrupted the detective, with another incredulous laugh. "I'm not so sure about that, Mr. Hetherwick. Baseverie is evidently an accomplished scoundrel, and full of all sorts of tricks! I'll tell ye what I'm wondering – will that parcel ever get to Southampton post office, where it's to be called for?"

"Whatever do you mean?" demanded Hetherwick. "It's in the post! Posted this morning."

"No doubt," agreed Robmore dryly. "By special delivery, eh? And when it gets to Southampton Station, it's got to be taken to the head post office, hasn't it?"

"Well?" asked Hetherwick.

"There's many a slip twixt cup and lip – so the old saying goes," replied Robmore. "That parcel may slip. But isn't this the number your clerk mentioned?"

The door of Mrs. Mallett's house looked more closely barred than ever – if possible. And no answer came to several summonses by bell and knocker. But presently Robmore tried the handle – the door opened at his touch.

"Hallo!" he exclaimed. "Open! Um! That seems a bit queer. Well – inside!"

For the second time that afternoon, Hetherwick walked into a place that seemed to be wholly deserted.

# WATERLOO

The detective, walking a little in advance of his companion, stepped forward to a hall-table and knocked loudly on its polished surface. No answer came. He went further along, to the head of a railed stair which evidently communicated with a cellar kitchen; again he knocked, more loudly than before, on an adjacent panel, and again got no reply. And at that, turning back along the hall, he opened the door of the room which faced upon the street, and he and Hetherwick looked in. A musty-smelling, close-curtained room that, a sort of Sunday parlour, little used, cold and comfortless in its formality. But the room behind it, to which Robmore turned next, showed signs of recent occupancy and life. There was a fire in the grate, with an easy chair drawn near to it; on the table close by lay women's gear – a heap of linen, with needle and thread thrust in, a work-basket, scissors, thimble; it required no more than a glance to see that the owner of these innocent matters had laid them down suddenly, suddenly interrupted in her task.

"I'll tell you what it is, Mr. Hetherwick!" exclaimed Robmore abruptly. "This house is empty! Empty of people, anyway."

"Silent enough, to be sure," agreed Hetherwick. "The woman—"

"You've frightened her by calling here," said Robmore. "Then she slipped round to Pencove Street. And there she found Ambrose dead! She's some connection with him and Baseverie, because she possesses a key that admits to that yard. And finding Ambrose dead, she came back here, got her things and cleared out. There isn't a soul in this house. I'll lay anything on that!"

"It struck me that this might be the place where the two ladies were detained," remarked Hetherwick.

"We'll soon see about that," declared Robmore. "Come upstairs – we'll search the place from top to bottom. But stop, downstairs first."

He ran down the stair to the cellar kitchen, with Hetherwick at his heels. And at the door he laughed, pointing within.

"Look there!" he exclaimed. "I told you you'd interrupted things. See! there's one tea-tray, laid out all ready for two – cups and saucers, teapot, bread and butter cut, cake. There's another for one. And there's the kettle, singing away like a bird on a bough. What's that mean? The woman was going to carry up tea for two, somewhere; t'other tray was for herself. Well, you nipped that in the bud; she'll have to get her tea somewhere. But – the others? Come upstairs."

Going back to the hall, he led the way up the main staircase. There were two storeys above the ground floor; on the first were rooms the doors of which, being opened, or being found open, revealed nothing but ordinary things: of these rooms there were three, opening off a main landing. But on the next floor there were only two rooms; one was unfurnished: at the door of the other, a few inches ajar, the detective immediately paused.

"Look you there, now, Mr. Hetherwick!" he said, pointing here and there. "Here's recent work! Do you see that a strong bolt, more like a bar, has been fitted on the outside of this door, and the door itself fitted with a new patent lock, key outside? And, good Lord! A chain as well. Might be in a gaol! But what's inside?"

He pushed the door open and revealed a large room, fitted with two small beds, easy chairs, a table on which books, magazines, newspapers lay; on the table, too, was fancy-work which, it was evident, had been as hastily laid aside as the sewing downstairs. Hetherwick bent over the things, but Robmore went to the one window.

"Gaol, did I say?" he exclaimed. "Why, this is a gaol! Look here, Mr. Hetherwick! – window morticed inside and fitted with iron bars outside. Even if whoever's been in here could have opened the window, and if there'd been no bars there, they couldn't have done anything though, for there's nothing but a high blank wall opposite – back of some factory or other, apparently. But what's this?" he added, opening a door that stood in a corner. "Um! Small bathroom. And this," he continued, going to a square hatch set in the wall next to the staircase. "Ah! Trap big enough to hand things like small trays through, but not big enough for a grown person to squeeze through. Well, I shouldn't wonder if you're right, Mr. Hetherwick – this, probably, is where these ladies were locked up. But – they're gone!"

Hetherwick was looking round. Suddenly his eyes lighted on a familiar object. He stepped forward, and from a chair near one of the beds, picked up a handbag of green silk. He knew it well enough.

"That settles it!" he exclaimed. "They have been here! This is Miss Han – I mean Miss Featherstone's bag – I've seen her carry it often. These are her things in it – purse, card-case, so on. She's left it behind her."

"Aye, just so!" agreed Robmore. "As I say, they all left in a hurry. I figure it out like this: the woman, who, of course, acted as sort of gaoler to these two unfortunate ladies, when she made that discovery round yonder, came back here, got her outdoor things, and cleared off. But before she went, she'd the decency to slip up here, undo that chain, slip the bolt back, and turn the key! Then, no doubt, she made tracks at express speed, leaving the ladies to do what they liked. And they, Mr. Hetherwick, having a bit o' common sense about 'em, did what I should ha' done – they hooked it as quick as possible. That's that, sir!"

Hetherwick thrust Rhona's handbag into his pocket and made for the door.

"Then I'm off, Robmore," he said. "I must try to find out where they've gone. I've an idea probably they'd go to Penteney's office. I'll go there. But – you?"

"Oh, I'm going back to Pencove Street," answered Robmore. "Plenty to do there. But off you go after the ladies, Mr. Hetherwick, there's nothing you can do round here now. I'll keep that clerk of yours a bit, and the Jew chap – they might come in. We shall have some nice revelations in the papers tomorrow, I'm thinking, especially if Matherfield has the luck he expects."

"What are you going to do about this house?" asked Hetherwick as they went downstairs. "Do you think the woman will come back?"

"Bet your life she won't!" answered Robmore. "Not she! I should think she's half-way across London – north, south, east or west, by this. House? Why, I shall just lock the front door and put the key in my pocket. We shall want to search this house narrowly."

Hetherwick bade him good-day for the time being, and hurried off to Victoria Street, to fling himself into the first disengaged taxi-cab he encountered, and to bid its driver go as speedily as possible to Lincoln's Inn Fields. He was anxious about Rhona – and yet he felt that she was safe. And he was inquisitive, too; he wanted to hear her story, to find out what had happened behind the scenes. He felt sure of finding her at Penteney's office; she and Madame Listorelle, once released from their prison, would naturally go there.

But the clerk whom he encountered as soon as he rushed into the outer office, damped his spirits at once by shaking his head.

"Mr. Penteney's not in, sir," he answered. "He was in until not so long ago, but he got a telephone call and went out immediately afterwards. No, I don't know who it was that rang him up, Mr. Hetherwick, nor where he went; seemed a bit excited when he went out, and was in a fearful hurry."

Hetherwick concluded that Madame Listorelle had summoned Penteney, and that he had gone to meet her and Rhona. He went away, somewhat at a loss – then, remembering that Matherfield had promised to wire from Southampton, he turned towards his chambers. At the foot of the stairs he met his caretaker.

"Been a young lady here inquiring for you, Mr. Hetherwick," said the man. "Been here twice. I said I didn't know when you'd be in – any time or no time. She said – but there is the young lady, sir – coming back!"

Hetherwick turned sharply and saw Rhona coming across the square. Hurrying to meet her and disregarding whatever eyes might be watching them, he took both her hands in his in a fashion that brought the colour to her cheeks.

"You're all right – safe?" he asked quickly.

"Sure?"

"I'm all right and quite safe, thank you," she answered. "I – I've been here twice before, but you were out. I came to borrow some money. I left my bag and purse in – the place where we were locked up, and—"

Hetherwick pulled out the handbag and silently gave it to her. She stared at him.

"You've been – there!" she exclaimed. "How—"

"Got in this afternoon, an hour ago," he answered. "Here, come up to my rooms! We can't stand talking here. Madame Listorelle – where's she?"

"I left her at Victoria, telephoning to Major Penteney," replied Rhona. "She, too, had no money. She wanted me to wait until Major Penteney arrived, but I wouldn't. I walked here. I – I thought you'd want to know that we'd got out – at last."

Hetherwick said nothing until they had entered his sitting-room. Then, staring silently at her, he put his hands on Rhona's shoulders, and after a long look at her, suddenly and impulsively bent and kissed her.

"By gad!" he said in a low voice. "I didn't know how anxious I was about you until I saw you just now! But – now I know!"

Then, just as suddenly, he turned away from her, and in a matter-of-fact manner lighted his stove, put on a kettle of water, and began preparations which indicated his intention of making tea. Rhona, from an easy chair into which he had unceremoniously thrust her, watched him.

"Liberty!" she said suddenly. "We're both discovering something. When you've been locked up, day and night, for a while—"

"How was it?" he asked, turning on her. "Of course, we know all about the kidnapping – but the rest, until today? Baseverie, of course?"

"Baseverie and another man," she answered. "A tall, clean-shaven man, whose name we never heard. But Baseverie was the chief villain. As to how it was, they met us at the sunken road at Riversreade, forced us at the point of revolvers into a car, and drove us off to London – to Westminster – and into a house there, the house you've been in. There —"

"A moment," said Hetherwick, who was finding cups and saucers. "The driver of that car? He must have been an accomplice."

"No doubt, but we never saw him again. We only saw those two and a woman who acted as gaoler and brought our meals. We were fed all right, and they gave us books and papers, and actually provided us with fancy work. But they were inexorable about madame and her jewels. They must have known all about them, because they got her own notepaper—"

"I know all about that," said Hetherwick. "I'll tell you my side of it when you've had some tea. Forced her, I suppose, to write the letters?"

"They forced her to do that just as they forced us into the car," said Rhona, "with revolvers! And – they meant it. I suppose they've got the jewels now?"

"Remains to be seen," replied Hetherwick. "Did Madame Listorelle happen to tell you what those jewels were worth?"

"She talked about little else. Between eighty and ninety thousand pounds. She's in an awful state about them. But it was literally a question of her life or her jewels. I don't know what they'd have done with me. But now – I'm all right!"

Hetherwick opened a tin box, and producing a plum cake, held it up for Rhona to inspect.

"What d'you think of that for a cake?" he asked admiringly. "Present from my old aunt in the country – real, proper cake that. Yes," he went on, setting the cake on the table, "yes, yes; you're all right now. But, by George—"

Rhona said nothing; she saw that his relief at seeing her was greater and deeper than he cared to show. She poured out the tea; they sat discussing the recent events until dusky shadows began to fall over the whole room.

"I ought to be getting back to Riversreade," she remarked at last. "It's late."

"Wait a bit!" said Hetherwick, who by that time had told her all he knew. "There'll be a wire from Matherfield before long. Don't go down to Riversreade tonight. Telephone to Lady Riversreade that you're staying in town. Her sister will be there by now, and will have told her everything. Wait till we get the wire from Matherfield; then we'll go and dine somewhere, and you can put up at your old hotel in Surrey Street for the night. I want you to know what's happened at Southampton and —"

He broke off as a knock came at his outer door.

"That'll be Matherfield's wire," he exclaimed "Now then—"

A moment later he came back to her with the message in his hand.

"It is from Matherfield," he said. "Handed in Southampton West six-nineteen. Doesn't say if he's got him! All he says is; 'Meet me Waterloo, arriving eight-twenty.' Well—"

"I wonder?" said Rhona. "But Baseverie is—"

"Just what Robmore says," muttered Hetherwick.

"However – " he looked at his watch. "Come along," he continued. "We've just time to get some dinner – at Waterloo – and to be on the platform when the eight-twenty comes in. If only we could see Baseverie in charge of Matherfield and Quigman first it would give me an appetite!"

The vast space between the station buildings and the entrance to the platform at Waterloo was thronged when Hetherwick and Rhona came out of the restaurant at ten minutes past eight. Hetherwick was inquiring as to which platform the Southampton train would come in at when he felt a light touch on his arm. Turning sharply he saw Robmore. Robmore gave him a quiet smile, coupled with an informing wink.

"Guess you're on the same job, Mr. Hetherwick," he said. "Wire from Matherfield, eh?"

"Yes," replied Hetherwick. "And you?"

"Same here," assented Robmore. "Just to say I was to be here for the eight-twenty – with help," he added significantly. "I've got the help; there's four of us round about. Heard anything of those ladies, Mr. Hetherwick?"

"Here is one of them," replied Hetherwick, indicating Rhona. "They're safe. You'll hear all about it later. But this business – what do you make of Matherfield's wire? Has he failed?"

"I'll tell you what I make of it," answered Robmore. "I think you'll find that Baseverie is on the train, with Matherfield and Quigman in close attendance. For some reason of his own, Matherfield means to arrest Baseverie here – here! That's how I figure it. They've seen Baseverie there and decided to follow him back to town. As soon as that train's in—"

A sudden, sharp exclamation from Rhona interrupted him and made both men turn to her. She clutched Hetherwick's arm, at the same time pointing with the other hand across the space behind them.

"Baseverie – himself!" she said. "There – under that clock! See! He's going towards the gates!"

With a swift and unceremonious gesture Robmore laid a hand on Rhona's shoulder, twisted her round and drew her amongst a group of bystanders.

"Keep out of sight, miss!" he muttered. "He'll know you! Now, again – which man. That with the pale face and high hat? I see him. Good to remember, too. All right! Stop here, you two. If he moves in this direction, Mr. Hetherwick, move away anywhere. Wait!"

Robmore slipped away. A moment later they saw him speak to a couple of quiet-looking men, who presently glanced at Baseverie. Hetherwick was watching Baseverie, too. Baseverie, quiet, unconcerned, evidently wholly unsuspicious, had taken up a position at the exit through which the Southampton passengers must emerge; he was smoking a cigar, placidly, with obvious appreciation.

"You're certain that's the man?" whispered Hetherwick.

"Baseverie? Positive!" declared Rhona. "As if I could mistake him! I've too good reason to remember his whole appearance. But – here! Daring!"

"Well," said Hetherwick, "something's going to happen! Keep back – keep well back! We can see things from here without being seen. If he caught sight of you—"

Robmore came strolling back and joined them.

"All right!" he murmured. "Four pairs of eyes, beside ours – that's three pairs more – on him! My men are close up to him, too. See 'em? One, two, three, four! All round him, though he doesn't know. I shan't let him go, whether Matherfield turns up or not. Cool customer, eh?"

"The train's due," said Hetherwick. He had Rhona's hand within his arm, and he felt it tremble. "Yes," he whispered, bending down to her, "that's how I feel. Tense moment, this. But that scoundrel there—"

Baseverie was glancing at the big clock. He turned from it to the platform behind the gates, looking expectantly along its lighted surface. The others looked, too. A minute passed. Then, out of the gloom at the further extremity of the vast station, an engine appeared, slowly dragging its burden of carriages and came sighing like a weary giant up the side of the platform. The passengers in the front compartments leapt out and began filing towards the exit.

"Now for it," muttered Robmore. "Keep back, you two! My men'll watch him – and whoever's here to meet him, for he's expecting somebody."

Nothing happened for the first minute. The crowd of discharged passengers, men and women, civilians, soldiers, sailors, filed out and went their ways. Gradually it thinned. Then Hetherwick's arm was suddenly gripped by Rhona for the second time, and he saw that she was staring at something beyond the barrier.

"There!" she exclaimed. "There – the man in the grey coat and fawn hat! That's the man who drove the car! See! Baseverie sees him!"

Hetherwick looked and saw Baseverie lift a hand in recognition of a young, fresh-faced man, who was nearing the ticket-collectors, and who carried in his right hand a small, square parcel. But he saw more. Close behind this young man came Matherfield on one hand and Quigman on the other. They drew closer as he neared the gate, and on its other side the detectives drew closer to Baseverie.

"Now then," whispered Robmore, and stole swiftly forward.

It was all over so swiftly that neither Hetherwick nor Rhona knew exactly how the thing was done. Before they had realised that the men were trapped, or the gaping bystanders had realised that something was happening under their very noses, Baseverie and his man were two safely handcuffed prisoners in the midst of a little group of silent men who were hurrying both away. Within a moment captors and captives were lost in the outer reaches of the station. Then the two watchers suddenly realised that Matherfield, holding the square parcel in his hand, was standing close by, a grim but highly satisfied smile in his eyes. He held the parcel up before them.

"Very neat, Mr. Hetherwick, very neat indeed!" he said. "Uncommonly neat – eh?"

But Hetherwick knew that he was not referring to the parcel.

# THE ASSURANCE

Rhona went back to her old quarters at the little hotel in Surrey Street for that night, and next morning Hetherwick came round to her, with an armful of newspapers. Finding her alone, he laid them on the table at her side with a significant nod of his head at certain big black letters which topped the uppermost columns.

"Matherfield must have given plenty of informing news to the pressmen last night," he remarked with a grim smile. "It's all in there – his own adventures at Southampton yesterday; mine and Robmore's in Westminster, and all the rest of it. I believe the newspaper people call this sort of thing a story – and a fine story it makes! Winding up, of course, with the dramatic arrest of Baseverie at Waterloo! I'm afraid we're in for publicity for a time, worse luck!"

"Shall we – shall I – have to appear at that man's trial?" asked Rhona.

"That's unavoidable, I'm afraid, and at other things before that," answered Hetherwick. "There'll be the proceedings before the magistrate, and the adjourned inquest, and so on. Can't be helped; and there'll be some satisfaction in knowing that we're ridding the world of a peculiarly cruel and cold-blooded murderer! That chap Baseverie is certainly as consummate a villain as I ever heard of. A human spider – and clever in his web-spinning. But I wish one had a few more particulars on one point – and yet I don't see how one's to get them."

"What point?" asked Rhona.

"That sealed packet, containing the details, or formula, or whatever it is, of your grandfather's invention," replied Hetherwick. "Where is it? What, precisely, is it? Did Ambrose get it from him? Has Baseverie got it? So far as I can make out, the whole thing began with that. Whether it was really worth a farthing or a fortune, your grandfather brought to London something which he honestly believed to be of great value, and there's no doubt that he got into the hands of those two men, Ambrose and Baseverie, because of it. There's no doubt, either, that in conversation with them, he told them, perhaps jokingly, what he knew

165

about Madame Listorelle. Nor is there any doubt that these two murdered him. Nor is there any doubt, in my mind, as to *how* they murdered him! You must remember that both men were trained medical men, and, obviously of a scientific turn of mind into the bargain. Each had doubtless made a deep study of poisons. Such a knowledge is of value to such men as they were – men of criminal tendencies. Probably they knew of a subtle poison easily administered, the effects of which would not be evident for some hours. No doubt they *timed* their work, so that their victim should die swiftly and suddenly when well away from their laboratory. And, of course, they did the same thing in the case of Granett. Granett paid the penalty of being with your grandfather. But for what did they murder your grandfather? Did they get rid of him so that they could keep his secret about Madame Listorelle to themselves, and blackmail her and her sister, or that they could rob him of his invention and turn it to their own profit? If the latter, then—"

He paused, looking inquiringly at Rhona, as if he expected her to see what he was after. But Rhona shook her head.

"I don't follow," she said. "What then?"

"This," replied Hetherwick. "If their desire to get hold of your grandfather's secret was their motive, then that secret's worth a lot of money! Money which ought to come to you. Don't you see? Where is the secret? Where's the sealed packet? I suppose the police would search Baseverie last night – perhaps they found it on him. We shall hear – but, anyway it's yours."

Rhona made a gesture of aversion.

"I should hate to touch or have anything to do with it if it had been in that man's possession!" she said. "But I don't think there's any doubt that they murdered my grandfather because of that secret. Only, I think, too, they'd a double motive. The secret about Madame Listorelle was their second string. Probably they believed that Lady Riversreade would be an easy prey. And I think she would have been, if she hadn't had Major Penteney to fall back on. I know she was dreadfully upset after Baseverie's first visit. So I put it this way – always have done: they thought they could sell grandfather's invention for a lot of money, and get another lot out of Lady Riversreade and Madame Listorelle as blackmail."

"Black money, indeed, all of it!" exclaimed Hetherwick. "Well—"

A woman servant put her head into the little parlour in which they were sitting, and looked significantly at Rhona.

"There's a policeman downstairs, miss, asking for you," she announced. "Leastways, he wants to know if you can tell him if Mr. Hetherwick's here or been here."

Hetherwick went to the head of the stair; a policeman standing in the hall below looked up and touched his helmet.

"Inspector Matherfield's compliments, sir, and could you step round and bring Miss Hannaford with you?" he asked. "There's new developments, Mr. Hetherwick. Important!"

"We'll come at once," assented Hetherwick. "Ten minutes!" He went back and hurried Rhona away. "What now?" he asked as they hastened towards Matherfield's office. "Perhaps they've extracted something out of Baseverie? Or possibly the newspapers have attracted the attention of somebody who can give further news?"

The last suggestion strengthened itself when, on entering Matherfield's room, they found him closeted with two strangers whose appearance was that of responsible and well-to-do commercial men. All three were discovered in what looked like a serious and deep conversation, and Hetherwick was quick to notice that the two unknown men looked at Rhona with unusual interest. Matherfield made haste to introduce her as the late ex-Superintendent Hannaford's granddaughter, and Hetherwick as a gentleman who had been much concerned in the recent proceedings.

"These gentlemen, Miss Hannaford and Mr. Hetherwick," he proceeded, waving his hand at the others, "are Messrs. Culthwaite and Houseover, manufacturing chemists, of East Ham – incidentally, they've also a big place in Lancashire. And having seen this morning's papers, in which, as you've no doubt noticed, there's a good deal about our affair, they've come straight to me with some news which will prove uncommonly useful when Baseverie's put in the dock before the magistrate this afternoon. The fact is, Mr. Hetherwick, these gentlemen have supplied a missing link!"

"What link?" asked Hetherwick eagerly.

Matherfield nodded at the elder of the two men, Culthwaite, who produced a pocket-book, and extracted from it a sheet of paper. Silently, he passed it over to Matherfield, who turned to Rhona.

"Now, Miss Hannaford," he said, with a note of triumph in his voice, "I dare say you can positively identify your grandfather's handwriting and his way of making figures? Can you swear that this has been written by him?"

Rhona gave but one glance at the paper before looking up with a glance of positive assertion.

"Oh, yes!" she exclaimed. "That is his writing, without a doubt! Nothing could be more certain!"

Matherfield turned to Hetherwick.

"That's the formula for the ink!" he said. "Now we've got the big thing we wanted! And Mr. Culthwaite will tell you how he got it."

Culthwaite, after allowing Hetherwick to look at the paper, carefully replaced it in his pocket-book. There was an air of anxiety about him and about his partner concerning which Hetherwick began to make guesses – they looked as if they were uncertain and uneasy. But Culthwaite was ready enough to tell his story.

"We got it in this way," he said. "And I may as well say, as I've already said to you, Mr. Matherfield, that I don't think we should have got it at all if you police people hadn't been so reticent on that one particular point – if you'd noised it abroad about Hannaford's secret we might have been forewarned. However, some little time ago, a man whom we knew as Basing, and whom I firmly believe to be the Baseverie that we've read about in the papers this morning – a man, mind you, that we'd done business with now and then during the last year or so – came to us and offered us the formula for a new black ink which he asserted would drive every known ink off the market, all over the world! He made extravagant claims for it; he swore it was the first absolutely perfect writing fluid ever invented. He brought a sample of it which he'd made up himself – he put it to various tests. But he did more – he offered us the use of the secret formula so that we ourselves could make and test it before deciding whether we'd fall in with his suggestion, which was that we should offer him a lump cash sum for the formula. Well, we did make the ink, from the formula, and we did test it, and there is no doubt about it – it is all, and perhaps more, that Basing, or Baseverie claimed for its excellence. I needn't go into the drawbacks attaching to most well-known inks – this has none of them. And when Basing came back to us, a few days ago, we decided to buy the formula from him. We agreed upon a cash price, and day before yesterday we paid the amount over – at our office in East Ham."

"Yes?" said Hetherwick quietly. "And – what was the price agreed upon?"

The two partners exchanged a glance; it seemed to Rhona, who was watching them intently, that they looked more uneasy than before. But Culthwaite replied with promptitude.

"Ten thousand pounds!"

"How did you pay him?" asked Hetherwick. "In cash?"

"No – by open cheque, at his own request. That, of course, was as good as cash. But," continued Culthwaite, "as soon as we read the newspapers this morning, we – that is, I, for I read the whole thing on my way to business – went at once to our bank to see if the cheque had been cashed. It had – an hour or two after we'd handed it to Basing. He'd taken the amount in Bank of England notes."

Hetherwick looked at Matherfield.

"Of course," he remarked, as if he were asking a question, "that formula belongs to Miss Hannaford? Baseverie had no right to sell it – he stole it?"

"That's the fact, Mr. Hetherwick," assented Matherfield. "These gentlemen, innocently enough, bought stolen property. But I've just told them something that I'll now tell you. We found the money – notes – on Baseverie, last night. Intact – in his pocket-book. Of course, with that, and the jewels which his accomplice succeeded in getting at Southampton, he'd got a nice haul. But now we can easily prove how he came by that ten thousand – and it'll go back to Messrs. Culthwaite and

Houseover there. We can prove, too, from their evidence, that Baseverie poisoned Mr. Hannaford for the sake of that formula. Baseverie's done!"

"These gentlemen will recover their ten thousand pounds, then?" said Hetherwick. "In that case" – he turned to the two partners – "I don't see that you've anything to worry about?" he suggested. "The formula, of course, must be handed over to—"

"Well, now, that's just it, Mr. Hetherwick," interrupted the partner who until then had kept silent. "The fact is, sir, we don't want to lose that formula! We gave this man Baring or Baseverie ten thousand pounds for it, but—"

"But you really believe it to be worth more, eh?" said Hetherwick with a smile. "I see! Then in that case—"

"If we get back our ten thousand, sir, we shall be pleased to discuss it with the rightful owner," said Culthwaite, after an exchange of looks with his partner. "In the meantime, the formula is safe and secret with us. We are well-known people—"

"We'll leave it at that, just now," answered Hetherwick. "Miss Hannaford will trust you to keep your word about safety and secrecy. And later – business!" He got up, and Rhona rose with him. "Shall you want us today, Matherfield?" he asked. "If not—"

"No!" replied Matherfield. "Merely formal business today – then, this afternoon, he'll be brought up. Only evidence of arrest and application for adjournment. You can go away, Mr. Hetherwick – we'll let you both know when you're wanted."

Hetherwick led Rhona out, and once clear of the police precincts, smote his stick on the pavement.

"When we're through with this business I'm hanged if I ever dabble in crime affairs again, personally!" he exclaimed. "Baseverie has been a pretty vile example to tackle! And that you should be dragged into it, too!" he added, suddenly. "That upset me more than anything. However, it's getting to an end, and then—"

He paused, while she looked up at him with a little wonder at his vehemence. Then, and as they were at that moment walking along a quiet stretch of the less frequented side of the Embankment, she timidly laid a hand on his arm. He turned sharply, laying his hand on hers.

"I think you've been very considerate and thoughtful for me," she said. "After all – it wasn't quite mere interest in crime that made you—"

"Good Lord, no!" he exclaimed quickly. "At first, perhaps, half that – half you! I felt – somehow – that I'd got to look after you. And then – and when you disappeared – but I believe I'm a bit muddle-headed! I'll tell you something – all that time you were lost, I – well, I scarcely ever slept! Wondering, you know. And when you turned up yesterday afternoon – but I want to ask you something that I'm not quite clear about – I was certainly muddled just then!"

"What is it?" she asked.

Hetherwick bent down to her and dropped his voice.

"I was so glad, so relieved to see you, yesterday afternoon," he said, "that – that I felt dazed – eh? And I want to know – did I kiss you?"

Rhona suddenly looked up at him – and laughed.

"Oh, really, how amusing you are!" she said. "Why, of course, you did! Twice!"

"That's good!" he exclaimed. "I – I thought perhaps I'd dreamt it. But – did you kiss me?"

"Do you really want to be dead sure?" asked Rhona mischievously. "Very well – I did!"

"That's better!" said Hetherwick.

## THE END

Thank you for choosing this book – I hope you enjoyed it. Please be sure to visit oleanderpress.com to sign up for our infrequent, non-spammy Newsletter and get:

> A free classic text
> Updates on new LONDON BOUND titles
> Complete list of all LONDON BOUND titles
> Pre-order discounts
> Special Offers
> Exclusive Offers

As well as news of other Oleander titles.

For further benefits:

> facebook.com/oleanderpress
> Twitter.com/oleanderman

I'd also appreciate any comments – good and bad – on the current list and welcome ideas for new classic titles to publish – info@oleanderpress.com

I look forward to hearing from you!

Jon Gifford

Publisher,
Oleander Press

Printed in Great Britain
by Amazon

14224676R00103